WYNTER WAKENETH

SUSANNA M. NEWSTEAD

HERESY PUBLISHING

First Published in 2022
by HERESY PUBLISHING
Newbury RG14 5JG
www.heresypublishing.co.uk

Cover design by Charlie Farrow

A CIP catalogue record for this book is available from the British Library.

ISBN 978-1909237-13-1

Savernake Forest c.1200

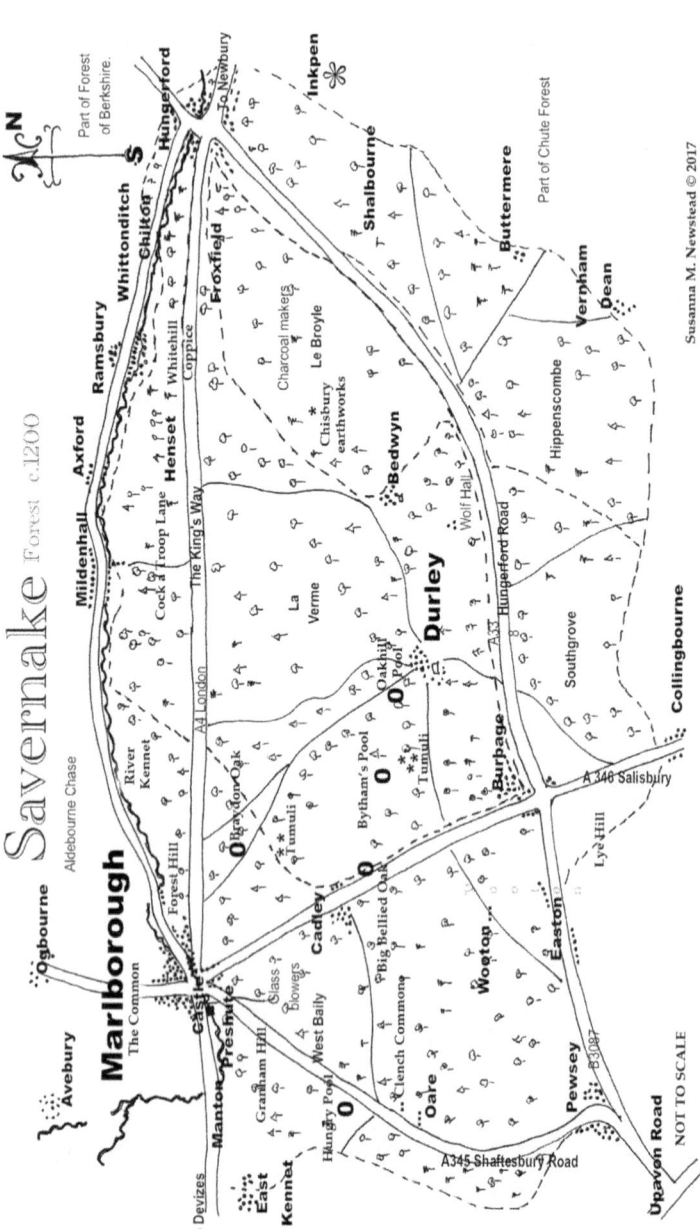

N

Part of Forest of Berkshire.

To Newbury

Inkpen

Part of Chute Forest

Susanna M. Newstead © 2017

Hungerford

Whittonditch

Chilton

Froxfield

Shalbourne

Buttermere

Ramsbury

Axford

Henset

Whitehill Coppice

Le Broyle

Charcoal makers

Vernham

Dean

Mildenhall

Cock a Troop Lane

The King's Way

Chisbury earthworks

Bedwyn

Hippenscombe

River Kennet

Aldebourne Chase

Ogbourne

Avebury

Marlborough

The Common

Forest Hill

A4 London

La Verme

Oakhill Pool

Durley

Wolf Hall

Hungerford Road

Southgrove

Collingbourne

Manton

Presh ute

Castle

Glass ?

Bowers

Braydon Oak

Bytham's Pool

Tumuli

Tumuli

Burbage

A 346 Salisbury

A345

East Kennet

Gramham Hill

West Baily

Big Bellied Oak

Clench Common

Cadley

Woottop

Easton

Lye Hill

p o o l s

To Devizes

Hungry Pool

Oare

Pewsey

B 3087

Upavon Road

A345 Shaftesbury Road

NOT TO SCALE

Marlborough and Savernake Forest c.1200 (1)

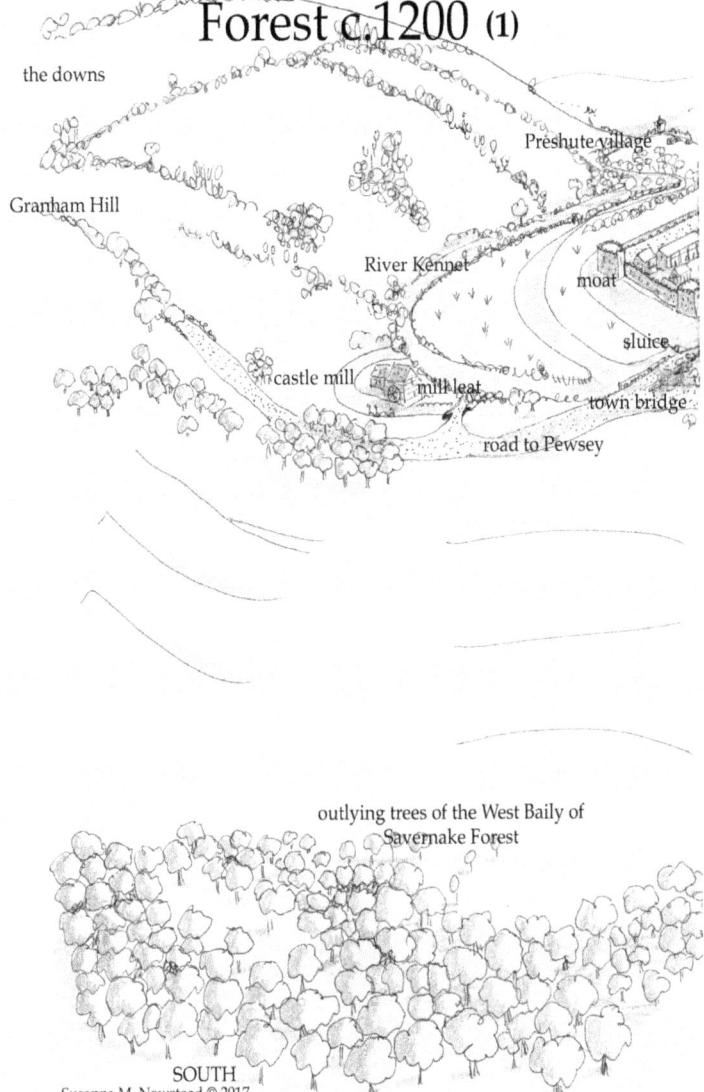

the downs

Preshute village

Granham Hill

River Kennet

moat

sluice

castle mill

mill leat

town bridge

road to Pewsey

outlying trees of the West Baily of Savernake Forest

SOUTH

Susanna M. Newstead © 2017

Marlborough Town and the forest c.1200 (2)

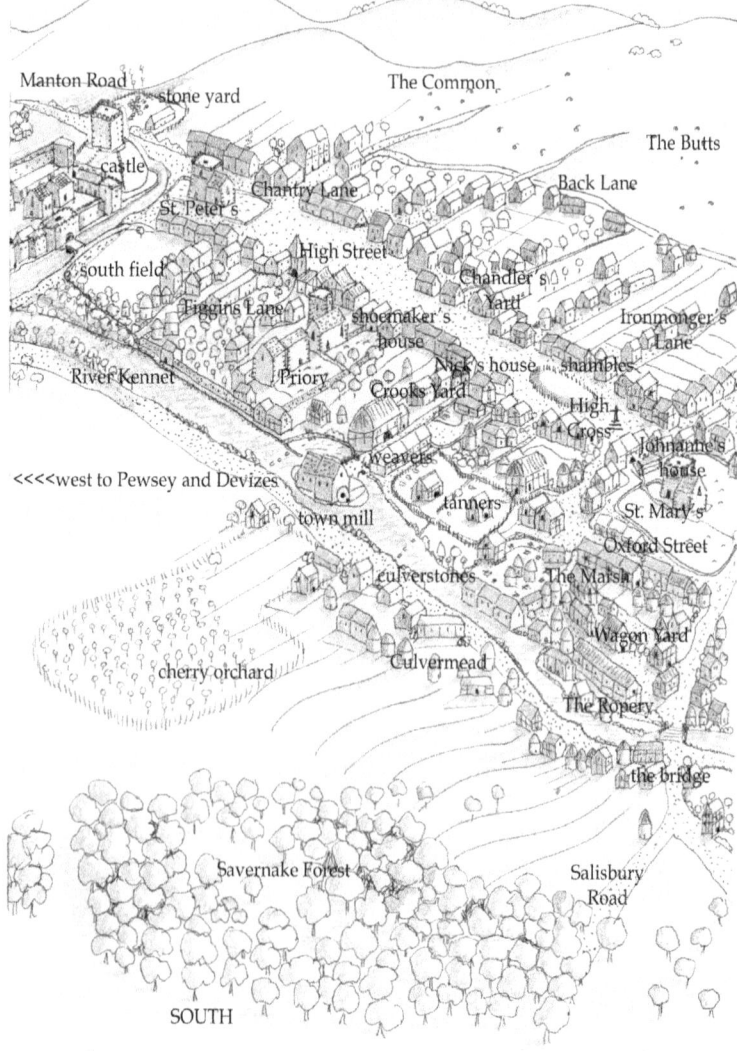

Manton Road
stone yard
The Common
The Butts
castle
Chantry Lane
Back Lane
St. Peter's
High Street
Chandler's
south field
Yard
Tiggins Lane
shoemaker's
ironmonger's
house
Lane
Nick's house
shambles
River Kennet
Priory
Crooks Yard
High
Cross
Johnanne's
weavers
house
<<<<west to Pewsey and Devizes
tanners
St. Mary's
town mill
Oxford Street
culverstones
The Marsh
Wagon Yard
cherry orchard
Culvermead
The Ropery
the bridge
Savernake Forest
Salisbury
Road

SOUTH

not to scale

Marlborough and the forest
c. 1200 (3)

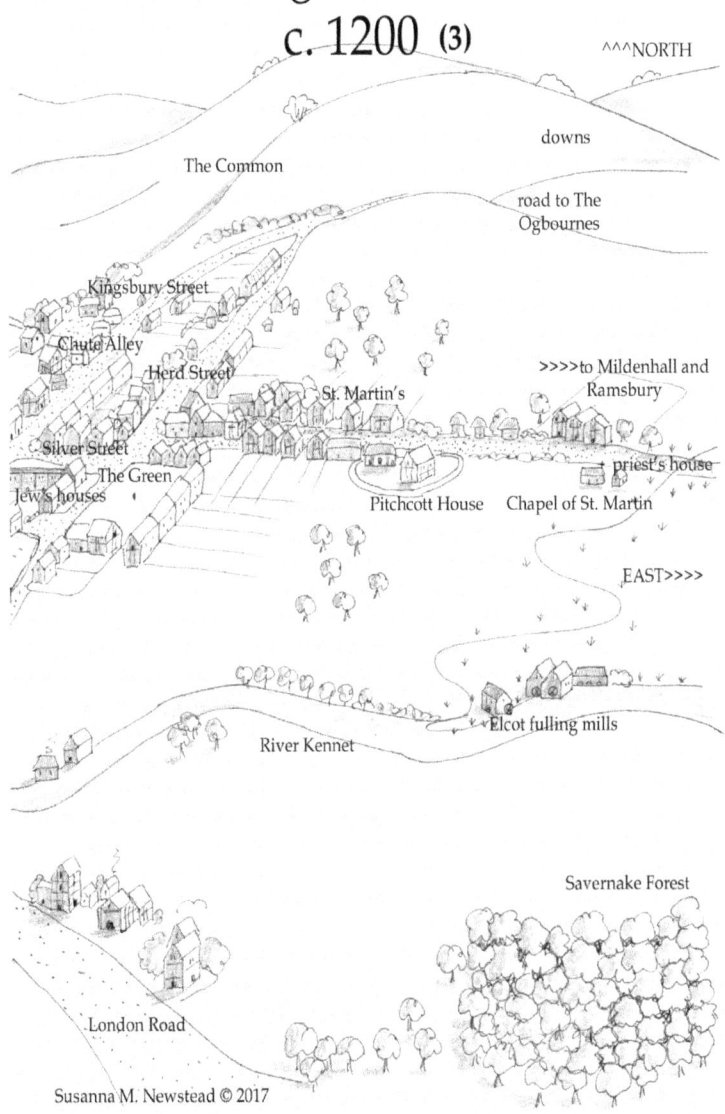

^^^NORTH

downs

The Common

road to The
Ogbournes

Kingsbury Street

Chute Alley

Herd Street

>>>>to Mildenhall and
Ramsbury

St. Martin's

Silver Street

priest's house

The Green

Jew's houses

Pitchcott House   Chapel of St. Martin

EAST>>>>

River Kennet

Elcot fulling mills

Savernake Forest

London Road

Susanna M. Newstead © 2017

WYNTER WAKENETH

Wynter wakeneth al me care
Nou this leves waxeth bare;
Ofte y sike and mourne sare
When hit cometh in my thoht
Of this worldes joie hou hit geth al to noht

Nou hit is, and nou hit nys—
Also hit ner nere ywys;
That moni mon seith soth hit ys:
Al goth bote godes wille;
Alle we shule deye us like ylle

Al that gren me graueth grene;
Nou hit faleweth al by-dene
Jhesu, help that hit be sene
Ant shild us from helle!
For y not whider y shal ne hou longe her duelle

Winter awakens all my sorrow,
Now the leaves wax bare.
Often I sigh and mourn sorely
When into my thoughts come
This world's joy, how it all goes to naught.

Now it is, and now it is not,
As if it had never been, truly.
What many people say, it is the truth:
All passes but God's will.
We all shall die, though it please us ill.

All the grass which grows so green,
Now fails all together.
Jesu, help this to be understood,
And shield us from hell!
For I do not know where I shall go,
nor how long I shall dwell here.

Anon.
Possibly from Leominster Herefordshire around 1310.

Chapter One

"It's like looking up the devil's arse in 'ere, I can't see a damned thing," said Hal of Potterne, my man at arms as his head poked out of the undercroft door. "Someone get me a candle or somethin'."

I looked up at the sky. "It's uncommon dark today Hal."

Indeed on that day Tuesday the 22nd of January 1208 there was a louring brown, grey sky and a biting east wind.

I was standing outside, at the edge of the courtyard waiting to help my old retainer fetch out the Belvoir cradle from its resting place in a corner of the undercroft to my little manor house. My manor, which lies in the village of Durley, deep in the forest of Savernake, in the county of Wiltshire.

What, Paul my scribe? Why was it there? Because my elder son Simon was now two and a half and we had put it away, for he had outgrown it. The cradle had been getting in the way in the solar. You can write that down if you like. I don't mind. If you think it explains things for my readers.

We had need of it again for my wife Lydia had gone into her labour that morning and God willing, it would soon have a new occupant.

Hal rooted around a little more.

"Nope... I can't see. I'll 'ave to..."

"Allow me Hal," said a voice. I turned to see Henry Pierson, my steward, a rushlight held above his head, coming around the edge of the steps.

"I've had to work with a lit candle all morning, it's been so dark. I've been lighting some candles in the hall. Here take this, sir." He handed me the light. "Might we have some snow?" he added, looking up at the sky himself.

"I'm not sure. I truly hope not. Thank you Henry." I ducked under the undercroft door lintel. This was quite an exercise for I am a full six feet in length and the opening was a mere five feet and I must hold the rushlight high or I would be in peril of setting fire to my hair.

I carefully descended the steps, four of them.

Hal came into view, covered in cobwebs, his favourite kingfisher blue cotte dusty and disordered. He pulled at the foot of the cradle, his breath steaming before him in the gloom.

"God's ditties, I'd forgotten how 'eavy this is."

"That's why you shall need help to carry it up the stairs. Sturdy Savernake oak that is and a good hundred and fifty years old too."

"Aye, it's seen generations of Belvoirs."

"Me included," I laughed as the light from the flaring rushes held by Henry, spiked up the undercroft wall.

Hal turned the cradle round with a scraping sound.

"Right... 'ead or foot, sir?"

I smiled. "Head I think"

Together we manhandled the heavy cradle up the four stairs, out of the undercroft and to the base of the twelve steps which led up to the first floor and the hall of the house.

We stopped at the first step and put it down.

"Phew!" said Hal. "I'm gettin' too old for this sorta thing, I think."

"Nonsense, Hal!" said Henry, coming out of the undercroft and locking the door. "You can't be a day over forty!" His mouth tried not to smile.

"You watch it young man..." chuckled Hal, "you're scarcely outa breech clouts!"

Henry was twenty-seven.

"My Lord Belvoir," came a voice from the gate arch.

I turned to see Aolfe Midwyfe, the woman who helped in most of the birthings in the forest, coming through the gate.

"Aolfe, welcome," I said.

She trotted up to the steps and curtsied.

"I see, my lord, you are preparing things."

I smiled and nodded. "You have come from Buttermere?" I asked. This was a small hamlet to the east of Durley where the woman lived.

"No, my lord, from Bedwyn. I delivered a girl child there to Matthew Farmer's wife this morning about the third hour."

"All's well?"

Aolfe nodded. "Sturdy stock they are, sir," she smiled. "And then I had the summons to come here."

"Aye well... follow us up, Aolfe."

We took up our heavy burden again and step by step struggled up the stone stairs, round the door jamb, into the screens passage and out into the hall.

Henry opened the door and held it so it wouldn't foul our way. Aolfe followed, curtsied and was gone up to the solar.

Menfolk had been banned from thence since the morning.

I saw my housekeeper Agnes Brenthall, the wife of my chief wood warden John, supervising the scouring of the hall trestles and asked her if we might get someone to dust down the cradle and make it fit for its new inhabitant.

"I'd be pleased to do it, sir," she smiled. "Then when the child is born you can get it up the solar steps." She peered at it. "We shall need to set it before the fire to force the damp from it a little."

I glanced at the furthest end of the hall. Twelve steep steps there too. We'd be glad to have it rest here for the while.

"Where is Hawise?"

Hawise was my eight year old daughter, the progeny of my first wife Cecily and I, who had been murdered in 1203.

"In the chapel with Father Crispin, sir."

I looked up at the chapel door, on the mezzanine floor above the end rooms and the screens passage. It was open and I heard Crispin and Hawise talking quietly. I heard her giggle. At their lessons, no doubt.

Hal had gone to the fire to throw on another log and poke the flames.

Matthew Cook came in from the kitchen to ask about food for supper.

I sat down and poured myself a mug of ale.

"Just a little repast, Matthew. No one will have much of an appetite until...." My words trailed off. "Until this is over and then we shall feast."

He smiled. "What a time for a child to come... End of January, m'lord."

"Yes, I'm sorry. Well... we shall feast as well as we are able. At least this winter is not a season of hardship."

Hal looked up and out of the window. "Can't tell what the time is, can we? It's so dark."

"I think it's about the second hour after sext." I said.

"Hmm… Oh no!"

"What Hal?"

"It's damn well snowin' that's what!"

*****

It snowed all afternoon and evening.

It was still snowing the next morning when my second son, whom we called Phillip for Lydia's father, came into the world.

He was silent and sleepy from the first, this son, small and perfect. Hawise took his tiny hand in hers and looked up at me with eyes full of love.

"He's much prettier than Simon was," she said.

I chuckled. "And much quieter."

At that moment the object of our conversation was riding his cock horse around the little nursery room at the end of the solar. Felice, the children's nurse, smiled and closed the door and we left Lydia to sleep and then to feed Phillip, for Lydia preferred to feed her children herself, as the Church actively encouraged.

The snow fell all day and into the next day. We began to wonder if we should have a winter much as we'd had in 1204 and into 1205 where the land was locked up in ice for five months. That had been a terrible time; a time of famine and sickness. Please God this was going to be a short blast of cold.

We dug our way out of the courtyard and piled up the snow into huge walls outside the manor. The weather turned even colder. Everything froze. We stayed huddled by our fires. People began to be bored and fractious and of course folk remembered the terrible winter of just four years ago and worried that we might come as close to starvation now, as we had then.

We'd had my mother in law, my first wife's mother, staying with us from the summer of 1207. Since her husband had died that summer, she had been failing in her wits and had been unwell. A congestion took her off one early February morning and she slipped quietly away to God.

We all cried, for we had loved her dearly and we prepared her for a lengthy wait in our mortuary, a small building close to the western walls of the manor courtyard and by the privy, until the weather was not so cruel and we could venture out to Bedwyn and inter her beside her beloved husband Toruld, in the church there.

On February the eighth the weather warmed. We all heaved a sigh of relief. It was to be a premature sigh for the sky dumped more snow on us and froze solid that evening and the icicles began to form on the manor eaves and the other buildings.

Then came a week of thaw and freeze.

Once more as we had done in that year of the great winter, we knocked off the long sword like icicles from the roofs of the manor so that they should not fall and injure anyone.

They came crashing down like trees in the forest to powder on the cobbles of the yard, now swept of the snow.

Icicles too had formed on the church tower and roof and on the barns. We had no way of getting these down save we get up ladders and crawl onto the roofs and that I would not allow.

Finally on the 20th day of February the sun shone and the snow and ice began to thaw for good.

The next day one of my tied villeins from an outlying farmstead at Braydon in the forest near the village of Cadley, which was three miles from Durley, struggled into the courtyard and asked to see me.

He came up the stairs sweating with his exertions and banging his boots on the outside wall to free them of slush, he entered the screens passage.

He bowed and snatched down his hood.

Henry ushered him in.

"Alwyn Cottar, sir. Of Braydon."

The man bowed again and caught his lip with his teeth.

I stood up. "Come on in, man, warm yourself at the fire. We shan't eat you."

His eyes grew as round as a cheese when he spotted the fire, a modern 'chimneyed' piece which allowed the smoke to be vented through a hole in the outer wall. I'd had this built a few years ago.

He staggered up to the hearth and bowed again, pulling off his woollen mittens.

"God's Grace on you, m'lord. I come from Braydon, not for myself but for my neighbour, Mistress Lea. She cannot come, being big with child."

"Why has she asked you to come to see me, Cottar?"

"She wants me to tell you, sir, that her husband, her husband and my neighbour too, Bordern Lea has gone missing."

I came up to the fire and stood over the small man.

"Missing? Has he been swallowed up in our terrible weather perhaps?"

"He went out to see to the kine and he never came back sir."

"When?"

"When the third or fourth thaw came."

I looked back to Hal who was a mine of information about these things.

"Which was Hal?"

"When poor Lady Evisa got worse, sir. About two days before she died."

I thought back. "So, around the 5th of February. St. Dorothea's Day.

"That's about it, sir," said Hal.

"Ten days or so ago. Why did you not report this earlier?"

"We thought that he would come home having taken refuge somewhere from the cold and then when we thought about it Mistress Lea was unwell and could not come and then the weather was too bad and so I said I would walk here."

"So the man went out, what—to feed the cattle?"

"Yes, sir. Make sure they were all right in the barn at Luton Lye sir. He's a cattle man as am I. I struggled back to my home but Bordern..."

"Didn't return."

"No, my lord and we have since been out to look for him."

"The cattle?"

The man nodded, "All is well with them. We have cared for them."

"So his wife hasn't seen him for ten days?"

"No, sir and no sign of him anywhere."

"Have you told Artor Hayward?"

"Aye sir. We have."

Hayward was my senior herdsman in the area and he lived in a cottage in a forest meadow at the very edge of Cadley village.

"He told us to come up to you soonest. He would go to Mistress Lea's to see what might have happened. Then to the barn."

"He's there now?"

"Yessir."

"Then let's waste no more time. We shall go out to Braydon and speak to this Mistress Lea and learn all we can."

I called for my cloak. Then I had a thought and turned back to Alwyn Cottar.

"Cottar, Lea is a tied villein is he not?"

"Aye sir. He is your man tooth and toe as was his father before him. As am I."

"Might he have absconded? It's not unknown. In this weather folk think they can disappear and never be searched for."

Alwyn Cottar looked frightened. "Oh no sir. Why should he do that? He has a nice wife and a child on the way, a good house—and forgive me, sir," he looked a little embarrassed, "—a fair master, why should he run away?"

"Has he ever said he is discontented with his life out at Braydon?"

"No, sir. And he knows that we should all be fined if he was to go missing. He's a good enough man not to cause us woe like that sir."

"Hmmm."

He referred of course to the fact that in the tithing, a group of ten men local to each other or of a family group, each was responsible for his neighbour and would be amerced should one of their fellows break their frankpledge.

"Warm yourself for a while, take some ale and then we shall go out and see what can be done."

What, Paul? Yes, many men would ask what I was doing investigating the disappearance of a serf; a man tied to the land and myself. They were thought to be men of little worth. Freemen and noblemen were protected by the law. Serfs had no such rights. However these were my people and I considered their lives as important as any. These men and women were

7

threads in the larger pattern woven into the cloth of life in Savernake. I was not about to let their disappearance or death go unremarked. Besides, if the man had simply run away, he was my tied man, I would fetch him back. I remembered my father doing this once; searching for a missing serf without success. At least he'd tried.

You remember the tale of when she was eventually found don't you Paul?

It was just after noon before we arrived at the home of Mistress Lea.

She was a tiny, mousey woman with a huge belly close to her time. She waddled out of the cottage, watching our horses splashing up the slushy snow and melting ice as we arrived.

She looked up at me with watery grey eyes as I dismounted and she made what approached a curtsey.

"Good woman, let us go into the house out of the cold. You should be taking care of yourself at this time," I said.

Alwyn Cottar stepped down from Hal's horse where he had been riding pillion and went to the woman.

"This is the lord, Ellen; he will see if he can find Bordern."

He ushered her into the house.

It was the usual type of cott; a living space with a place for sleeping and an animal pen to the side.

I looked around. There was a pallet rolled up by the wall. I thought perhaps that Mistress Lea could not climb the ladder to the loft in her advanced stage of pregnancy and so she slept by the fire.

A wide bench might provide a base for the mattress to be laid, otherwise there was a single stool and a table and two small chests.

All the pots and pans and treen were laid tidily on shelves fixed to the daub walls. One of the small chests stood under the single window upon which was laid several blankets and a pillow. Leaning against the wall was a stripped blackthorn stick. I picked it up, scanned and replaced it. A small barrel of water stood by the door. The rafters were hung with a few vegetables, a little goat's meat and hard baked flat bread. There was no sign of any other occupants.

Hal came to stand in the doorway. My large wolfhound Ben had come out into the forest with us. He sat by Hal's feet and yawned.

8

I motioned for the woman to sit.

Mistress Lea lowered herself to the bench and shrugged on a large rough dark brown blanket shawl.

"Thank you for coming, my lord. I just do not know what to do."

"Ten days ago your husband went out to his work at Luton Lye. That isn't too far from here."

"No, sir, and it was in one of the thaws so we could get around a bit more."

"What time did he go out?"

"A mite after dawn, sir."

"What time did you expect him home?"

"Just on dusk."

"Which is early at this time of year."

"He didn't come. I thought maybe he'd stayed on in the barn because it was freezing again. He sometimes stays with the animals."

"Sensible men would. They're warm," said Hal smiling.

Mistress Lea gave Hal a small smile in return. "But he always said he might do it. So I knew, you see."

"If he didn't come home you weren't too worried?"

"No, sir."

"However?"

"He would never stay out so many days." Her eyes filled with tears, "he would never stay away so long."

I sat down on the small stool. I smelled the goat in the pen behind me.

"Tell me what happened when he left."

"The day he went out, sir?"

"Yes. Was he all right? Did he seem his usual self?"

The woman shrugged. "He was a little worried, I think, about the weather as we all were."

"Aye well—now the thaw has come—," said Hal leaning on the doorpost.

"Things will get better from now on," I added, smiling.

Alwyn Cottar came up behind Hal.

"The hayward has come back from the barn, m'lord. Do you want to speak to him?"

"In a moment, Cottar. So nothing seemed to be worrying him? It was a normal day?"

"Except for the snow sir—yes." Mistress Lea began to cry silently; tears tracked down her face.

"He's gone isn't he, sir? Gone?"

"Now we don't know that. Let's keep our minds open."

Cottar squeezed past Hal in the doorway. He came to the stricken woman and pressed her shoulder.

"Shall you come to me and Freya? You can't stay here. She can't stay here alone can she, sir?"

"When we have finished, it might be a good idea to go to Alwyn's home, Mistress Lea."

"No. No!" she cried "I must stay here in case he comes home."

"It's not far, a matter of a few hundred paces Ellen. I'll know if he comes home and then..."

"No. No."

Mistress Ellen Lea wiped her sleeve over her nose. "He'll want his supper."

We all looked at each other.

"Get her a drink of ale if you can find some, Cottar," I said.

The man searched around and found a jug and a small beaker.

"Oh..." said Mistress Lea looking at the fire, a catch in her voice. "The potage."

Hal leaned over the central fire and took off the pot swinging on its hook. He stirred the mixture with the wooden spoon, which had been left on the top.

"It's alright. It's not spoiled," he said smiling. "Not stuck to the bottom yet."

He set it down on the floor and Ben, my wolfhound, came up and sniffed.

"Out Ben!" I said severely, pointing to the door hole and my hound trotted off obediently, into the yard.

"So did your husband tell you definitely ten days ago that he wouldn't be returning that night?"

"No, m'lord."

I leaned over and folded my arms.

"You and your husband are my tied people. Has he ever voiced discontent about that, do you know?"

The woman's eyes rose slowly to mine "You mean, m'lord, did he think of running away and becoming a wolfshead....a hunted man?"

I shrugged, "It's not impossible, mistress."

"I think if he was going to go, he'd go in better weather, sir." She made a small rather hysterical giggle and burst into tears. "And he wouldn't leave me, sir—not now." She rubbed her enlarged belly.

Alwyn jumped forward. "Now, now Ellen." He patted her back as she lay with her head on her arms on the trestle and wept.

"Sir, I really don't think he's run off. He isn't the type, sir. Besides, as I said, he's a happy man," he said.

I patted Mistress Lea's hand and she looked up at me, her face ravaged with worry and crying.

"Was he a happy man, Ellen?"

"Aye sir," she sniffed. "As happy as any of us can be on this earth. He was looking forward to being a father, having a son maybe."

"Yes, of course." I thought of my own little bundle back at Durley.

"Well, then—send in Hayward, Cottar," I said.

Artor Hayward was a small man with a round cheerful face. His cheeks were red with the cold and his eyes watered in the wind, or I imagined that was what had happened. He wore a rust coloured cloak over an undyed wool tunic and cross gartered hose to the knee with small brown boots.

He wiped his eyes with his hand. "I've searched the barns, both of them, Luton Lye and Red Vein Bottom. No sign of Lea, m'lord, and I've searched this one too." He gestured to the barn which lay in this glade, a large cow barn from which came the noises of mooing and shuffling.

"How many men were there on the day he left?"

"Three, sir," answered Cottar. "Me, Bordern and John Mount."

"Mount? Mount? Thin man with a slight limp, light brown hair?"

Cottar looked impressed. "Aye, sir. Fell off a roof when he were a young'un."

"Hmmm, I recall him. You all remember Lea being there that day?"

11

"Aye, sir, we do. He left before us to walk home through the snow," said Hayward.

"Did anyone stay behind?"

"Aye sir, Mount did that night."

"He reached his home safely the next day?"

"Aye sir, he did. His cott's next to mine. I went out to do the next night."

"When your husband left, what did he take with him, Mistress Lea?" I asked standing and pacing around the little room.

"Take with him? Oh... erm... a sack with food for his dinner, sir. His cloak and hood and his stick."

"Nothing else?"

"No, sir. His dinner in a sack and his clothes. He wore his cloak and hood."

I looked at a peg driven into the cob of the wall. "This cloak?"

Mistress Lea smiled. "No, sir. That's mine."

"Ah."

On the small chest in the room's corner was a sack.

"This sack, mistress?"

"One very much like it, sir."

"There's dozens like that about," said Hal, picking it up and stretching it out. "Just an ordinary sack."

"Hmm."

"Well, mistress. I know that a search has been made...."

"Of the immediate grounds around the barn and the route home, m'lord," said Hayward. "Nothing."

"I will get my foresters out and we shall search further afield."

I stood in the doorway. "Meanwhile, we'll continue to ask questions. See if anyone has seen your husband in another place?"

The woman's head flew up. "Another place, sir?"

"If he has absconded then he may have made his way to the town, either Hungerford or Marlborough or maybe further afield."

"Oh..."

Hayward came forward. "He's a simple man, Bordern, sir. I really doubt he's gone far. If he has gone, that is."

"We shall look. Good day, mistress. I would go and stay with someone as requested. You're near your time. It's not good for you to be alone."

Hal nodded to her and we exited the small cottage.

I grasped Bayard's reins with my gloved hand and whistled.

"Ben...here, come on we're going home."

The dog was nowhere to be seen.

Alwyn Cottar and Ellen Lea came to stand in the doorway. I heard him say to her. "You get yourself a few things and then we'll take you to Freya."

I looked over the small glade in which three houses stood. Where was that dog?

I called again.

Hal bellowed, "Ben yer pest where are ya?"

I moved back towards the house. I heard a scrabbling and whining coming from the back of the building.

"Stay here," I said to the three occupants. "Hal...I think he's round the back."

Hal jogged past me and disappeared round the corner.

I went back to Bayard, my roan gelding.

After a heartbeat Hal came up holding Ben by his collar.

"M'lord, I think you'd better come and 'ave a look."

I sighed and, shrugging my cloak tighter around my chest, I walked with him and my errant dog to the back of the cottage.

Here was a small outhouse, tucked onto the back wall of the cott. It projected out from the main cottage by about six feet. The door was closed.

Hayward had followed me. "It's Lea's little store, sir. Wood and such like. A bit of herbs hanging from the rafters, that sort of thing."

"Hmmm."

Hal let go of Ben and he scrabbled to the right hand side of the store whimpering and pawing the ground.

"All right lad—we hear yer!" said Hal.

Ben had managed to dislodge some of the snow piled up at the back, where it had fallen in lumps from the roof as it thawed. There were still a few small dripping icicles on the eaves.

Sticking out from the pile was a piece of brown material.

Hal bent and pulled. It was still quite stiff and rimed with frost. The sun didn't really reach the ground here.

I looked over my shoulder. "Hayward, find a shovel," I shouted.

He opened the door of the shed with a squeak and a shudder, leaned in and came out with a wooden shovel. He began to dig the pile of snow and ice.

Ben sat back looking up at me with expectant eyes.

I patted his head. "Yes, you're a good boy, a very good boy." He wagged his tail. I took out a small piece of dried liver which I always kept rolled in a scrap of waxed cloth in my purse and he took it gently from the flat of my palm.

I heard Hal take in an audible breath, "Ah..."

Hayward ceased his shovelling and crossed himself.

"God in Heaven," he said quietly.

A face stared up at us. Its eyes were open and glassy. Well, I say eyes. One was missing all together and was merely a bloody hole.

"The man we seek?" I asked Hayward.

"Aye, sir. That's Bordern Lea, God help him."

Suddenly there was a shriek. Mistress Lea, helped by Alwyn Cottar, had come round the corner of the house. Naturally she saw the head of her husband poking out from the pile of snow.

"Nooo! Bordern!" she cried, folded and crumpled onto Cottar's shoulder like a dropped sheet. She was as white as a sheet too.

Hal bent to the corpse and sighed.

"Straight through the brain sir."

"Aye, Hal." I too sighed.

"Get her to your wife, Alwyn. And Hayward, ride to the coroner at Ramsbury. Send someone from there to the doctor in Marlborough."

I provided all my major woodsmen with ponies with which to ride about the forest at their duties.

Hayward nodded and turned on his heel.

Hal looked up seriously.

"Murder then, sir?"

"Looks like it, Hal," I said. I swung my cloak from my shoulders.

"C'mon, let's dig him out."

Chapter Two

So there we are Paul my scribe, we have the makings of another tale of murder. Another murder which I, as Constable of the county, was bound to look into, for the King himself had appointed me his investigator and had given me a warrant ratified by the great seal of England in the year of our Lord 1204, which entitled me to question anyone I suspected of a misdeed.

This was certainly a misdeed, though it was hard to see what had happened and why. I'd had a deal of experience in the past four years, investigating murders which had taken place in my county of Wiltshire and you have been kind enough to write them down for me, for as you know I can no longer hold a pen. I'm an old man now but then I was a vigorous knight of some thirty or so years, with a willing body and an inquiring mind.

It's good of the prior of St. Margaret of Antioch in Marlborough to let you come every so often to Durley to be my scribe. Ha, ha, yes Paul, I know you love the stories. Shall we continue then and write a little bit more before we have our supper and you must go back to the priory?

Prime your pen. Now next on that day....

A sobbing Mistress Lea was taken away by Cottar and we watched as they walked slowly to the cattle man's cottage a hundred paces away.

Then we turned back to the work of freeing Bordern Lea from the icy pile.

Hal and I carefully scraped away the snow making sure that no evidence was lost. We found no weapon, no cloak, no stick and no sack. Bordern Lea lay on his back with his head to the western most end of the cottage, his feet to the corner made by the outhouse and the cottage wall.

I stood looking down at the body for quite a while. Something was bothering me but I couldn't put my mind to it.

Hal stood the shovel up against the cob wall and replaced his cloak.

"What's puzzlin' you then, sir?"

I frowned.

"The man has returned home. He's within a few yards of the cottage door. His wife does not see or hear him and yet if he hasn't been into the house place, where is his cloak, his sack and his stick?"

" 'Is cloak might have been taken by the murderer, sir."

"Hmmm."

"The stick too and the sack, well 'e might 'ave left it at the barn."

I looked down again. Still there was this feeling of disquiet.

"They have no dog?"

"No, sir."

"If they had a dog the man might have been found earlier." I looked up at the steeply pitched roof of the cottage.

"Snow has fallen on him. Both from the sky and with the thawing, from the roof, I think."

" 'Is wife didn't see him 'ere?"

"Has she a need to come to this part of the cottage, Hal?"

"No, I suppose not. It's the wrong side of the place. The path goes the other way and nothing faces 'ere. It's the most secret side."

"But why kill him so close to home?"

Hal shrugged.

"We must speak to his wife again."

We trudged across the glade.

"Mistress?" I said ducking under the door lintel of the first cottage. This one was considerably larger than the other two with several out houses and a substantial plot at the back.

A younger woman with curling light auburn hair under a white head rail turned quickly to look at me. She pushed the curl decorously back into the headdress.

"This is my wife Freya, sir," said Alwyn Cottar swiftly. "This is our lord, Freya. He is also the Constable of the county and it's his job to look into murders and such."

The woman curtsied. She was small and shapely with a pale oval face, green eyes and a sweet expression and I snatched in an involuntary breath, for she was very beautiful. She was not what I had expected to find here in this lowly cott. And she was at least fifteen years the junior of her husband.

"M'lord," she said as she curtsied lower.

"I'm sorry to burst in on you like this," I said. I saw her eyes enlarge; it was not every day the lord of your life came into your cottage and apologised for the intrusion. "I have a few more questions for Mistress Lea. Are you able to answer me, mistress?"

Ellen Lea turned her red face towards me and sniffed. "Yessir," she said.

"You heard no commotion behind your cottage the night your husband disappeared?"

"No, sir."

"Why would he go that way? Why would he be behind the cottage? Surely he would approach from the front and come to the door?"

"I don't know, sir."

Mistress Cottar came and rested her hands on Ellen Lea's shoulders.

"Bordern kept a few things in the shed at the rear, my lord. He might have gone in there to store something and been surprised. My husband tells us that he is dead of a head wound. Perhaps the murderer struck him as he left the shed."

"We shall naturally search the shed," I said. "Ellen, ten days ago was anyone with your husband at the back of the shed at any time that morning?"

She shook her head.

"But sir, it cannot have been so, for we all saw Bordern that day with the cattle. He *must* have been killed as he came home," said Cottar. "Later."

"Hmmm. None spoke to him as he came home, Mistress Lea?"

She looked up at me puzzled. "He didn't come home, sir."

"The snow. Hal, when did it last snow so that the man may have been covered by it?"

"Well, we've 'ad bits almost every day for a week and thaws in between. If 'es bin there ten days, he's bin snowed on a few times and then when the thaw came the roof slid on 'im too."

"You have no cause to go to the back of your cott, mistress?"

"Not to that bit sir, no," she wailed. "I don't go there only into the shed."

"If the weather had been warmer," said Hal, "'e mighta stunk 'igher than a dead mole on 'is 'ill. We'd of found 'im then, right enough."

I shook my head. "What I can't understand is, why leave him there? Right by his home."

Mistress Lea cried louder.

"You are sure, mistress, that you can tell me nothing more? For example, where is his cloak, his stick and his sack?"

She shook her head. "I don't know. To think he's been there all the time... Oh Bordern!"

"And before you ask, sir," said Alwyn, "I have no need to walk that way either. There's no track into the forest that way."

"Master Mount's cottage is further along. He too would see nothing?"

"No, sir."

"Thank you for your help. The coroner will come and look at the body. You will have to answer his questions. I have asked my friend Doctor Johannes of Salerno to come and look at the corpse. He will study it and help to decide how Bordern met his end. Meanwhile no one must touch the body or move it. If you do, you will be fined. Do I make myself clear?"

They all nodded.

"You may cover the body with a cloth and keep a watch against animals but that is all."

I made for the door. "I may need to talk to you all again." We left them staring at each other in shock.

Back at the little shed, we opened the door. It stuck on the beaten earth floor and stuttered and squeaked as we pulled it, much as it had when Hayward had opened it. That would certainly have been heard from the cottage, I thought.

Inside the shed was some wood, a small tub which I judged contained cider to only a third full, a few old cloths covering some wizened apples in a wooden box, a ladder and some pottery jars of preserves laid down for the winter. Amongst the stored tools was nothing we could judge which might have made the wound received by Bordern Lea. Nothing here was out of place or odd. Hal returned the shovel to its home leaning

18

up against the wall.

"I think we shall return to Durley, Hal. We can do no more here. The coroner will be told you are the first finder and he'll have to seek you out at home. Johannes will come when he has time. We cannot hang about in the cold waiting for him."

We mounted our horses and made for home.

*****

The sun was setting late that afternoon as Dr. Johannes of Salerno came clopping into the courtyard having been to the little glade in the forest to look at the corpse. Johannes was family for I had married his niece Lydia who had been the widow of the lord of Wolvercote near Oxford. The coroner Sir Hugo Ramsbury had not yet arrived, he said, but as usual he had made notes about the murder which he would share with him.

Johannes was a tall man, muscular, for one who was not a fighting man; though I know he had once wielded a sword, for he had been out in the Holy Land on crusade with our last King, Richard Plantagenet. He had shoulder length brown hair, now greying a little at the temples, scrupulously clean and shining, which he often wore tied back in a queue. He was clean shaven, unlike me who went with the current fashion for a small clipped beard. His eyes were an amber brown, clear and direct of gaze and he had a fierce intellect.

He had learned his doctoring in Salerno in Sicily, the best school of learning in the world for doctoring, he assured me. Though he had some odd ideas, as far as the rest of the profession believed, he lost fewer patients and cured more people than others could ever hope to send their bills to. Not only this, but he had learned his surgeon's craft on the field of battle and under one of the acolytes of the famous surgeon Rogerius of Salerno. Cleanliness and orderliness was paramount to Johannes. He had been born in Oxford of a parchment maker and a seamstress but, upon his return from Italy, finding it hard to pursue doctoring in his hometown had packed his bags, changed his name to honour the place in which he had studied and fetched up here in Marlborough. We were most glad he had.

Johannes shook the slush from his boots and pulled them off, helped by Peter, the sixteen year old son of my senior wood warden John Brenthall, and from his pack he picked out some soft soled felt ankle boots and donned them. Peter set his riding boots to dry on the hearth.

Now sitting before the fire in the hall he told me what he had discovered.

"I found no other wound but that dreadful gouge to the man's eye, Aumary," he said, warming his hands over the flames. "No disabling wound to the back of the head. No other bruising, no other knife wound. I made a search, as no doubt did you, but I could find no weapon. Nothing underneath him."

"What kind of weapon made that terrible wound Johannes? I asked. "Some sort of thin knife?"

"A weapon wielded with deadly accuracy. The point entered the eyeball and punctured it, travelled back and into the brain. The man will not have known what had happened to him."

"Dead in a blink then?" said Hal offering Johannes a beaker of warmed wine.

"I measured the length of it; the wound."

"Ah yes, with one of your little metal probes?" I had seen Johannes at work with one of these before. He often inserted it into a wound to ascertain the size of the weapon used—the width of the blade, the depth of the wound.

"And?"

"Well, it's an odd wound but as I say the point goes back into the brain a full four inches. The blade is quite narrow at the tip and widens. I would say we are looking for a knife two inches in width at its widest part."

"The ice has made the job of working out when the man was killed very difficult has it not?" I asked.

Johannes shrugged. "Ten days you say he was missing? Then I would guess that he was killed ten days ago. There has been no putrefaction as there would be with a body lying in the open at another time of the year. I've noticed before that bodies which lie in ice or snow do not rot, though I have no idea why."

"The trail, forgive me, is cold then," I said with half a smile. "No footprints, nothing clasped in the man's hand as we have had before?"

"No motive, sir," said Hal "Your *cui bonies*—who might 'ave a reason to kill the man."

A long time ago my deceased brother's tutor, a Master Quimper, had debated with me about the Roman philosophers of old. He was a very learned man and he told me about a lawyer called Cicero who, when defending a man in court had come up with the phrase '*cui bono*'—who benefits. Who has a motive for a crime? It was a phrase that was used either to suggest a hidden motive or to indicate that the party responsible for something might not be who it appears to be, at first.

"As yet we do not know if the man had enemies who might seek to destroy him. We must ask those who knew him. Why might someone wish to kill a simple cowman?"

"It's certainly not for money," said Hal.

"No, they are a poor sort. Though might we be right in thinking that he was robbed for he has no scrip, no weapon and no cloak with him?"

"Right by 'is 'ouse sir? That's a mite dangerous."

"Hmm. I remember I asked you before Hal, a few years ago and I shall ask you again, what makes a man murder? Why might someone plunge a knife into the eye of another?"

"If you want to kill someone and be sure about it, you don't go trying to 'it 'im in the eye, sir. Most inaccurate way a goin' about it. Knife in the guts or up into the 'eart if you can."

"Or as we've seen before, a knife wiped across the throat from behind," said Johannes.

"An 'eavy object like a branch and struck from behind?"

"Hmmm."

"As to why? Well, folk kill for money. There's no doubt 'e didn't 'ave much of that. Land, he didn't 'ave any of that either. A woman?" added Hal.

"Ah, jealousy?" said Johannes.

"Looking at 'is missus sir, I don't think anyone wanted to get rid of 'im to get their 'ands on 'er!"

"Ah! Ahem... no Hal!"

"And by all accounts they were a devoted couple. I can't see her

21

looking at anyone else. Besides..." said Hal.

"She is with child, yes."

We sat in silence for a moment, the flames crackling in the fire.

"It cannot have been an accident Johannes? Is there some way he might have stumbled onto something, been pierced and... Ah no." I finished as I saw my friend's face.

"If that was what happened then we would have found the offending article there, behind the cottage," said Johannes.

The fire spat and spluttered. Holdfast my little white gazehound lying at my feet, twitched in her sleep in front of the flames.

"There is one thing., said Johannes.

"Oh?"

"I have a feeling the body was moved."

I sat up straighter. "Oh?"

"There is no blood at the site, well very little. Blood would have pooled into the snow where he lay. The man was lying tidily on his back with his arms to the side as if someone had placed him there."

"Ah! I knew something had bothered me about how he was found," I said, slapping my knee.

Hal looked up at the rafters. "No man I've ever seen stabbed has fallen so tidily—so tidy they don't have to set 'im straight for his windin' sheet.' "

"He was dragged, I think," said Johannes.

"Dragged from where?"

"Ah, that I can't say, for the ground is so hard and covered in snow and slush that all traces will have disappeared."

"So how do you know he was dragged?"

Johannes smiled. "His tunic and belt was pulled up to his arm pits at the rear and not straightened again. He was dragged by the feet into that corner."

I sighed. "Why did I not see that? I knew there was something strange...."

"I suspect you didn't move the body as I did to examine it."

"Nah we just dug 'im out," said Hal.

"So killed elsewhere and dumped there. Why?"

Johannes shrugged. He drained his pot.

"I can't say," he said. "Is there anything to eat....I'm starving?"

*****

On the next day I rode out with Hal to examine the barn where some of my cattle overwintered at Luton Lye. I had several barns like this scattered about the forest glades and in the meadows close to the River Kennet.

The forest was not just a thing of trees as far as the eye could see. Savernake was made up of glades and meadows, bogs and small river beds, coppices which had been managed for the wood and shrubby heath left much to its own devices. Commoners grazed their animals on the lush pastures.

Here was a glade of several large meadows where, in spring and summer, grazed my little red cattle.

A few of the best beasts remained now to breed. The rest had been killed and salted down for the winter, their hides sold to the town for the leather trade. The remaining beasts shuffled about in their stalls, their breath steaming in the cold air. Two men were raking out the old straw from the ground under their hooves and piling it close by the barn. Soon, we hoped they would come out onto the fresh grass of the pasture.

"Ho, Cottar!" I shouted.

"Ah m'lord, it's you," said my cowman tugging his forelock. "This is John Mount, sir."

Mount turned and leaned on his rake.

"Yes...I remember you, Mount."

"Aye, m'lord," he said, wiping his nose on his grubby sleeve. He was a young man of middling height with light brown thinning hair and a short, straggly beard. I looked him over. His right leg was twisted and the foot pointed inwards much more than was normal. I supposed his leg had been broken and imperfectly set.

He bowed low. "Very sad about poor Bordern, my lord," he said.

"You both saw him on that last day?"

"We did, my lord," said Mount. "I stayed behind that night, 'twas not my turn but I'm not married and I let the others go home early to

23

their wives."

Alwyn Cottar put his arm over Mount's shoulder. "He's a good man, sir, is John."

"I've no doubt. You saw Lea stride out for home?"

"Aye, we both did."

"Tell me, had he a cloak, a scrip, a stick upon which to lean?"

They looked at each other their brows lined in thought. "Aye, no man would go out without a cloak that day. It were dammity cold," said Cottar.

"And only a fool would take no stick sir... in that snow," added Mount.

"What did he carry... anything?"

Mount turned to his work again. "Nothing I can remember, my lord."

"His purse hung from his belt sir," said Alwyn Cottar, "but no, he carried nothing... Ah except his old dinner sack."

I nodded. "I'll leave you to your work." I turned to the outside and breathed in the cool air of the day.

"Anything you can see, Hal?" I asked.

Hal was scanning the glade with practiced and narrowed eyes. "Three paths. The one by which we entered the glade, from Durley. The one which the men take for 'ome which goes to Braydon and the one which winds down the 'ill to Milden'all."

"All of them searched?"

"Just the one from here to the Braydon Oak, sir."

"So we must search the other two roads."

"He can't have gone that way...."

"Ah no, but someone may have *come* that way and followed him. Or seen him."

"Bit late, sir. We'd not find anything so late."

"Nevertheless we shall make a search and question folk along the way."

I went back into the barn. "Who else knew Bordern Lea, Alwyn, John? You three lived together in the same glade but who else do you see regularly?"

"The Haywarden, sir," said John, flinging his burden of dung onto the pile outside the door.

"Bouvery, sir," said Alwyn.

"Ah, one of the cowmen from Red Vein bottom?"

"He comes now and again. Kineman used to come before he got killed sir... and of course Wilkin Chetel, he comes too."

"Another herdsman?"

"Yessir. We see the riding foresters and the walking ones."

"We see some of the woodsmen of course, about their business," said Mount.

"Master John Brenthall, and the like," said Alwyn Cottar. "We exchanges the time o' day with them."

"We don't see too many folks here," said John.

"All of you tied men. All of you, my cattle men, are serfs." I said almost under my breath. This meant that they were tied to the land upon which they lived and worked, my land and must have my permission to travel elsewhere. "Some of you farm hereabouts too?"

"Aye, sir. We have fields out there." John Mount threw his hand in a northerly direction. "That's where most of the womenfolk hereabouts are to be found."

"We'll soon be spreading this lot on the strips. We'll be out next with the ploughing," said Cottar, smiling.

"Of course if we were up on the downs, it would be the lambing which would be taking up our time now," chuckled Alwyn, scuffing up the earth of the stall which was now devoid of straw and dung. "Some of us are blessed with a few sheep too."

"Some of us have a few beasts around and about," said Mount. "We all pull together to make it work. It's a case of all the neighbours lending their muscles to..."

"I know. Yes..."

"And now we're one good man short," he added, looking me in the eye.

I cleared my throat. "Tell me and speak truthfully, was there anyone with whom Bordern was at loggerheads? Was there anyone with whom he had quarrelled or who bore him ill will?"

Mount leaned on his rake again. "Bordern, my lord? Nah," he chuckled. "Not Bordern."

"Cottar?"

"No, sir. Bordern wasn't the arguing kind. He was a mild man, content with his lot, his home, his wife and his cows. He had no enemies, sir."

"Every man 'as enemies," said Hal folding his arms over his chest. "No man living can be liked by every man 'e meets."

The two cowmen shared a look.

"He was generally liked. Though like I say, we don't see too many folk hereabouts," said Mount, "and well, you asked us to be truthful, sir." Mount looked sidelong at his companion. "We are generally kept so busy, my lord, we don't have time for quarrels and arguments."

I stared at him. He stared back.

"I am very glad to hear it," I said at last.

I joined Hal at our horses.

"Hmm. Something funny there," he said.

I looked back at the two men working in the barn.

"It was more in what they *didn't* say than what they did say, Hal."

"They were lyin' or I'll pull out me own teeth!"

I just had time to chuckle before a scream rang out and echoed round the glade.

"The side of the barn..." said Hal, dropping Grafton's reins.

We ran around the end of the building as the two cow men rushed from their work inside.

There was Mistress Lea, her face white and horrified, pointing at the side door which was closed.

"Whatever's the matter, Ellen?" cried Alwyn, dropping his fork. "Have you walked all this way?"

The woman staggered and pointed further. Her voice was shaky and weak with shock. "The cross... The cross... it's gone!"

"What...?"

Both cowmen looked to where she pointed. It took me a while to work out what she was saying and I too looked above the small door of the barn.

Alwyn Cottar came up and took the woman in his arms, turning her away.

"It's fallen off, that's all, in the snow. We shall find it on the ground."

"The devil has it..."

26

"How can the devil have it?" asked Mount. "It's been blessed by the priest. The devil wouldn't dare touch it."

"The devil I tell you...that's why these awful things have happened."

Hal stepped forward. "Mind tellin' us what's missin'?"

Alwyn hugged Mistress Lea to his chest.

"Every year we have a cross made of spent candle wax and the priest of Cadley..."

"Father Justin?" I asked.

"The same, sir, he blesses it for us. It keeps our barns and houses safe."

I came forward and scuffed up the melting snow. "I can't see it."

"The devil...the devil..."

"Hush now Ellen, it will do you no good to fret so. What were you doing here anyway? You should be in the house place with Freya, not wandering around the forest."

"She..."

"Never mind... let's go back." He looked up to me, "I shall take her back, sir. If you have finished with us that is?"

"Aye for the moment," I said.

*****

As I sat long that evening over my wine in my little office off the screens passage and thought about the murder of Bordern Lea, I vowed to ask about and see how much more information I could gather about the man and his lonely life out in Braydon and his work at Luton Lye and elsewhere.

He frequented the church at Cadley, his nearest place of worship. Perhaps the priest there, Father Justin, would know something about him.

Little Father Justin was round and cheery and he made the sign of the cross over me as I approached him the next morning. "God's greeting to you, my Lord Belvoir. What brings you to my little abode?"

"For one thing Justin, I am come to see how well the building of the new church is going?"

"We have no complaints, m'lord," he said. "It goes. Of course as you know we had to move it but... the building progresses."

27

I looked over the flattened ground between the man's little house and the new church building, rising fifty yards away from the site of the old church destroyed by fire almost a year ago.

The ground where the little wooden Saxon church once sat was growing now with dog's mercury, cleavers, nettles and all those grasses which had instantly sprung up from the barren ground where we had filled in the pit.

"Ah yes, not long now to completion, I think."

"Come in, sir and take some ale with me. I have a feeling that you have not just come to talk about the building works."

"No indeed. You will have heard," I said, as we walked to his humble one-roomed cottage, "that the body of Bordern Lea was found yesterday, buried under snow at the back of his cottage."

Father Justin crossed himself. "Aye, I'd heard it. News like that flies like fire across dry bracken, Sir Aumary."

"It's murder, sir priest, and I am investigating as is my responsibility. The man was one of my herdsmen. I was wondering if you could tell me aught about this Lea and his wife."

Father Justin opened the door to his house and ushered me inside.

"They are my parishioners, it's true. I haven't seen the wife for some weeks. The snow has no doubt kept them at home and her condition..."

"Yes, I know."

"The woman is a creature of good habits, I hear. Quiet, obedient, diligent. One who keeps a tidy house and looks after her husband well."

"They have no children... no other children?"

"God has seen fit to give them no offspring who survive my lord, though they have been married nine years I think."

"Ah, I see."

"Of course we have no church at present and so church services here are held in the churchyard."

"I understand but can you tell me what the man was like when you did meet him at church, Father?"

Father Justin made a moue. "A man like any other. Hard working, quiet, a slow man in thought and deed."

"Enemies?"

"Oh no. I doubt it."

"Have you any idea why he might have been killed, father?"

Father Justin sat slowly at his table shaking his head and poured some ale into two beakers. "It was not robbery, then?"

"Robbery?"

"I heard that his cloak and purse are missing."

"There are no masterless men in the forest, sir priest. I do not allow it. My foresters are out in the trees every day. I would know if we had any outlaws roaming the woods."

"But sir, this past month? Perhaps a man with wickedness in his mind and evil in his heart has come into the forest and since your men have been unable to go about their normal duties?"

"You believe they have failed to find him, arrest him or drive him out, because of the snow?"

"Just so, sir."

"I think he might have been noticed by the other inhabitants, Justin. A man like that steals where he can. No other man has come to me with tales of food, livestock or possessions gone missing."

"Hmm."

"So you say, as does everyone else, that Bordern Lea was a popular man and that..."

"Oh no, sir. I didn't say he was popular. Well..."

"Come Justin, what are you saying?"

"The seal of the confessional, my lord. I cannot, as you know, break it." He looked up at me from under his dark brows. "I cannot tell you what I know but I'm sure someone else will."

"I have already met the stone wall that is his fellow cowmen."

Justin nodded. "They are a close knit lot."

I rubbed my forehead distractedly. "So, who might I speak to who will tell the truth about Bordern Lea?"

Father Justin shook his head.

"His sins are known by one or two. Dig sir and I am sure you'll find what you need. I fear, however, that it will not help you find his murderer."

"Oh...?" I sat down at his table. "Tell me, how did the man look? What were his traits? All I have seen is a frozen corpse and I cannot for the life of me come upon a picture of the living man in my mind." I took a sip of ale.

Justin smiled. "A man straight of back and wide of shoulder. Long brown hair to the neck in the Saxon fashion. Brown eyes with a look in them that was like a dog sir, docile and dependable. Good skin and teeth." Father Justin stopped to think. "Tanned with wind and weather but not unpleasantly so."

"How old?"

"Thirty or thereabouts I believe."

"Hmm. Still a relatively young man then?"

"Yes, and a young man good to look upon or so I'm told." Father Justin cackled. "But what would I know, eh?"

I smiled. "I'm told he was a happy man."

"As happy as any under Heaven I think. He was not one who sought riches or advancement. I would say sir that ... well... Bordern was a rather dull man. He was one without ambition. He knew his place in the world."

"Dull?"

"He was a man who on the outside looked full of God's beauty m'lord but on the inside, he was quite, erm... well..."

"Slow-witted?"

"Oh no, sir—not in that way—just boringly dull."

"And dull men do not get murdered, is that what you are saying, Justin?"

Father Justin put down his ale pot.

"That he was not interesting enough to have someone murder him?" I added.

The priest looked me in the eye.

"No one who knew him well could wish him harm. He was simply...."

"Not worth murdering? That's a strange thing to say, sir priest."

Father Justin shrugged. "I think my lord you are looking for an outsider. Someone who killed him for the cloak on his back and the money in his purse."

I stood and replaced my riding gloves.

"Thank you Father. Good luck with the church. God keep you."

Why was it that everyone seemed to be obstructing me?

*****

I returned home that afternoon and went straight up to the solar to see my wife and my children. Lydia was in the room sewing. I pecked her on the cheek and she looked up at me with tired violet blue eyes.

"I'd go and lie down for a while if I were you," I said. "The sewing can wait. Get Felice to do it. You look exhausted."

"No, it's alright. It's just the feeding of Phillip. And I have been watching him..."

"He's not as greedy as Simon was. That's all."

"No," chuckled Lydia, "but he simply does not move."

"And that keeps you awake? He suckles well?"

"Oh yes. But I watch him and I listen for the little grunts and mewls which babies make and so I can't sleep for thinking that, that he..."

"Oh Lydia! He's simply not a bawler for feeding like Simon."

"I keep listening and looking at him for fear he has died. He's so quiet."

I smiled and patted her shoulder.

"He is fine I'm sure. Look, I'll go down to the hall to give you some peace. You rest here." And I jogged down the stairs again.

*****

Hal and Simon, my elder son, were playing on the hall table with some wooden soldiers which Hal had carved over the winter. I joined in the game for a while until Felice came to take Simon away for his afternoon rest.

Hawise, my daughter, I was told, was in the kitchen with Matthew Cook and Agnes Brenthall. Heavens only knows what she was up to.

I sat at the hall table with Hal and we chewed over the fat over what I had learned at Cadley.

"So in conclusion Hal, there is no reason I can think of why Bordern Lea should have been poked in the eye."

"That puzzles me, sir."

"What does?"

"The eye.... well.... Why the eye?"

"And what do you think, old Hal?"

"It's as I've said an odd way to kill someone. Not easy to do. Is it maybe kinda symbolic somehow?"

"You mean that the eye was targeted because he saw something?"

"That's it, sir."

"What can he possibly have seen?"

"Hmmm."

"By all accounts he was a rather dull man. I doubt if he did see something untoward he would make anything of it."

"They all tell you 'e had few friends. Went to 'is work in the cattle barns and the meadows, farmed his plot, came 'ome to 'is wife and went to church. That's all. So it must be something in that dull life which got 'im killed."

"Hmmm."

Try as we might, we simply could not come to any conclusion about the death of Bordern Lea.

Until a while later.

I remember it began the day that Lydia was churched so it was a month or so after Phillip was born, Paul my scribe.

We were walking back from the church in the village after giving thanks for Lydia being safely delivered of our son and from the churching of my wife. We chanced to meet the midwife Aolfe walking hurriedly through the village on her way to a birthing.

Good wishes and a little gossip were exchanged.

She was on her way, she said, to Mistress Lea for she was about to give birth in her little cottage in the glade at Braydon and being a woman alone with few female neighbours Aolfe was asked for specially.

She walked back that evening and met Agnes who was told that the woman had been delivered of a girl child and all was well.

Five days later in the late afternoon a man came panting into the manor courtyard.

I looked up from the work I was checking in Hubert Alder's forge;

a pair of sluice gates which I had commissioned from the blacksmith and my wood worker Alfred. This was to dam the small river which ran through Durley and which joined with the River Og further on in the forest.

Artor Hayward had left his small pony outside the gates and had run into the courtyard. I heard my name called loudly.

Poking my head out of the smithy door I hailed the man.

"Oh my lord!" he yelled "Calamity sir. My Lord Belvoir!"

"Whatever is it, Hayward? Has the devil been seen in Savernake?"

"The devil is about his work in the forest, certainly," he stuttered. He screwed up his coif and mopped his forehead with it. "Another body sir."

"Another murder, Hayward?"

"Aye sir... Oh it's too awful to contemplate."

"Come up to the hall and tell us."

Hal had now been alerted and was striding from his room in the south range towards the smithy. He shepherded the perspiring and muttering man up the steps and into the hall. A few people were there, Lydia, Agnes, Father Crispin and John Brenthall and the kitchen girl who was about to take some dishes down the stairs after dinner.

"What has happened, Hayward?"

"Terrible sir... just terrible. The head all mangled. Must have been blow after blow. Found by the stream. No doubt killed fetching the day's water."

"Who Artor? Please tell us who has been killed."

"Didn't I say, sir? Oh, it's Mistress Cottar, sir. Freya Cottar, Alwyn Cottar's wife. She's dead. Dead as yesterday's dinner, sir!"

There was absolute silence in the hall.

Then the kitchen girl Maud screamed and there was a clatter of plates and beakers.

Chapter Three

Hal jumped up and caught the girl as she fell and gently laid her down. Agnes went straight down to her knees before her. Father Crispin prevented the crockery from rolling about further and picked up the wooden tray.

"Maudie... Maudie... Oh dear. It's her sister isn't it? Freya is Maud's sister," said Agnes.

I pictured the lovely young woman I'd seen at my herdsman's house; her angelic face, her glorious copper hair.

"There's no resemblance I can see, are you sure?" I said coming up to the three of them on the floor as the girl began to stir from her faint. I looked at the mousey hair, the thin features and snub nose of Maud the thirteen year old kitchen girl.

"Well, half-sister really. Freya's mother was Aelfiva of Cadley, sir. Their da married again. Maud's ma is Cicely Swyre."

"Ah yes. I remember now."

Maud shook her head and moaned. "I feel sick, mistress," she said to Agnes.

Hal picked her up and sat her down on a bench. "Just you take in some deep breaths Maudie and we'll get you a drink of ale."

"I don't want no ale. I...." She started to sob and retch.

"I think she should go home, Agnes," I said. "It's been a great shock."

Agnes looked to Lydia.

"Yes, take her home," said my wife. "It's late now and she would be going home soon anyway. Her father will have to know that his eldest daughter is dead."

"I'll take her sir," said John. "It's not far."

I nodded as my chief wood warden put his arm around the weeping girl and ushered her out of the hall and down the steps. I heard the outer door close.

I sat down heavily on a bench and exhaled loudly. "Well! You had better tell us the story, Artor," I said. "From the beginning."

Artor Hayward ran a shaking hand across his brow and through his thinning hair.

"I can't tell you very much my lord but what I do know is that as the sun was beginning to dip over the forest this afternoon, Alwyn, Alwyn Cottar came running up to my cottage. He was in such a state, sir. Such a state..."

"In what way, Hayward?"

"Disordered and blabbering, bloodied and shaking. Shaking, sir."

"It was he who found his wife?"

"Yes, sir. He got home this afternoon and found the fire cold on the hearth with no warm supper in the pot. The pottage was prepared on the table but it hadn't been cooked, sir. That was most unusual, most unusual."

"What did he do?"

"He looked round—well his house isn't a small one as you know, sir—and he could not find his wife anywhere about."

"He searched the barns and outbuildings?"

"Yessir." Hal handed the shaking man a pot of warmed ale and he gratefully upended it with two hands. It was hot and he slurped it carefully and, wiping his mouth with the back of his hand, he carried on.

"He went back into his cott to wait a short while wondering if she had been delayed somewhere and then he tells me he thought to go to Mistress Lea to see if she had seen Freya."

"Had she?"

"No, sir. Not all day."

"Did she not think that was odd?"

"Odd it was, sir, for Freya had been in and out since the babby had come—well you know what these women are like."

I saw Lydia give a small smile and look down at her hands.

"They can't keep away when there's babbies to be looked at, especially if they don't have none themselves."

"So Mistress Lea wondered where Alwyn's wife had gone because she hadn't seen her?"

"Yessir. Ellen said that Freya was a good friend to her what with her being alone now and all." Hayward coughed as he finished his ale in one huge gulp, gasping at the heat of it.

"Then Alwyn thought to get himself a drink of water for he was sore thirsty with worry and with racing around. There was no ale see. No ale."

"Yes?"

"The water barrel was empty sir. His missus normally filled it in the morning if things were running low. The big pail she took to the river was gone and there was no water. No water at all."

"So Alwyn went out to look for the pail and his wife, by the river?"

"Yes sir he did. He did."

"And sadly he found her?"

"Aye sir. Her head bashed in so as her pretty face was all...."

"Yes, Artor. We can imagine. Thank you. We shall go out to Braydon tomorrow early and speak with everyone."

"Thank you, sir."

"We shall also inform the coroner and the doctor. The priest too will have to go there. The body must not be moved..."

I saw my haywarden's face and stopped. "You have left the body where it lay?"

"Well, no, sir. It were half in the water—and of course when Alwyn saw Freya there he pulled her out and..."

"I see. Well, that can't be helped. Let no man go down to the river until I get there tomorrow. Leave everything as it is. You may keep a watch on the body but touch nothing and do not go near it only to cover it perhaps. Get the priest of Cadley to go and make her soul safe."

"All that's been done, sir. I thought to do it."

"Where is Cottar now?"

"At my house, sir. When he'd done blubbering and shaking and telling me between sobs sir, he just sat and stared at the wall. I can't get any sense out of him. It's like he's a deaf and blind man, sir. Marion my wife, she's tried to get to him but it's like he's behind a wall and he can't see or hear us."

"Shock," said Hal with authority. We all looked up at him. "Dr. Johannes says that's what 'appens in shock."

"Who else is at home? Your sons?" I asked.

"Yes sir."

"Will you stay here the night and travel back with us tomorrow?"

Hayward looked up out of my hall window. It was fully dark now.

"I should go home, sir, by rights...I don't like to leave the wife with all this misfortune....and Alwyn will be there still. I should..."

"Go then with care. We'll see you tomorrow. God keep you in his hand."

Artor wiped his coif over his sweating face again and nodded. He began to back out of the room. "Thank you, sir. Thank you. God keep you too."

Hal closed the hall door after him and we heard in the ensuing silence the man's voice boom into the echoing screens passage. 'The devil... the devil is about in the forest...' then we heard first, his quick running tread across the courtyard and then the clop of his pony's hooves as he returned to Cadley.

Lydia looked up at me with her beautiful violet blue eyes. "What *is* going on, Aumary?" she asked.

I came to the chair on which she sat and took her hand. "I don't know. Two people who have nothing in their ordinary lives which might be considered extraordinary—nothing to get them killed—I cannot imagine what, if anything, is the connection."

"The one stabbed, sir. The other bludgeoned," said Hal.

Agnes came forward. "Sir, are we looking for two murderers? God forbid."

I shrugged. "I really do not know, Agnes."

Agnes Brenthall shook her head. "You know, sir. I heard that... No, I mustn't say."

"What have you heard, Agnes?"

"That Freya, the girl who is dead, sir—God hold her in his hand—dropped the mistletoe she was pinning to the door at Christmas. Well, we all know that if the mistletoe touches the ground it loses its power to protect..."

"Oh Agnes, really!"

"No, sir. It's true. She just hung it up again laughing saying it was nonsense."

"It is nonsense," I said. "This death can have nothing whatsoever to do with mistletoe, dropped or not dropped."

"The Lord Aumary's right, Agnes," said Father Crispin. "It can have nothing to do with a flesh and blood person taking a blunt object to Freya Cottar's head."

"She might have been protected if she..."

"Do you really think that Agnes?"

Agnes sighed. "Well....I'm only telling you what I heard."

"Mistletoe drops all the time to the forest floor, Agnes from many an oak tree. It's nothing but a berry," I said. "The birds eat the berries all the time but they do not protect them from the forest falcon, now do they?" I said.

"No, sir. I suppose not."

"Well, we must go out to Braydon tomorrow morning and check on our corpse. I'll write a note to the coroner and to Johannes. Perhaps they will meet us there. Agnes do you think Peter will deliver my note to Johannes early?"

"I'm sure, sir."

"Good. I'll send Bill to Ramsbury tomorrow to the coroner."

Everyone was silent.

The door opened and my blacksmith poked his head around the door. "Sir? Are we finished for the day only Alf and me want to...?"

"Yes, Hubert, for today. Now we are all for our supper."

But few of us could eat much that night.

*****

We looked down at the body of Freya Cottar under her hempen cloth. My eye raked the bank of the small stream. Even though the woman had been moved a short distance, it was possible to see where she had fallen.

" 'Ere," said Hal, bending his back and putting his hands on his knees. "She was leanin' here, I think, and a-bendin' over the water."

"The pail is there, Hal."

Hal leaned out over the stream and grasping onto an overhanging alder branch to steady himself, he hooked the handle of the wooden bucket with his knife in his extended hand and lifted it. "Dropped and it floated out a bit to be stuck there in the gravel."

I stood where the murdered woman had been standing, careful not to obliterate any footprints and mimed the action of dipping the bucket. "So, leaning like this and struck from behind first."

There was a rustling of bushes and Johannes came into view, his medical pack slung over his shoulder.

I straightened. "Good day, Johannes. Thank you for coming. It looks fairly easy to work out how the woman died but, I'd like you to see if there's anything we're likely to have missed."

My friend smiled and stooping pulled the cloth from the body of Freya Cottar. Her head was turned to the right hand side.

He grimaced. "Merciful Jesu!" He slowly put down his pack.

I came to stand beside him. "Aye. Not a thing of beauty though in life, Mistress Cottar was good to look upon."

Johannes hunkered down.

"There's a good deal of hatred in this, Aumary." He lifted what was left of the woman's chin.

"Repeated blows long after the woman was dead—this wasn't accomplished by one or even two blows—there are perhaps five or six, maybe more."

I leaned in. "So there at the back was perhaps the first blow?"

"Causing her to fall forward...."

"And drop 'er pail," added Hal, "where it floated out and was stuck just there."

"And then when she was down, more blows."

"Her head rail is 'ere," said Hal lifting it from the yellowed grasses with the point of his knife. "Close by." The white linen was stained brown-red with blood.

"Footprints here, sir," said John Brenthall, who was the best tracker we had in the forest.

"Aye, John. That's Mistress Cottar's shoe."

"And this one?"

"Master Cottar, I suppose."

"Maybe Master Hayward."

"We shall look at their boots."

Hal started to search the grass and muddy bank and his eyes

narrowed. " 'Ere's another boot all together."

I stood up and went to where he pointed. "Ah yes, a third man stood here."

I turned myself about and took up the position in which the man must have stood. There was something familiar about the pattern of the boot but I passed it by for the moment.

"So, a man stood here in the bushes watching. Did he move forward? Did he pick up a stone and strike the woman repeatedly?"

Hal scoured the ground. "No more footprints."

"None coming closer," added John.

"But that doesn't mean he didn't."

I called to Artor Hayward. "Hayward, where did you stand to view the body when you came with Cottar?"

Hayward came through the riverside bushes. He'd not joined us at first; the sight of Mistress Cottar's body upset him too much, he said.

"Here sir. I think that is my foot. Yes, my foot."

"Put your boot beside it and we shall see."

Hayward carefully placed his boot by the muddy indentation.

"Aye, your print," said Johannes.

"And this one is Master Cottar perhaps?"

"Well, sir, he did stand there but he fell to his knees soon enough and these two small holes are where his boot toes gouged the mud. The second time he came here," said Hayward.

"His wife was not far into the water?"

"No, sir. I came later to the scene but I think that Master Hal has the right of it. Yes, the right of it. She lay there and Alwyn dragged her a little way up. He lifted her head I think as he pulled her up from the water but didn't alter her lying position. No, he didn't."

Johannes turned the body slightly. "See, drag marks here and mud caught on her belt and dress."

There were signs of blood and other matter in the mud closer to the river.

"Have we the weapon used?" asked John.

"We searched the immediate place sir but could find nothing."

Hal's voice came from deeper in the bushes. "Well, you should'a searched a bit further out for 'ere it is, I think."

Johannes and I walked into the tangle of riverside plants. The old plants which had died down at the end of last year were lying at the water's edge, brown and soggy. New plants were springing up from the bank. A large willow tree hung out over the edge of the stream and under it, plants of the riverbank were greening the mud.

"Tossed 'ere, I think," said Hal, "for there don't appear to be any footprints just 'ere."

"Thrown from beside the body...?"

"Quite a way!"

I ran my hands through my curly black hair.

"In anger again, Aumary?" said Johannes.

Hal carefully put the stone into my hand.

I lifted it to my eyes.

Johannes peered at it.

"Yes, blood, skin and hair." He looked down at the woman, "Red hair. It is the weapon used to kill her."

"And a thread or two of her head cloth, Johannes."

He looked further. "Yes...that I think *is* linen."

"Where does it come from, this stone?" My eyes raked the river bank and the waters. "There's none like it here."

"We need to search for its companions, sir," said John.

"Aye we do. If there is no stone here then someone brought it with them and intended to use it."

"Sir?"

"It means that the murderer intended to kill...this was no spur of the moment thing."

I gazed over the scene before me. The water, about twelve to fifteen inches deep, ran over a gravel bed and was clear enough to perfectly reflect the blue sky above us and the dark trunks of the alder and willow trees. There was a slight ruffling breeze and the river burbled on, oblivious to the terror enacted upon its bank. There were no large stones in the water. Soon the pond skaters would be active on the river's surface. Now all was quiet.

"Cottar. Where is he, Hayward?"

"In his house sir. Still he doesn't speak or move."

"We'll try to have some words with him."

We walked back the few hundred yards to the clearing where lay the three cottages and ducked into the first house. Cottar sat on a stool, his hands flat on the table and he stared at the wall.

Mistress Hayward, a short, tubby woman of about thirty five stood by him.

She curtsied. "No change my lord. He is still away in his head."

I nodded. "Cottar. This is the Constable Lord Aumary Belvoir. Can you hear me?"

There was no response.

"He hasn't moved since we fetched him here sir, and he hasn't spoken. He won't eat or drink," said Hayward.

"Cottar. Speak man, tell me what you found."

"I don't think he slept last night either, m'lord," said the woman. "He was on the floor downstairs with us and we were up in our loft. I left the night candle burning and there were a couple of times when I woke and I could see the glint of his open eyes just staring up at the rafters."

Johannes moved forward and made to examine the man. He submitted and did not move, speak nor blink.

"He's docile enough but it's like he's lost himself, sir...just gone," said Hayward.

Johannes straightened. "It's the shock of finding his wife...."

"Or it's guilt..." said Hal folding his arms across his chest.

"Not uncommon," said Johannes again, looking sidelong at Hal.

"Hmmm. Make a search hereabouts for a similar stone Hal."

"Right you are, sir."

"I don't think there's any point in you trying to get some sense from the man for a while, Aumary."

"He will come back anon?"

"He will. It must run its course," said Johannes.

"Can we look at his boots at least?"

Johannes gently lifted the man's foot. I bent to look at the shape and configuration of the sole. It was the sort of boot which moulded to the shape of the wearer's foot. The leather was coarse and was folded over his instep where it was secured with large stitches in the middle. The boots were then threaded with a leather thong and pulled tight around the ankles. His knees were muddy as were the palms of his hands.

"Thank you. There's blood on his tunic?"

Johannes pinched a fold of the red brown material between his fingers.

"He lifted Freya's body, sir. He's bound to be bloodied," said Hayward. "Bound to be."

"Johannes...?"

"Hmmm? Oh yes. Blood on his fingers where he took hold of her head I think. And yes, on his tunic where he wiped them and a little on the sleeve where he passed over her head to fetch her out of the water."

"But not to hit her with a stone from behind...and be in line for the spurting of blood which..."

"No, Aumary. I don't think there's anything like that."

"The person who has done this...they would be covered in blood?"

"Not much blood for the first blow. The front of their tunic would be splattered after the second blow. The sleeves too. Five, six or more blows would spot them here and there, particularly on the chest as blood flicked from the stone and the woman's head. Naturally their hands too would be bloodied. But they can be washed."

"Could a woman do it?"

"A strong woman, yes. But they'd need to have some weight to them."

"Right. We must look for clothes which are bloodstained."

Mistress Hayward looked at me oddly. "He hasn't changed his clothes, sir. He don't have many anyway."

"Those he does have we must examine and the clothes of all who live in this glade and elsewhere close by."

The woman looked at her husband. "Us too sir?"

"Anyone who knew them well, knew both Mistress Cottar and Bordern Lea."

Her eyes widened. "You think the same person killed them both sir?"

"Don't you, mistress?" I asked.

*****

John and Johannes went about looking at clothes. They found none that were bloodstained. Hal searched for stones. I went to speak to John Mount.

I found him in the closest field by the clearing occupied by the three houses. He was moving the thorn hedge gate out and scanning the ground about.

"The cattle come out today, do they, John?" I asked.

John jumped. "Oh, m'lord. I didn't hear you come up. Aye they come out now. The weather is better and there's grass for them."

He bowed. "The cows are in calf sir. They will drop soon. We have one or two who will drop later so our milking can go on further into the year. If you look well to your cows sir, you can keep them milking into next winter."

"Good. I am glad to see that it all goes well."

"You are here about poor Freya, sir?" he said with a long face.

"Yes, I am. Did you see her at all yesterday?"

"No, sir. Not yesterday. I had no cause to speak to her."

"So the first you knew of her death was...?"

"When I heard Artor talking to his wife, sir, last night."

"You saw Cottar?"

"Later at his house today. He wasn't at home last night."

"He stayed with Hayward" I said.

"Ah."

"Did you go to the river yesterday, Mount?"

"The river, sir?"

"Did you fetch water or go there for some other reason?"

"No, sir. Not yesterday."

"You have no wife you say, so you must fetch your own water?"

The man's eyes narrowed. "Yes, sir. But not yesterday."

I walked closer to him. He shifted on his stick.

"Might I look at your boots, Mount?"

"Boots, my lord?"

Hal came up behind me with a stone in his hand. It was, however, not the stone which killed Mistress Cottar.

"Sir, I found these...." I put up my hand to quieten him.

44

"Boots please, Mount."

Mount laid down his stick. His eyes never left my face as he sat on a dry tussock of grass and began to pull off a boot.

"Right boot please, Mount."

He stopped for a fraction of a heartbeat and then moved to his other foot. Off came the brown leather boot which was much the same in construction as Cottar's.

"Hmmm. Your foot turns in, John."

He grimaced. "I broke my leg when I was young ...the lower bone never set properly..."

"Yes. I can see that." I showed the sole to Hal.

"Well, I'll be bugg... bagged like a bird...'tis..."

"You were not by the river yesterday, Mount? How do you account for your footprint being found in the bushes to the rear of where Mistress Cottar met her end?"

John Mount turned pale but didn't speak up.

"We found your footprint. A mark which turns inward with the right foot and a heaviness to the inside of the tread."

"This too, sir."

"Hmmm, Hal?"

"A whole load of them in the plot at the back of his 'ouse."

"Ah, stones similar to that which killed Mistress Cottar, are they?"

"Yessir, made into a little pile like those you'd collect to make a small wall of."

I hefted the stone in my hand. "Were you making a small wall of these flint stones, Mount?"

"Aye, sir."

"And did you pick one up, go down to the river and...?"

"No! No sir!"

"No, you say?"

Mount's lips formed a thin line.

"You have some explaining to do, my lad," I said.

Mount swallowed. He took back his boot, jammed it on his foot and jumped up. "That print might have been made at any time. I often go there."

"You go there but you don't go up to the water's edge? Nah!" said Hal.

"I looked. All up and down the river. There's no more prints of your turned-in right leg. You stood there behind the bushes."

"What are you building at the back of your cott with these, Mount?" I asked, showing him the stone which was jagged on one edge and about six inches long.

"I was going to put them on the top of the cob wall I was making to my vegetable plot. Stop Lea's bloody goat coming in and eating my shoots. I have permission sir."

"The small stones are quite common hereabouts, Mount."

"Aye, sir, they are."

"Not usually as big as this."

"No, sir. Mostly smaller on the surface. Dig and you find the bigger ones."

I stared at the man. There was a frightened flicker in his eye instantly gone. "I wouldn't kill Mistress Cottar sir." He stepped forward a pace.

"Nor Master Lea?"

"No, sir."

"You had no quarrel with him, you say?"

Mount caught his lower lip with his teeth and looked away.

"None, sir."

"And yet his goats eat your crops, Mount?"

Mount laughed. "If that was all it was going to take to make me want to kill him, then I'd be wanting to kill a few others too."

"Ah. Such as?"

Mount scratched his head and disordered his already tousled hair. "Mistress Lea's cat—well it isn't her cat but she pets it—we keep it about to see to the vermin in the barn. It shits in my plot, sir—and I…"

"Ah, I see. And you say you'd no reason to dislike Mistress Cottar?"

The answer came back quickly, too quickly. "No, sir. Why would I? She was a lovely woman."

I walked around him. He shifted uncomfortably.

"The coroner will be here shortly, Mount," I said. "You had better have your story straight before he comes or you might find yourself tied and walking behind the tail of his horse, off to Marlborough gaol."

He turned to look at me, "I've told the truth."

"We shall see what the coroner's jury says.

"So, let's go and speak to Mistress Lea. You Mount, will go to your home and stay there until the coroner arrives."

Lea touched his head and turned, quite nimbly considering the state of his bad leg and limped away.

Johannes and I watched him go.

"Think he's guilty?" he asked.

"Hmmm. I am not sure. He is certainly hiding something."

"He's lyin' sir, lies like a tooth drawer. Or I'm a Welshman," said Hal.

"But lying about what, Hal?"

*****

We walked across the clearing from the field and past the barn. The toe of my boot stubbed against a partly buried stone. I kicked it free of the ground and then dug it out with my fingers. I then examined it and with my hand against my forehead to shield my eyes from the sun, I looked over the ground round about.

"Show me this pile of stone, Hal."

We walked round the edge of John Mount's cottage just as he disappeared inside.

"There, sir."

"Hmm." My gaze circled the garden. "Now let's go to Mistress Lea's."

Hal made for the door of her cott but I carried on walking to the small plot beside it.

"These stones are as plentiful in this glade as fleas on a beggar, Hal. Look."

In the corner of the garden plot was a pile of stones.

"Looks like they bin takin' them out of the ground when they dig and they just throw them in a pile, sir. Everyone has a pile it seems."

"Exactly, and not just Mount." I dropped my stone on the top of the pile. "C'mon."

We scratched on the door of Mistress Lea's cottage. There was some scrabbling inside and a voice said, "A moment."

The woman came at last and opened the door. "Forgive me, my lord. I was feeding the babe." She was ordering her kirtle about her body.

I looked towards the centre of the room where a sheepskin lay on the floor by the fire. On it was placed a very small swaddled baby.

"Mistress Lea, might we ask you some questions about your neighbour, Freya Cottar?"

"I can't tell you anything, sir. I didn't see her yesterday."

"But she has been to see you upon every other day, mistress? Did you not think it strange that she failed to visit you yesterday?"

Ellen Lea wrung her hands before her. "Well yes, I did and so I walked over to her cott and called out to her. I opened the door and looked in. She wasn't at home."

"What time of the day was this, madam?"

"It was the morning, sir. The sun had been up a while but the day was still cold. My breath streamed out before me and the sun had not yet warmed the air."

"You expected her early?"

"She usually came early."

"Did you see anyone else?"

"No one, my lord."

"You heard nothing?"

"No, sir. When I realised that Freya was not in the glade, I walked home again."

"Tell me, Mistress Lea, did you leave your child at home when you walked to her cottage?"

"Yes, sir. Tilda was asleep on her sheepskin. Much as she is now and so I left her for a short while."

I nodded.

"Oh my lord. Whatever is happening in this village? It used to be such a happy place, so happy and now? It's evil... evil."

"You can think of no reason why Mistress Cottar should be killed in this way?"

"Artor tells me she was struck on the head with a stone, my lord. Is this right?"

"When did you hear this?"

"I heard him speaking when he told his wife and John Mount, my neighbour this afternoon. Some wicked, wicked person is coming into the glade and killing us one by one. Ooh..." Mistress Lea began to sob, "I may be next."

"You have no idea why this little cluster of houses should be so targeted, mistress?"

"Red hair, sir. Red hair. It's always a bad thing."

"I beg your pardon?"

"A red haired woman first thing in the morning betokens something unlucky befalling the beholder during the day." The woman's eyes grew huge. "*The rede mon he is a quet for he wole the thin uvil red.*"

I folded my arms over my chest. "The red haired man...?"

"Or woman... is a wicked one for they will give you ill-counsel. That is a proverb of Alfred, our Saxon king," said Mistress Lea, her face serious.

"Come, mistress, you don't believe this. It's nonsense. The woman Freya, you say, was your friend."

"Aye she was... but... we all know that red hair is unlucky. Many believe it so."

"It was unlucky for her," said Hal under his breath.

"How long had Mistress Freya lived here, Ellen?" I said, the annoyance in my voice making Hal raise his eyebrow and look at me askance. My first wife had had red hair and my daughter Hawise had inherited it.

"Three months or so. They were married in January. Just after Christmas—a bad time to marry."

I sighed. "Where did she live before her marriage to Alwyn Cottar?"

"Henset, sir, I believe."

This was a very small village in the forest not quite two miles from Braydon.

"Have you a family locally to whom you can go, Ellen?"

The woman crossed herself. "You think, my lord that we are in danger?"

"In truth I don't know. Best that you have folk around you. If you can go to your family...better still."

"My folk are in Cadley, sir."

"Then pack up anything you don't wish to lose, mistress and go. You

49

have my permission to leave your home, until the danger is past."

An unfathomable expression flitted across the woman's face.

"Lord above! God Almighty save us from the devil," she said, crossing herself vigorously.

"God's peace on you," I said, turning away.

I muttered disagreeably under my breath as we walked back to Cottar's house.

Johannes was there waiting for us at the door.

"Hayward, I want you to stay here with Cottar until he regains his wits. I have told Mistress Lea that it's wise for her to go to her family in Cadley."

"Mount, sir?"

"He is a young man and will be much on his guard. If the coroner is satisfied with his words then he will not be marched off to the castle. I think he will be safe."

"If not, sir?"

"Then he will be safe in the gaol at Marlborough."

Mistress Hayward came forward. "John Mount is not the culprit sir. I know it."

"Marion," said Hayward with a warning note in his voice.

"Well, Master Hayward," she said to her husband truculently, "it will do no harm to tell the truth."

"Be quiet, woman."

"And what truth is that, madam?" I asked.

Marion Hayward looked at her husband and opened and closed her mouth like a stranded fish.

Artor Hayward hissed at her.

"No, Artor, I *will* speak. Mount would not have harmed a hair on the head of that girl, my lord."

"Why's that?"

Artor Hayward continued to whisper to his wife. "You don't say anything, hear me."

"Because, my Lord Belvoir, he loved her with all his heart, that's what," she said and she folded her arms under her ample bosom with a jiggle.

"Aw!" said Hayward in annoyance.

Chapter Four

Yes, Paul, you're right, our suspects are dwindling... it was a small community, even if we added those who lived and worked further out in the forest. However, we are about to add one or two new people to our tale.

I rode home quietly thinking about what Mistress Hayward had told us. John Mount and Freya of Henset as she was then, had been childhood sweethearts. It was expected that they would marry one day. However Freya's father had other ideas and he prevailed upon the girl to marry Cottar. Alwyn was more wealthy and had better prospects, he said.

Sometimes people, especially those from the town, find it difficult to understand the complexities of our rural life. They imagine that all villeins are poor and live frugally in their one roomed cottages, eking out a thin existence with no chance of betterment. Not so. Some villeins are landholders themselves. They have servants, money, good possessions, cattle and sheep: Alwyn Cottar was one such. John Mount simply could not compete with him.

I had asked Mistress Hayward if Mount and Freya had carried on a clandestine liaison under the nose of her husband.

"Bless me, sir, no. John wouldn't do that. He's too upright a man."

"Aye well. Now you have spoken, wife," said Hayward, "I'll add my penn'orth." He looked daggers at his spouse who simply stared back. "Mount accepted it, sir. Accepted Freya's will. It was what Freya wanted and so that was that."

"He never tried to persuade her to…?"

"Oh no, sir. John wouldn't. He is a pious man. Religious man. The sanctity of marriage is to him as..."

"No reason for Alwyn to kill his wife then?"

The two of them looked shocked. They stared at me and then their eyes slid to each other.

"No, sir," said Marion Hayward. "Alwyn would never kill Freya."

"No, it's unthinkable," added her husband. "Unthinkable!"

"Someone did," I said.

"Well, if you want to look for someone who might have killed Freya you need only look to…"

"Wife! Be quiet!" shouted Hayward.

Putting her hands on her hips Mistress Hayward turned on her husband. "Hayward, the lord needs to know all the things that have been going on in order to get the man responsible…or woman," she said.

She turned back to me. "Cottar's daughter, sir."

"Cottar's daughter? I thought they had no children. They've only been married…"

"Ah no, sir. This would be with Cottar's first wife. She died in the outbreak of dock fever a few years ago. She left Alwyn with a littlun. I looked after her for quite a while when she was small. Little madam she was. Still is."

"How old would she be now?"

"Sixteen sir, come July," said Hayward.

"And as sore about her da and Freya as it was possible to be."

"She's not at the house?"

"No, sir. She moved out when Freya came. She lives with the Chetels at Henset, sir."

"Wilkin Chetel? The cowman at Red Vein Bottom?"

"Aye, sir."

"She milks the cows and helps around the house and farm and with the childer, sir," added Mistress Hayward.

"You think things were so bad between them that this young woman might take a stone to the back of her stepmother's skull?"

Again the two exchanged a look.

"Well, sir. There were some awful arguments between her father and her when she still lived here," said Mistress Hayward. "It wouldn't surprise me."

"Why didn't they get on? Was it mere jealousy on the part of the girl?"

"Well, I've no doubt there was a deal of that but no—it was all about who would inherit. Cottar is not without wealth sir, as you know. The girl knew that with a young wife, Alwyn might have further children, and if one was to be a son..."

"The daughter would inherit much less of the wealth?"

"Yessir."

"Thank you for your frankness, Mistress Hayward."

The woman preened herself. "It's only fair you know, sir."

My silent ride home was not unproductive. I thought everything over. Now I realised that for the first time, I had a believable motive for the murder of Freya Cottar.

What I did not understand and could not connect to this murder was that of Master Lea. I still had no idea why anyone would wish to kill him. I must go out to Henset, to the home of Wilkin Chetel and speak to Cottar's daughter.

*****

That night there was a terrible storm in the forest.

The wind rose to a howl. The rain poured from the heavens. We all closed and barred our doors and windows, secured our shutters, banked up our fires and wrapped ourselves in blankets.

For those of us lucky enough to live in a stone house with a good solid roof, it was the noise of the storm which kept us awake. For those unfortunates who lived in daub and cob houses with thatch for a roof, it was a night of wakefulness, misery and fear. Fear of the loss of a roof and the collapse of a wall.

At just after midnight the rain ceased and hail followed, clattering on the stone roof like gravel poured from a bucket. I began to believe that we should not have, thankfully, the flooding of the village such as we'd had in the previous year. I vowed to push on with my project of the making of the sluice gates for these would protect the homes nearest to our small river.

We heard the wind reach its peak the hour after Lauds. It rattled the tiles on the house roof and we heard the banging of shutters which had become unlatched in the nearer village and folk yelling as they helped each other to secure their homes, livestock and goods.

The morning dawned grey and damp and the miserable light showed us the damage which had been done to village houses and to forest trees.

The tree behind my forester Bird's house had been uprooted and had come crashing down on his outhouse a foot or so away from the roof of the loft where he and his family slept.

The large oak tree by the cottage up by the copse lived in by Thomas Field, had a branch down perilously close to his roof. And the thatch had been damaged by another.

Martyn and Janet Peddler's house had lost part of their thatch and Rob Hartshorn's house had a huge hole in the wall where a branch had fallen and taken the daub with it. We had only just finished rebuilding his house after a fire in the autumn.

Several houses were minus small amounts of thatch. Our half-wit Dysig's bothy had collapsed altogether and another home must be found for him. Luckily he was cowering in fear with his great aunt, Old Joan in her own house that night and he escaped injury. Debris was everywhere. Branches, indeed whole trees had come down, fouling the roadways and paths and smaller twigs littered the ground. Folk were about early picking them up for this was an unlooked for bonus. I gave permission for them to be gathered for firewood, for all fallen wood belonged to me.

We took stock.

None had been seriously hurt in the storm but there was much work to be done. Out in the forest I knew that damage would be serious. John organised groups of foresters to go out and clear paths, to fell dangerous trees and to plot where the worst of the damage had been done. We had a responsibility to keep the king's highways open.

We had trees in Savernake which were many hundreds of years old. Two of these had been felled by the wind. The stately Braydon Oak, close by the clearing where lived Cottar, Mount and Lea, was stripped of several of its larger branches and it lay with its roots bare and open to the air.

The huge oak at the area known to us as the Vaunt had also toppled over to lie at a jaunty angle amongst its fellows. I had known this massive tree all my life and a lump came to my throat as I passed it that next morning on my way from Durley to Henset. With it had gone part of my childhood.

Henset was a small village of ten houses set along a track and the final house was that of Wilkin Chetel.

The folk of Henset too were not without damage.

People were going about clearing the spaces of fallen trees and gathering together possessions which had broken loose.

As I rode up the main track an argument had broken out between two housewives who both claimed a basket which had been rolling around in the roadway. As I approached they dropped into silence and curtsied and when I had passed, their screeching broke out again.

A hen house had been destroyed and the chickens were being gathered up by a small young woman whose figure was straight up and down. Indeed if she hadn't been wearing a long kirtle, I should have thought her a young boy. Her hair was shorn and she wore no head cloth.

"I am looking for the home of Wilkin Chetel and for Tova Cottar in particular," I said looking down at her from the back of Bayard.

"I am Tova Cottar."

I introduced myself. "Is there somewhere where we might go to have a private word?"

The girl looked surprised but led me to the cottage by the roadway which was mercifully intact.

She pushed open the door and once inside she gestured for me to follow her into the right hand room, quite a large space open to the rafters. The fire was burning in the central grate and water was bubbling in a pot.

A large dog lounged in the corner and Tova shooed it out of the back door.

It was a dark space and so I opened the two shutters to let in light.

"I am your lord, Tova. You may not know that I am also the Constable of the county. This means that the King has given me the power to search out those who have committed a crime."

One dark eyebrow flew into her hair and her mouth twisted but she said nothing. Her face however said, 'what has this to do with me?'

"You will know by now that your stepmother Freya has..."

"Yes, I know."

"I hear that you and she didn't get on."

She scoffed loudly and looked away.

"Where were you yesterday morning before the second hour?"

"Here as I always am."

"Can anyone vouch for you, Tova?"

She looked at me with hostile eyes. "I don't know. They were all at their work. The children can. The dog can."

"Mistress Chetel. Was she here with you?"

"She was out with Wilkin with the cattle, I think, later when I got back from the milking. I didn't see her early yesterday."

"Tell me Tova, are you always this surly?"

The question puzzled her and she moved back a pace. "No, my lord."

"Then I would be grateful if you could be a little more helpful and less disrespectful. It will do you no good to be rude. I am your master and I can have you flogged should I wish it."

Tova Cottar sighed and bowed her head. "Yes, my lord."

I walked about the cottage looking round at the furniture and possessions.

"You came here shortly after Freya married your father, I hear?"

"Yes, sir. I could not stand to be with them in the house."

"Ah..." I smiled. "Difficult for you. Freya was not much older than you are and it must have been onerous for you to obey her and..."

"No. It wasn't that."

"No?"

"I couldn't bear the constant attention my father gave her. He was totally besotted with her. Pawing her all the time and 'sweeting this' and 'sweeting that' and always trying to please her, his 'dearest one.' "

"And you...suddenly you were not his dearest one any longer?"

"No, my lord. I was just a useful slave."

I sat on a small bench. "What did you think of your stepmother, Tova? I will know if you lie so speak the truth."

Tova sighed again and fiddled with the woven belt around her long cotte of faded red.

"She was beautiful and had all the men gazing after her. She loved it. She loved the attention. Of course my father couldn't see it. She'd trapped him as soon as he set eyes on her."

"I thought that she wished to marry John Mount, Tova. I have been told that they were childhood sweethearts."

"I have heard that too but I don't know. What I do know is that she set her cap at Da, knowing Ma was in her grave."

Tova went to the central fire and poked it angrily with a twig. She hunkered down, her face sour and vexed. Then she removed the boiling pot with an irritated, "Oh".

Her manner and posture was not dissimilar to that of a bad tempered young lad. No wonder I'd thought her of the male sex when I'd first seen her.

"You gave permission for them to be married and that was that."

"I did?" All my tied villeins must ask me if they wished to marry anyone themselves or marry off their daughters.

I searched my memory but I couldn't remember having approved it. Ah well. I was a very busy man. My steward Henry will have dealt with it.

"So you should by rights still be living with your father at Braydon. He is your guardian till you marry."

"He didn't care that I left."

"You left with his permission?"

"He didn't care, I tell you."

"Neither did you have my permission."

She stared at me angrily.

"Your arguments with Mistress Cottar...?"

"Do not call her that!" She jumped up and spat at me. "My mother was Mistress Cottar, that woman will always be Freya of Henset."

"It seems you enjoy arguing with people, Tova?" I smiled falsely.

She stood in front of me and fumed.

"So we have established that you hated your stepmother and that you were jealous of the attention your father lavished on her."

"I didn't kill her."

"You have a powerful motive."

"If I had stayed at Braydon then I might have done it. I removed myself so that I was not tempted," said the girl with an angry tilt of the head.

"Ah, but there is the matter of what happens when your father has an heir, Tova."

"An heir? Well, he won't now, will he?" she sniggered.

I shrugged. "He may marry again."

She looked at me sidelong and there was disbelief in the look.

"Whilst there were just the two of you at Braydon, it was you who would gain if your father died."

"I didn't kill her."

"Perhaps your father will be next and then..."

"No!"

"You dislike him too. It seems to me that..."

"I haven't and I never would kill anyone." The venom was back in the gaze, if it had ever left. "Certainly not Father."

"Did you know Master Lea well, Tova?"

"We lived within spitting distance of his cott. How could I not know him?" She turned her back to me and folded her arms and looked at the sky out of the window.

"He too is dead of course."

"I didn't kill him either."

I stood. "You will come here and stand before me, Tova Cottar, and you will look at me in respect as I question you and you will answer me using my proper title. I am your lord. Do not forget it."

The girl blanched, swivelling her eyes to look at me. She blinked. I could see her face in a shaft of light slanting through the open window. She turned and marched up to me still truculent. I towered over her for as I've said I am a full six feet and Tova was not a tall girl.

"Now, Master Lea. Tell me what you know of him."

"He was an idiot....my lord."

"He was a handsome idiot I hear?"

Tova Cottar tried not to smile and her lip twitched. "He was good to look upon and he knew it."

"Ah. He was a proud cock, was he?"

"No, not particularly, just that he knew his pretty face would get him what he wanted. With some. He had a sweet way with the fairer sex, sir."

"But not with you?"

"Not with me. My lord."

"Did he try?"

She hooked her upper lip with her bottom teeth and pulled.

"He did. I gave him short shrift."

"Did he try it with your stepmother?"

"I don't know."

"What did he want?"

"Not that...if that's what you think, sir."

"Oh? And what do I think?"

"He did not ask me to lie with him."

"Then what did he want?"

"He wanted me to lie *for* him."

"Lie? About what?"

"About where he'd been one day. He wanted me to say I'd seen him when I hadn't."

"And when and where had you ...not seen him Tova?"

"In the large barn at Braydon..." she said.

"And where was he really?"

"I don't know. But I wouldn't lie for him."

I looked out of the window and saw two children of about seven and nine years of age walking down the main road chatting animatedly. They were struggling with a large bucket of water between them.

"Your charges return, I think, Tova."

She stood on tiptoe and looked out of the window.

"Alfred and Thomas, sir. They return from the well."

I turned back to her. "So Master Lea asked you to lie for him, to give him an alibi?"

"Yessir."

"Who were you to tell?"

"His wife, my lord. His wife Ellen."

The door opened with a bump.

"When was this, Tova?"

The children came through the hole and stopped dead, eyeing me with distrust.

Tova Cottar turned to me and said, "The day he died, m'lord. Just the morning of the day he went missing. It was here at the house in Henset."

*****

59

Back along the track through the forest I went, turning over this new information in my mind.

I made a detour and came to the Braydon Oak, that venerable old tree I had climbed in my youth.

I dismounted and walked around the upended oak.

The red soil of the forest clung to the roots like ivy to the trunk. Now there was a huge hollow where the tree had been fixed. The hole was damp and the soil friable and mixed with many tiny stones and flints. The trunk of the tree bore holes at the bottom of the magnificent bole where badgers had dug and rabbits had made their homes. These animals were long gone; now the rotten core was visible and I could see why the tree had toppled.

I brushed my hand over the tiny rootlets which stuck out like hair from the larger twisted supporting roots. There was one other large oak in the glade. This would be our Braydon Oak now. Looking about me, I found a scion of this great toppled oak, already grown to six feet and vowed that I would tell John to nurture it as the future Braydon Oak. There must always be a Braydon oak in Savernake.

Donning my gloves again I rode on to the three cottages at Braydon.

*****

The Cottar house door was open and I yelled as I dismounted and strode up to the house.

"Ho, Artor! 'Tis the Lord Belvoir, again!"

"My Lord. God keep you. We have no change here."

I ducked under the lintel and threw off my cloak. "But I might have some news which will bring him out of his stupor, Artor."

I watched Alwyn Cottar as I came to stand in front of him.

"I have today learned something very interesting."

"Oh, my lord?" asked Artor.

"That his daughter, Alwyn's daughter, Tova, did indeed wish her stepmother dead. I am considering taking her up for the murder. I think I have enough evidence to suggest that she hit her from behind with a rock. She has no one to vouch for her at the time of her death. She was alone and no one saw her. Tova is a singular girl, more boy than girl I think and more than capable of delivering those blows…. She is a very angry young woman with every opportunity to take out her venom on Freya. Yes, I think Tova did it."

I watched Cottar's face. At first his expression was blank. The more I spoke the more animated his face became until it bore an expression of disbelief. Upon my last utterance of the girl's name the man grimaced.

"She also tells me that she disliked Bordern Lea. I wouldn't be at all surprised to find that Tova had dispensed with him too. We have but to search and find the knife she used to strike him through the eye and we have her…."

"Nooo!" said an agonised voice quietly. "No, it cannot be. It cannot be Tova."

"Ah, Master Cottar, you are back with us?"

The eyes focussed on me. "No, my lord…it cannot be." His voice wavered and was croaky.

"Why can it not be, Alwyn my friend?" I said.

Artor Hayward jumped up and produced a beaker of ale for the stricken man.

"Here Alwyn, drink—your throat must be as dry as a walnut." The beaker was thrust into his hand and Alwyn Cottar put the cup to his lips and drained it.

He blinked several times and then took in a shuddering breath.

"My daughter would not kill her."

I sat down on the nearest stool.

"Artor, will you go and fetch Mount, wherever he is? I wish to talk to you all. I suppose your wife is back at Cadley?"

"Aye sir."

"Then John Mount will suffice."

When he'd gone I leaned closer to Cottar and whispered.

"I am told, Alwyn, that your wife Freya liked to flirt with the village men?"

"Who told you that? It's not true."

"First she is enamoured of John Mount, then she marries you. Then she makes eyes at many men in the villages hereabouts. Oh it's not hard to do, for she was very beautiful and many would desire her."

"No, sir. I suppose my jealous daughter told you these things." Alwyn Cottar rubbed his hand through his hair and then his eyes. "It's difficult to bring up a girl child all on your own sir. They get so attached to you. No matter what you do to make them see that you must have a life too..."

"Aye I know it, Cottar. I too was a father alone for some years. Though I am lucky in my own daughter."

"They are so easily moved to jealousy."

"A jealous child may kill, Cottar."

"No, sir. No. Tova would never kill. It would be her idea of punishment to *torment* and to torment *me*, not her stepmother. Killing her would be too easy."

"It would hurt you. Freya's death *has* wounded you greatly."

"Yes. I am lost sir, without her, but Tova is the sort of girl who would enjoy my pain in another way."

John Mount came in through the door. He froze, slightly stooped and with an uncertain look in his eye.

"Ah...so now we are all here and I will have the truth. Mistress Lea cannot be found? She has gone to Cadley already?"

"She left early this morning, sir," said Hayward.

"So be it."

I raised myself and went to stand at the back of the cottage.

"I am hearing many things about the people involved in this strange series of events. Firstly I hear that this person or that has a motive for wanting Mistress Cottar dead. No one will tell me anything about Bordern Lea and no one admits having disliked him....and yet...yet he lies dead for more than one week before someone reports him missing."

"We explained that, my lord," said Hayward. "We simply could not get to you to report it. Nor to the town nor to the coroner in Ramsbury. The snow had..."

"And yet, there were thaws in which you could all get about to and from your work at the barns."

They all looked at each other with worried expressions.

"Mistress Lea was convinced, sir, that Bordern was lying at the barn, waiting for better weather or that he had gone out to Red Vein Bottom. So we naturally did not worry about him until..."

Hayward saw my face and stopped speaking, licking his lips, he looked away all of a sudden adding, "We did not know where he was."

"I have asked you all and I will ask again. What kind of man was Bordern Lea?"

The three men looked, one at another.

"I must go out to piss sir," said Cottar, wiping his hand over his nose.

"Then go—and Mount go with him—do not leave him alone."

"Yes, sir."

There was silence as Cottar struggled to his feet and made for the door. Not far away we heard the hiss of someone urinating into the grass.

Mount and Cottar returned.

There was an uncomfortable silence as the three of them found seats as I requested.

"Answer my question. What kind of man was Bordern Lea?"

John Mount sighed. "He was as we have described him. A good friend and a hard worker. We three here have no complaint of him."

"But...others have?"

"It was said..." whispered Cottar, "that he was over fond of a particular lady."

"No, no," said Artor. "Bordern was a bit of a lad. Yes, he was a... playful sort. Playful. Only playful."

"Aye, that's all," said Mount. "There was no harm in it and no truth in any rumours of seduction."

"Whom was he supposed to have seduced?"

"No one...it was mere gossip, my lord," said Hayward.

"No substance in any of it," said Mount. "No, truly nothing, sir."

"Answer me true. Did his wife know?"

"Bless you, sir," said Hayward, "No. She had not the slightest inkling. They were a devoted couple. Truly. I have never seen a pair so....all together...."

"Together, my lord," said Cottar, rubbing his forehead.

"It was not your wife?"

All three men cried out as one, "No, sir!"

"It was not Freya...Lea had the sense to play his games away from home, my lord," said Mount.

"Freya would have boxed his ears, sir," said Cottar sadly.

"So when Lea went missing you, all three of you wondered if he was with this other woman?"

Three shifty expressions exchanged between their eyes. "Well, we couldn't be sure, sir. Naturally we would not reveal our suspicions to Ellen," said Mount.

I sighed in irritation. "Do we know who this woman is?"

"No, sir."

"It's not known."

"Not for sure, my lord," said one man after another.

"But gossip has it that it's...?"

"No sir...truly...we don't know," said Hayward.

"And there was nothing in it. Bordern would never take his silliness so far, sir. He loved his wife with all his heart. It's just he liked to...play about. It was all a joke...a bit of fun," added Mount.

"I think if a woman were to take him at his word and fall before his blandishments...he would have run a mile, sir," said Hayward, smiling.

"Hmmm. If I find this is not the truth I will not let you forget my anger," I said.

"No, sir."

"Please sir....you won't mention this to poor Ellen will you?" asked Cottar. "She has enough to deal with. Enough."

I pushed off from the back wall where I'd been leaning. "Someone killed Bordern Lea. I now find that he was playing with the affections of forest men's wives. You don't think this is a good motive for murder?"

"And then why murder my poor Freya? She can have nothing to do with it," said Cottar, his face creasing in agony.

"I don't know. For the life of me I can't find a connection but there is one...I'm sure. My thumbs are pricking and when my thumbs prick...I cannot ignore the..."

The three men were staring at me horrified.

Cottar surreptitiously made the sign against the evil eye.

I nodded to them "I have not finished with this," I said as I grabbed my cloak, ducked out of the door and strode to Bayard.

As I mounted and turned his head for home I heard Cottar weeping again.

"And I have not finished with the three of you!"

*****

My journey took me back round the Braydon oak.

I stared down into the pit where the tree had once grown. In the distance I heard the voices of my foresters laughing and talking. I was almost past when something caught my eye.

Suddenly it began to hail and I wiped the melted droplets from my eyelashes as I looked.

I turned Bayard again and we approached the old oak from the side. I looked down into the pit where the roots had once nestled.

Had this earth been so disturbed when I had last come this way? The hail was pitting the soft soil with small holes, shifting it.

I dismounted and told Bayard to wait and jumped into the hole, oblivious to the hail now turned to rain coming down in rods and the mud forming in the bottom of the pit.

With my gloved hand I brushed the pile which I had thought looked unusual from the height of my horse's back.

I blinked.

I brushed some more.

Into view came a white object which seemed very foreign to the red earth.

I dug with my gloved nails.

At last I saw the four fingers of a hand.

A woman's hand.

I jumped out of the hole, scrabbling for a purchase on the muddy earth and cupping my hands around my mouth, I yelled.

"Belvoir to me...to me!" This was the rallying cry of the Belvoir family and had been used down the ages to summon aid and to stir up Belvoir retainers.

I called four times before I heard a crashing of boots through the emerging undergrowth.

John Brenthall's blue tunic and black boots came into view followed by Drogo of Ladywell and a few paces behind, Walter Watson, the eldest son of my old manor reeve.

"Sir, are you all right?" yelled John over the hissing of the hail and rain. It bounced around us from leaf and frond and struck our clothes and our heads with an audible tap.

John put up his hood.

"John, have you a shovel? Can you dig here?"

"Aye, I have, m'lord. Drogo!"

Drogo ran off into the undergrowth, pulling up his hood. Wat bent to the hole and stared down.

"There, sir?"

"Yes, Wat. Someone is buried—a woman I think."

He jumped into the hole and cleared a little more of the wet red earth.

"Woe sakes, sir! It *is* a woman!"

"Not buried too deeply," said John.

We stayed there looking at the hand for a few more moments until Drogo came back with a shovel.

He jumped into the hole and began to dig, Walter helping him with his hands.

"Gently now...." I said. "I think I know who this is and she is deserving of our care. And I think her small child too..."

The woman lay on her side, her lower limbs tangled in her skirts, one hand raised up above her head. Eventually they freed her from the earth. There was no body of a baby.

John teased the pale red-gold hair from the soil and removed the head cloth which had become pushed over her face.

I took in a surprised breath.

"Oh. It's not who I thought it would be."

"Head bashed at the back sir," said John, "one blow there I think."

"Enough to make her fall into the hole left by the tree," said Walter, crossing himself.

"Then she was covered over. There's enough soil dislodged and it's easy to dig just here" said Drogo.

Wat gently lifted and turned the head.

"Do we know her?" I asked, for the face was not familiar to me.

"Yes, sir, I do," said John. "It's Wilkin's wife, Wilkin Chetel of Henset. It's Emma Chetel, sir."

Chapter Five

"Right. Come out of the hole." I extended my hand to Drogo and John lifted Walter from the mud.

"Drogo. Go to the town, fetch the doctor."

"Yessir." The man ran off in the direction of the road as the hail ceased.

I shouted after him "And on your way tell Father Justin at Cadley. We need him here too."

"Yessir," came the reply.

"John, Wat, help me to make a search of the glade. Anything which might be odd, out of place. Oh and we are looking for a large stone I think. About...oh, yea big," and I held out my hands.

"With which she was struck, sir?" asked John.

"I am thinking that it's the same as Mistress Cottar. Struck from behind with a large stone, one with the sharpness of flint in it."

"There are many flints around here." John gestured to the uprooted oak, "You can see smaller ones lodged in the roots of the old tree."

"I go south. You go north. You Walter, go east."

We parted and fanned out into the glade. The Braydon oak had been the largest tree in this glade. As I've said before, there was one other oak of probably two hundred years' growth and several smaller ones. One large ash tree marked the edge of the thin growth. A holly had been growing right up the back of this fallen tree.

My eyes scanned the ground as I walked. A stone with blood; the stone used to kill Mistress Chetel should be lying tossed somewhere here, if history was repeating itself.

"Aye sir....here!" yelled Walter.

"Do not touch it," I answered quickly and leapt diagonally through the brush.

"Here sir!" shouted John also.

"What... two stones?"

"No, sir. The shovel. The shovel lies here—the shovel used to bury her."

I bent to pick up the stone carefully and took it over to where John stared at the base of a small beech tree, still bearing its old leaves, shrivelled and rust brown.

I nodded and gently John bent to pick up the shovel.

The wooden handle was old and cracked. The blade of the shovel was ancient and worn.

I frowned. "I'm sure I've seen this before but for the life of me I can't think where," I said.

*****

Now Paul, I must take us from our tale a little. All this as you know took place as I have told you, at the end of February and into March. Great and ugly things were happening in the realm at that time which had a profound effect upon the church, upon our monarch John and the people of this kingdom.

I will go back and explain what had been happening and try to set out the history in as truthful a way as possible for there has been much talk and a deal has been written about that year and the breaking with the church which we endured for six years. I have said before that the church is the body which writes down our histories and, forgive me Paul my scribe; the church is not always truthful for its own reasons.

What's that? Well, for example they are bound to think unfavourably of our monarch, aren't they, when he confiscated some of their wealth and curbed their power in the land? It was tantamount to war. I'm not saying that this was right, just that it was so.

For the time of the Interdict may be regarded, I think not merely as a period when England was subject to ecclesiastical censure, but as a period of war, between Pontiff and King.

The trouble went back some way.

When Archbishop Hubert of Canterbury died in 1205, the monks of the abbey elected one of their own to succeed him.

John and the English bishops refused to support their election. Naturally John wanted a man he could trust, one of his own supporters in the role and he favoured John de Gray. De Gray was about to be installed when Pope Innocent the third refused to accept either man.

Of course John was furious. This was a blatant attempt by the papacy to undermine the monarch's control of his church.

Yes, Paul, it was history repeating itself - or almost, for a similar situation as we know, had arisen under John's father Henry which culminated in the murder of Thomas Becket, the archbishop of Canterbury in December 1170.

Innocent wanted his friend Stephen Langton to succeed to the post and to this end consecrated him. John would not recognise him nor allow the man into the country, even though Stephen was an Englishman.

The king declared that he should have been consulted prior to the man's consecration and that he did not feel him fit for the role.

Arguments raged. Innocent threatened to cut off the land from Holy Mother Church.

At last, after much toing and froing, worn out by John's contumacy, Pope Innocent III declared that the kingdom of England and Wales, be placed under an Interdict.

This, though it was by no means a thing of absolute clarity, meant that no church services might be celebrated.

The church doors were to remain firmly locked.

The Interdict not only deprived both guilty and innocent alike of spiritual consolation, it was designed to make folk angry and hostile to the man who had triggered it - John. Innocent had used it as a diplomatic weapon and I think he believed that John would be forced into an early capitulation.

He badly misjudged John and the English people.

*****

The weather had warmed as I have said and so we were now able to travel to bury my mother in law Evisa Congyre in the church at Bedwyn.

I'd had a double skinned coffin made so that Evisa might lie at Durley until the weather improved and we could get a cart to Bedwyn. All was ready on March 22nd when we trundled the coffin to Bedwyn and Father Godfrey would bury Evisa the next day in the nave of the village church next to her husband Toruld. We would all travel to the manor to take part in the service.

That day, the day the coffin left for Bedwyn, Father Crispin came running up to the hall, breathless and flushed.

"Crispin, whatever is the matter?"

"It's happened, Aumary. As threatened, it's happened. A letter from Salisbury. As of tomorrow no one will be buried with Christian rites, no one properly married and I am unable to open the church for services, no communion. I cannot give solace except to the dying. I can baptise children behind closed doors perhaps."

"Confession?"

"No. I cannot do that. For the moment. It's only for the dying. I can only celebrate a form of mass in the churchyard. No taking of the sacrament."

I grasped my friend's shoulder. "Crispin. It's not perhaps as bad as it seems."

We had talked about this often for there had been the rumour of a threat to cut off England from the Christian church since 1205, when John first refused to appoint Langton.

John had fallen foul of the papacy for he had expelled the monks of Canterbury when they defied him at the end of August 1207. He had also deprived the Archbishop of York of his lands. Innocent had ordered the bishop of Rochester to immediately excommunicate the knights who'd taken part in the raids, Reginald of Cornhill and Fulk de Cantiloup amongst others; men close to the King. At that date, the Pope was not yet completely without 'affection' as he called it, for John. John had, in his opinion, acted ungratefully and had followed imprudent advice.

These words were not addressed to John himself. A letter had been written to the bishops of Worcester, London and Ely - so chosen because they had acted as papal agents before and had not been especially favoured by John.

I'd heard that the bishops had not immediately approached the King but that they did so in October and they begged him to reconsider.

John would not be moved.

Yes, Paul, I know that it's said that the King threatened to send any Roman clergy found in England back to their master with their eyes put out and their noses slit. However I have no doubt the report was more lurid fiction than balanced truth. As I've said those already hostile to the king were those to write of it. Whatever it was that John did say, there is no doubt that he refused the bishops' request.

Why, you ask, did they not enforce the interdict then?

Well, it's my belief that they had a better grasp than the papacy, of the feeling in the country at the time. It was true that John was then beginning to become unpopular particularly with some of his lords. However, when it came down to it, most men here would choose King over Pope. People thought that John should indeed have a say over who was appointed to that most important role of the see of Canterbury. The man chosen would not only be a churchman but a force in the country, a political force whose grand estates drew him level with the great men of England.

You ask me if I still think that John was right to defy the Pope?

Oh my lad, I don't really know. I had sworn my oath to him and as you know, I am not one to renege on my promises. However one must remember that John had sworn, in his coronation oath, to uphold the rights of the crown, those rights as set down by his father, Henry and those before him. He would be forsworn else.

Yes, Paul, he was unpopular, you're right and became more so as his reign went on. The forest eyres had squeezed money out of rich and poor alike. We suffered here in our forest of Savernake, despite my careful intervention. Sir Hugh de Neville, the chief forester, launched the eyre in the spring of 1207. They didn't get round to us until later but still it was a costly time for us all. However still folk favoured John over the Pope.

In his hand Crispin clasped a letter of closely written lines. "It's all in here. From the Bishop. Though how I am to baptise children with chrism when I am not allowed to consecrate that chrism, it doesn't say."

I took the letter but the churchly Latin was beyond me, all but a few phrases.

"Is there no room for doubt anywhere?"

Crispin shrugged. "All over the place Aumary but the fact remains...."

"Yes?"

"No one may enter the church."

"No one at all?"

"Only the priest. The church is closed. After vespers tonight when I have read this letter to all, the church doors will be shut."

I looked at him seriously. "Crispin, no. This means that we cannot bury our dear Evisa in consecrated ground!"

"She can't be buried, Aumary, in God's ground, no service to send her soul onwards. Nothing. No burial service. No mass can be said for the repose of her soul."

I sat down heavily on my chair.

"This is terrible, Crispin. Is there is no getting round it?"

He shook his head. "I wish my friend that there was."

"Unless Crispin... We shall do it now. It's the last thing we shall do before the doors are closed. Pray to God Father Godfrey at Bedwyn will do it."

"Surely he cannot refuse the lady Evisa this one last boon?"

"We must hurry...if we are to be finished and all are to be returned before vespers so that you may read out the terms."

And so it was that our family managed to escape the rigours of the Interdict by the skin of our teeth.

*****

That night everyone was quiet. There was little talk at the supper table. Lydia toyed with her food and Hawise kept snivelling into her cup, Thomasina her cloth doll clasped firmly to her breast and under her chin. All those who ate at the lower table ate quietly and disappeared about their own business. Evisa's funeral had upset us all. That and the war with the church.

Crispin lounged back in his chair and stared into space.

Johannes had come back with us from the funeral of Evisa Congyre and stayed with us that Sunday night. He was trying to get Hawise interested in eating a few nuts which he had on his plate.

"Open your mouth Hawise and I'll toss one in. See if you can catch it."

"Uncle," said Lydia sternly.

"Only trying to..." he said and gave up as he saw her face.

"Ah well."

"Come..." I said. "Let's go into my office. We can discuss what you found at Braydon. You coming, Hal?"

I led the way and turned back to call our priest.

"Crispin, do you want to come and help?"

He shook his head. "I am redundant, Aumary. I have no job. No function. I cannot help."

"You have a good brain. It is brains that we need."

"No, I shall go home, Aumary and puzzle over my letter. See exactly what I can do and can't do. There must be some hole in it all somewhere. I shall draft a letter to the Dean of the Diocese. I have a few questions to ask him, things I need clarifying."

I nodded. "Then good night to you. God keep you in his hand."

Crispin tossed back the wine in his cup. "And you my friend though I must admit, tonight I feel that God has abandoned us."

"Not so. Crispin, God still watches over us," said Johannes rising. "If we keep Him in our hearts, He will not forsake us. The fact we can make no public declaration of our love for Him does not mean we are cut off from His mercy."

Crispin smiled. "You are as wise as ever my friend," he said as he rose shakily to his feet. "I think I have had a little too much of Aumary's excellent wine. I am maudlin tonight."

I had never seen Crispin drink as much as he did that night. He felt what had happened deeply, to the root of his soul.

Leaving our priest, we three walked the few feet to my office and closed the door.

"So what did you find, Johannes?"

I lit a candle and Hal stoked the brazier into life. Johannes lit tinder and touched it to the two lamps. Huge shadows leapt up the walls.

A screech owl lifted off with its unearthly scream from somewhere close by and I closed the shutter to the window.

"One blow to the back of the head. Another to the brow, I think," said Johannes. "The blow to the forehead stunned the woman, not a killing blow. She reeled and then when about to fall, another was delivered to the back of her head. This killed her."

"So two blows only. Not like Mistress Cottar whose head was beaten to a mash."

"No. There seemed much less malice in this attack."

"The woman was at the brink of the hole left by the tree... or was she dragged there and thrown in? We found no drag marks," I said

"I couldn't find any marks. There was a footprint, the deceased's at the very edge of the depression made by the fallen tree. I think she was facing her attacker, so knew them. I don't think she felt any fear of them and did not see the blow coming. As I said, the first wounded her, the second killed her."

"She fell..."

"Or was pushed," said Hal.

"Into the hole."

"Then the person took the shovel and covered her over. It would, as John has said, have been easy, for the soil had been disturbed and it was achieved without too much effort," said Johannes.

"There were no further footprints in the hole, except yours, Drogo's and Wat's, though it's hard to be sure with so much disturbance."

"Again we have a premeditated killing, for to bring a shovel with you, you intend to bury the victim do you not?"

"Not done in the 'eat of the moment then, sir?" asked Hal.

"No, Hal. The woman was lured to the forest and then calmly dispatched and buried."

We all thought about that awful fact for a while.

"We might not a-found 'er if you hadna spotted 'er hand," said Hal perching on the edge of my table.

I sat down wearily on my chair. "I cannot be sure that the body was not there when I first travelled the track from Braydon to Henset. I simply didn't look hard enough. The rain might have dislodged something I suppose."

"She died I think between dawn and the third hour," said Johannes, "by the state of the body, though I can't be absolutely certain."

"I must ask when she was last seen and where."

"You told me that girl, Tova, she hadn't seen her, sir," said Hal.

"No, that's right. She told me that Mistress Chetel went out to meet Master Chetel with the herd at Red Vein Bottom. Did she return at any time? I don't know. Tova didn't see her this morning."

"Hmmm," said Hal, " 'Ow did she end up at Braydon Oak? It's not a far walk, but still. She must 'ave got a message or summat."

"Someone—the murderer perhaps—walked her there? Or met her?"

"Or someone passed on a message. 'Meet me at the Braydon oak at...' that sort'a thing?"

I looked up at my man at arms. "Then that person—if it's not our murderer—is also in danger Hal, for they know who lured her there, by word."

"God's truth sir—that's not a pretty thought!"

"No, it's not. God, I wish I had a motive for these murders. They seem totally unrelated to me."

"Except that a stone was used twice," said Johannes.

"And we still haven't found the knife which killed Bordern Lea. The stones were tossed about freely but that knife has disappeared."

"It must identify the killer, sir," said Hal "It'll be cleaned up and back where it belongs, I bet."

"Not one of the people we questioned has such a knife, Hal. It's the sort of thing a man at arms might carry, not a herdsman or a farmer."

"You mean like this one?" Hal took out his long knife and we all looked at it glinting in the low light of the candles.

Johannes held out his hand. Hal passed it to him.

"It's a knife for fighting with, defending yourself. No one in Braydon has such a thing. Something like it, but more pointed might have made the wound in Bordern Lea, but where is it?" he said.

"Then we shall have to extend our search."

"Aumary, you can't search the whole forest," said Johannes.

I looked up. "No, no I can't but I can search Henset, Cadley and all points between. Ask all those who knew Bordern Lea. He didn't go much further than that. I'm told he used to flirt with the women around and about...oh not seriously they tell me, but someone might have become a little cross about his charming of their wife or daughter."

"His wife?"

"I'm told she thought the world of him and that their relationship was as perfect as a marriage can be. She knew nothing of his flirtatious nature and they were very happy."

"Who says this?" asked Hal.

"Her priest, no less, Father Justin and her friends in the forest, Mistress Hayward and all the cattlemen."

"She wouldn't want to kill him anyway, for it puts her in a very difficult position doesn't it?" said Johannes. "No man, a young child on the way. A plot to farm, no help, no protector."

Hal slid his knife back into its sheath.

" 'A course..." he said reflectively, "the weapon might not be a knife at all...it might be summat they use in the forest, a tool of some kind. 'Ave we thought of that?"

We looked at him.

And that was when we began to rack our brains and think larger and wider about this whole sorry business.

I went to the solar early that night, tired out with thinking and travelling about the forest.

Hawise was asleep in her bed, her hand draped over the edge of her mattress, Thomasina was laid over the top of her pillow. I looked in on her and tucked her hand into her coverlet. She stirred and moaned and I placed a soft kiss on her forehead.

Her nurse Felice was sitting by the light of a lamp, sewing and I bade her a quiet good night.

I looked down on my son Simon who slept in the corner of Hawise's room in his little box bed by the door. I watched him as his chest rose and fell then kissed him too on his pink cheek and closed the door.

Phillip slept peacefully in the Belvoir cradle by the side of the big bed. He was two months old now and growing finely. Lydia stirred in the bedclothes and sat up with wide violet eyes.

"Come to bed, it's been a hard day for you."

I sat on the edge.

"A hard day for us all."

Lydia smiled. "At least we managed to send poor Evisa into God's bosom properly. It will not be so good for that poor woman whom you found today."

"No, she must lie outside the churchyard at Cadley without the benefit of prayer or bell."

"When this is all over Aumary, the priests must surely make restitution."

I looked over my shoulder at my wife, her black hair falling free over her arms, her white shoulders above the counterpane which she grasped to her bosom, her violet blue eyes huge in the candlelight.

"I hope so, though in truth I don't know."

"The consequences are too awful to contemplate."

"Each man or woman must take their soul into their own keeping Lydia. God will see what's in someone's heart."

"He must or we are all lost."

I pulled my shirt over my head and threw it angrily onto a chest.

It missed, slid down and landed on the floorboards by Phillip's cradle.

I leaned down to retrieve it and caught sight of my second son. His large blue eyes were open and he stared at me as if I were a stranger.

He was not swaddled tonight but wore a tiny shirt of a cross shape and a simple breech clout. I offered him my finger. He grasped it and hung on blinking languidly.

"Are you still worried about Phillip?"

Lydia shuffled over to the edge of the bed and peered into the cradle.

"He is such a good child. Hardly ever cries. Worried? I just worry that he is not like his brother, that's all."

"Hawise cried. All the time. She cried to be fed. She cried for attention, she cried when she wanted cleaning. I remember Cecily and Felice being worn out by the attention they had to give her."

"Simon is full of life and has been so from the first moment he opened his eyes. This one, he is, oh I don't know. I have no words to describe him. I spoke to Phillipa Reeve the other day. You know their little lad Geoffrey is a bit older than our Phil?"

"Johnathan's second child yes, I know."

"And I saw Annot with little Algar."

"Ah yes, our orphan."

We'd had a child born on the manor in December 1207, to a girl who was simply passing through the village. Sadly she had died and so the newly married Henry, my steward and Annot Pierson his wife, had taken the child as their own, with my permission of course. Phillipa Reeve was suckling him. Thomas Potter, the man who made pottery and rented a workshop from me in the courtyard, was Algar's uncle.

"I asked them how their littl'uns are."

"And they said...?"

"As full of life as Simon was....at that age."

I looked down at Phillip. He stared back at me with that inscrutable expression and then his face creased into the sweetest smile I had ever seen. My heart took a lurch and I grasped his little hand in my large one.

"Hello my little man," I said. "Come let us take you up and your mother will feed you now you're awake." I knew it was about time he was fed.

I put my hand behind his head and lifted him with the other, cradling him to my breast, sitting on the bed edge once more.

I am not ashamed to say that I sat for a while and crooned to my second son with soft words and nonsense and he watched me carefully with his solemn eyes, smiling now and again.

After a while Lydia took him from me and set him to her breast. I pulled off my boot and walked the short distance to the fire which was clamped down for the night. I set one boot on the hearth and sitting on a stool pulled off the other. Tired as I was, I did not pay attention to what I was doing and the boot flew out of my hand and landed on the boards close by the bed with a bang.

Lydia jumped.

"Oh Aumary. You gave me a fright." She had been looking down at Phillip.

I chuckled. "I am too tired to undress."

"I hope you haven't woken the others."

I came back to the side of the bed.

"This one is unafraid of loud noises." I grinned. "Simon would have been yelling at the top of his lungs at this age."

"The other night when we had the loud winds, Simon crept into our bed."

"I didn't know."

"No. I put him back in his own bed before dawn," she chuckled.

I saw her look down at Phillip with a frown.

He sucked on oblivious to all this attention, his eyes wide and blue, his pupils tiny.

Lydia settled herself at the bed head, I lay on the coverlet propped on one elbow and watched them both. The manor lay in absolute silence. There was no noise from the hall below us; no sound came from the wind or from outside. The forest was quiet, the trees still. No owls hooted.

Suddenly there was a cry and a banging on a door. We both jumped.

I had been half asleep I think, staring at my son's adorable face. I watched him as the noise grew louder.

"Whatever is that?" mumbled Lydia.

"I don't know. It's the manor door I think. Someone is banging on it and shouting to come in."

I heard footsteps and mutters beyond the solar door, then more feet ascended the solar steps quickly and a voice cried out to me.

"My Lord Belvoir, will you come and speak to a messenger sir?"

"Aye, I will, Hal."

I threw on my cloak, wrapped it around me, opened the solar door and stepped out onto the top stair. Hal had descended again and I looked down at him.

"Hal, what is it?"

"Aelfnod, sir."

"Nod? I thought he'd gone home to his mother and father for a while."

"Aye sir. But he's ridden all the way from Cadley."

Aelfnod was one of my young grooms. His parents lived in Cadley and his mother had been ill of late. I had given him permission to go and stay with her for a while.

"He's not due back till - Tuesday, isn't it?"

"No sir, but he has news."

"All right. I'll come down." It must be something serious if Nod had ridden in the dark through the forest. He was only thirteen.

I closed the solar door and came down the stairs.

Nod was standing amongst a knot of folk who slept in the hall. Hubert Alder the blacksmith and farrier, the tallest man there stood beside him with his arm around the lad's shoulder.

"Nod sir, has ridden hard from Cadley."

"Aye, I hear."

Aelfnod had grown of late but he was still dwarfed by the huge frame of Hubert.

"Sir, I'm sorry to come so late."

"No, Nod, if it's important then I will listen."

"A fire sir..."

"A fire at Cadley?"

"Yessir."

I took hold of the lad myself and sat him down on a bench.

"What happened? Not your home I hope?"

"No sir...the priest's house."

"Father Justin?"

"Aye sir. I knew that Doctor Johannes was here and I knew too that he would want to come and see what can be done for....for..."

"Father Justin?" I repeated.

"Yes, m'lord."

"He's hurt?"

"Aye, sir. Sore hurt."

I turned to Hal.

"Hal, go down to Johannes' room and fetch him up. He'll need his pack."

"Right you are, sir."

"Tom, run down to the stable, will you, and get the boys to saddle the horses? Hal, Doctor Johannes and I will ride to Cadley."

Tom pulled on his jerkin and was gone.

"Tell me, Nod quickly. What has happened?"

"You know sir, how the house is now quite a way from the church and the plants and bushes have grown up a bit."

"I noticed when I visited a short while ago. The house will be hidden by it all when it all grows up."

"There's no house close by the Father's home."

"No, there's your house on that side of the road and what...two others? Quite far from Father Justin's."

"Yessir."

Most of Cadley lay on the western side of the road through the forest.

"I was out before going to bed sir, seeing to Old Farter—the pig, our old boar—when I smelled smoke and saw the flames coming out of the priest's house."

"How far gone was it?"

"Quite bad sir. So I got everyone out to the pond and did as you taught us...got da to get buckets going and that."

"Well, done, Nod."

"And got the reeve to collect some of the men and see if we could get into the house."

"Could you?"

"It were 'ard but we did it."

"And you took out Father Justin?"

"We got him out but 'tis bad for him, sir."

"Right Nod, go and help in the stable. Get yourself another horse."

"Yessir.

I flew back up the solar steps and threw off my cloak.

"I have to go. Trouble at Cadley."

"Oh Aumary, be careful."

"A fire at Father Justin's"

"Oh no. Poor man."

"At least the church is not a thatch as it was. Hard to burn down stone and there are no houses close by to catch fire."

"God preserve him."

Fire was a most feared thing in villages where the main building materials were wood and thatch—fire could rage through the forest too, if not checked.

I grabbed my recently discarded shirt and cotte.

"Lydia, I have noticed something—it may be nothing, but whilst I'm gone—think on it."

I struggled tiredly into my clothes.

"What?"

"Phillip, why he is so quiet?"

"Oh no, Aumary, please do not say..."

"No. No! The angels will not have him yet," I smiled.

I sat on the stool and pulled on my boots.

"I watched him, as the noise grew tonight. The disturbance and knocking at the door. Me dropping my boot."

"Yes?"

"He was totally undisturbed by it."

"I told you he is unafraid of noise—not like Simon."

I grabbed my cloak again and heard Johannes now in the hall calling me.

I went to the bed and pecked Lydia on the nose. "I'll be back as soon as I can."

"Aumary you haven't told me what…?"

"Ah yes."

I threw on my cloak, bent to my second son and clapped my hands loudly out of sight by my knees. He looked at me with his huge blue eyes. The pupils stayed small and there was no reaction.

"God save him Lydia. I think our Phillip is deaf." I touched her briefly.

I ran out of the door with Lydia's cry of, "No. Oh no!" in my ears.

I yelled up the stairs. "Fear not. He will not suffer for it. I promise you. We shall do all we can."

And I ran through the hall, gathered up Johannes and Hal and was off to Cadley.

Chapter Six

"So when you saw the flames they were issuing from the thatch?"

"And the doorway was on fire. There's only one way in, sir and that's why it was so difficult to reach Father Justin. I could see through the little window that he was lying on the floor in the corner."

"And you, being the clever lad you are Nod..."

"Well, sir, I thought...if we can't get in the door and we can't climb onto the roof to go through the thatch, we ought to try the wall."

"Nod, that was quick thinking."

"I got da to take an axe to the wall by the corner the furthest away from the flames that I could see."

"And then Alan, being a small person, the smallest man in Cadley, squeezed through the hole and handed the priest out?" I asked.

"Then we had to make the hole a bit bigger but, yessir...it worked."

"Well done, Nod."

I leaned over Johannes who had Father Justin face down on a pallet in Nod's parents' house.

"The flames are dying down now. The house can be repaired. I am not so sure about Father Justin," I said sadly.

Nod crossed himself. "No sir. He is badly burned and his head looks a mess."

"Hit on the back of the head, Sir Aumary. I think it's another of our stones. He fell in the corner and then the house was set alight," said Johannes.

"A flare perhaps, thrust into the roof and one left inside the door?" said Nod.

"So the attacker was inside the house?" I asked.

"Escaped and shut the door on it," added Aelfnod.

"Luckily Father Justin's back was to the door. The flames licked his shoulders and lower back and yes he's burned there. However I think I have said before..." said Johannes "that the worst thing about fire is the smoke. If you fall to the floor you are less likely to do permanent damage to your lungs."

"Aye the smoke rises to the roof."

" 'Twas the smoke I smelled, sir and then I saw the flames," said Nod.

"Your quick thinking may have saved Father Justin's life."

The boy crossed himself again and he looked worriedly at his priest.

"Right. I'll get to work on his head," said Johannes. "Nod, can you help me turn him slightly? We need to cut off his robe and I shall need to cut his hair a little more to get at the head wound."

"Good job he's a bit bald, sir," said Nod cheerily.

I left them to their work and went to look at the smouldering little cottage in which I had been made so welcome but a few days ago.

"What is it about this little glade Hal? Two fires in a year." I nodded to a couple of Cadley men still raking off the thatch.

"Ah well. This one didn't burn the 'ole place down like the last one did," said my man at arms, running a stick along the plants in the ground outside the cottage. "This one won't take much to restore."

"No, unlike the old wooden church. Find anything Hal?"

"Still looking, sir."

I stared up at the blackened thatch. "Why would anyone wish to hurt Father Justin?"

"Well, he'd just told everyone that he couldn't bury people properly hadn't 'e? Nor marry 'em. Nor relieve them of their sins. Maybe someone didn't like that very much."

"Humph," I said. "I can't imagine anyone in Cadley taking it out on their old priest, one they've known for years. Surely they realised that it wasn't anything personal."

"Who knows? Folk don't always think straight when there's family involved. Think how cross you might've bin if it hadn't bin possible to bury Mistress Evisa at Bedwyn properly."

"But I understand that it's not the clergy's fault, Hal."

"Ah well, sir, some o' these folk, well they're simple people. Him that shuts the church, is responsible for the shuttin'. That's maybe what they'd think."

"I can't believe that's it, Hal."

"Mark my words sir, there'll be a deal of trouble soon or I'll be buried..."

"In Burbage. Yes." This was Hal's favourite outburst.

"Folk's goin'a think what do we pay our tithes for? The priest i'n't doin' nothin'. Why should we pay fer nothin'?"

I took a deep breath and coughed as the residue of the smoke filled my lungs.

"Can we take a look inside yet?"

"Best we leave it a while, sir, it's still damnty 'ot. And besides it's mortal dark."

Hal hunkered down and peered at the place a little way from the jagged door, which now lay at a forlorn angle in the doorhole.

"Ah, here we are, sir."

He rose and in the darkness I could see a whiteness in his gloved hand.

I lifted the torch I had carried with me.

"The rock, sir. Used to bash Father Justin on the 'ead."

"Flint again, Hal. Do we know if these are as available here as they are further in the forest, at Braydon?"

"I'll ask, sir."

"Tomorrow will be early enough, old Hal."

"Right you are, sir."

"We should also ask who saw Father Justin yesterday and who was the last person to see him and when."

"Some folk have been goin' into town to the church sir, the freemen. Father Justin wasn't seein' anyone in the church yet. It's not consecrated."

I looked up to the grey shape, that was the new church, in the black of the night, its tower almost complete.

"A new church and the doors will be closed as soon as it's done."

"Sad that isn't it?" said Hal, following my gaze.

"I hope you are wrong about people being angry, Hal."

Hal shrugged but did not reply.

I rubbed my forehead, I felt as if I could fall asleep on my feet.

"Tomorrow can you organise a party to ask about Father Justin? Where he went, who he saw. I'll go to the castle and get some men out to comb the ground for anything that's out of place."

"Sir Aumary...."

I turned back to him.

"If he lives might be a good idea to leave a guard by 'im? Someone wanted Father Justin dead an' they i'n't managed it."

"They haven't yet, Hal. Can I leave that to you too?"

"Surely, sir."

*****

I returned to Johannes and Father Justin.

I put the stone down on the table with a thump. Nod looked up from his place squatting on the floor beside the priest. "The weapon used to strike Father Justin."

"Just as before, Sir Aumary?" asked Johannes.

"I cannot say, I dare not say that this is the same person but it does seem a coincidence."

Johannes rose from the small stool by the pallet. "There is something that bothers me about all this, Sir Aumary."

"Tell me."

"The first murder, that of Bordern Lea. That was a knife wound or something similar."

"Yes."

"And yet every subsequent death and now the wounding of Father Justin, has been by hitting the head with a stone. Why?"

"You are saying that if we are dealing with the same murderer, why have they not used the same weapon again?"

"That is what I'm saying."

I looked down at the stone.

"Nod, are these stones plentiful here in Cadley?"

Nod came and peered at the stone in the gloom of the poorly lit cottage.

"Aye sir. Just a flint. We get them all the time. Folk digs 'em up when they farms their plots and we use them to build with. The new church is built with some of them."

87

Nod's father Osmund who' had been silent till now, came up to look.

"Aye m'lord. These we find everywhere."

"Ah, perhaps that tells us where our would-be priest murderer got the stone."

"Anyone could've got hold of one sir," said Osmund, his face serious and troubled.

"Osmund, Nod—tell me—when Father Justin told everyone about the ban on church services...?"

"The Pope's instructions, sir?"

"Yes, Nod. How did he do it? He has no church to call you to? Yet."

"He told us at the churchyard, sir. Everyone gathered there to listen and speak to him and he told us there. We've had meetings in the open air in the churchyard."

"Was there anyone particularly...well...angry about it? Anyone voice dissatisfaction with the fact that the new church couldn't be used?"

Nod shook his head.

"Osmund?"

"No sir. Not that I can say."

"Some folks knew about it 'cos they have been goin' to town an' heard about it there." Nod chuckled, "And some were quite 'appy 'cos they don't have to go to church anymore."

"Ah yes, there is that."

"A few folks would rather stay in their beds of a Sunday than get up and walk to church."

"Can I ask you Nod... while you are here...yes please do stay and keep your eye on Father Justin for a while, can you keep your eyes and ears open?" I put my hand on his shoulder "You're a clever lad. If there's anything to see or hear, you will no doubt see and hear it."

"Count on me, m'lord."

I ruffled his hair. "Nod, I know I can," I said.

*****

Before I left Johannes took me aside at the door of the Hart's cottage, the home of Nod's parents Osmund and Godgifu.

"Aumary, I would like to remove Father Justin to my house. He can be better cared for there. And better guarded no doubt."

"You've spoken to Hal. Yes. Will he survive the journey down the hill?"

Johannes shrugged. "That is in God's hands. I'll do my best."

I nodded. "Do it Johannes and I'll ask Hal to get Jem from the castle to come and guard him. He's good and has done it before."

"Aye he's another clever lad," he smiled.

I looked back to Nod who sat by the bedside of his priest staring into space. "God knows where we'd be without that spirited young man. You know this isn't the first time he's proven his worth to me."

Johannes laughed quietly, "Aye. He's only thirteen but there's an old head on his shoulders..."

"As they say," I added and joined him in his whispering laugh.

"I'm for home now. I'll get a cart out first thing."

*****

I slept till late and rose to a grey day and an icy wind. It whipped through the courtyard and the emerging leaves of the rose which grew up the manor wall, tossed to and fro like the swish of a pony's tail.

Lydia was quiet and subdued and as I broke my fast up in the solar, I took her in my arms, embraced and squeezed her and planted a kiss on her raven black crown.

"I am sorry I had to leave you with those awful words last night Lydia. The thought had just come into my head and it had to come out."

Lydia sighed. "If the truth be known, Aumary, I was thinking something similar myself. It cannot be right that a child doesn't pay attention to the sounds around him yet focus on those sights he sees."

"He doesn't, does he?"

"No, he seems to pay more attention to what he sees. He seems to be concentrating on one's face."

Hawise came out of her room and bounced up to us. We took her into our embrace.

"Dada. I noticed that Phillip wasn't turning his head either. I come up on him in his cradle sometimes or once or twice when I sit on the floor with him to sing and he doesn't turn to look at me. Simon always did."

"Though he can turn his head, I know he can," said Lydia. "He's getting stronger every day."

"All babies are different, Lydia."

"I know but...in everything else he's just like Simon."

"Except he's not so greedy," laughed Hawise.

"I remember you when you were tiny. You stared at everything like your eyes would bore a hole through them," I said.

"Was I noisy like Simon?"

"No, not quite as noisy, but then you're a girl." I laughed, tickling her chin.

"What do we do?" said Lydia, catching her lip with her teeth in a worried expression.

"We ask Johannes what he thinks."

Hawise looked up at me with her intelligent green eyes. "We can't even go into the church to pray for him can we dada? To ask Father Crispin to pray to God to make things better for Phillip."

"No sweetling, we can't."

"Then I shall just have to ask God myself," she said. "Here."

I bent and kissed her cheek then.

"I love my brothers," she said. "Both of them."

Do you know what, Paul? She still does.

*****

Later that morning saw me at the castle at Marlborough rounding up a few of the soldiers to come out with me to the forest. I wanted to search the immediate area around Father Justin's house and ask questions about who'd seen him and where. Then I would send them to Braydon to ask questions there. I had no idea what I was looking for but the murders and attempted murder had happened in these two places and so I felt I must mount a search for anything which might give me a clue the direction my enquiries should take. The forest was growing up around us and soon it would not be so easy to search the ground for anything hidden there.

My old friend Andrew Merriman, who was one of the masters of the small permanent garrison at the castle, though off duty, came with me complaining that it was dull at the castle at the moment. The King had been in Marlborough castle from March 15th to the 17th and had rushed off to Clarendon near Salisbury, en route for Southampton. John was to make a tour of the southern counties and we'd not see him back until August. Andrew was bored.

Andrew and Hal took charge of the searches whilst I went back to Henset to talk to Wilkin Chetel.

The man was working at his plot at the back of his house when I arrived. He did not see me and I left Bayard in front of the cottage.

I watched him for a short while; a short stocky man with long straggly hair tied in place with a band around his brow. His beard was a yellow blond, his eyes bright blue. This man wore his Saxon descent visibly upon his features.

He was digging the ground with force, driving in the spade angrily and gritting his teeth, exhaling and moaning with almost every spade full of earth. He bent to remove a rock and threw it behind him. I watched as he wiped his eyes and nose on his sleeve, then dug again.

"Master Chetel. God's blessings on you."

He looked up, startled. His eyes were red rimmed and his nose runny. There was no doubt he had been weeping.

"My Lord Belvoir," he tugged his forelock. "You startled me."

"It was not my intention to worry you, Wilkin. Please accept my condolences upon the death of your wife."

He looked away and wiped his nose once more.

"Aye, aye. My thanks. Will you come in, my lord, out of the wind? It's a cold day today."

I smiled. "I think that would be a good idea."

We walked the few feet to the door and I followed him in.

"I wondered how long it would take for you to come, sir."

Wilkin and I knew each other vaguely. He had on occasions come out with me on searches of the forest when I'd need for extra men. He was the head of his tithing and a representative of his hundred.

"I am really very sorry about your wife."

"Aye..." The man's chest heaved and I could see that he was close to tears again.

"I'll find out who did it, Wilkin. You have my word."

He looked up at me with tear filled eyes.

"It's the boys, sir. The boys. How I am to manage them I don't know. Without Emma I...."

I touched my hand to his shoulder briefly.

"You will manage. And you have Tova's help."

He looked down at the floor.

"Maybe she'll return to Braydon now that her stepmother is gone."

"Back to her father?"

"Aye. She should never have come but Emma was kind and we gave her a home when..."

"When Cottar married Freya."

"Yessir."

"She tells me she was here alone with the boys when Mistress Cottar was killed. Where were you?"

Chetel moved about the cottage and lifted a cloth placed over a jug of ale.

He gestured for me to sit. I moved to a bench.

"Yes, Tova was here. I hear that Freya was killed in the early morning. Is this right?"

"Yes. Where were you from when you left this house to the fourth hour of the day?"

"I walked with Emma to Red Vein Bottom. Tova stayed here with the boys. Emma and I were letting the cows out to pasture sir, that day. Along with a couple of the others. She wanted to see how the cows in calf were faring sir. One had already dropped."

"And then?"

"Emma walked home and I stayed along with the lads to lay some more hedges. We wanted to be finished by the end of March."

"You were within sight of these other lads all day?"

"I was, my lord."

Wilkin poured ale for me. He did not pour any for himself.

"Where were you when Lea was killed?"

"Here, sir, with the family. And with Emma's mother too."

"You say Emma walked home the day she was killed. Tova tells me she didn't see her arrive."

"No, sir."

"I think she was waylaid on her walk and someone asked her to meet them at Braydon Oak."

"The murderer, sir?"

"Yes, I think so."

"But that means that she knew them!" His face was blotchy. He looked strange, his eyes red with crying, his cheeks draining of colour as I watched.

He sat down slowly, then jumped up again, aware that he shouldn't sit in the presence of his lord.

"No, sit Wilkin. You are distressed."

"I'm even more distressed to think that whoever killed my Emma was...known to us, sir. A friend. I thought...I thought we were looking at a masterless man in the forest, a stranger."

"Three people killed and a fourth wounded."

"No! I know about Lea and then Freya, now my Emma but who is the fourth sir?"

"The priest of Cadley, Father Justin."

Chetel crossed himself. "God's Almighty dust, sir. The priest?"

"He too was hit on the head and then his cottage was set on fire."

"But you say...wounded?"

"He survived, Wilkin. He lies sore hurt in the town at the doctor's."

He shook his head. "I cannot see why all these people should..."

"You can see no connection between them?"

"No, my lord."

"Neither can I."

I took a sip of the ale. It was sweet and good. Pleasure must have registered on my face because Wilkin smiled sadly.

"Emma was a good brewster, sir." His face creased again in agony.

"You loved her dearly?"

"Aye, sir. We were married at the age of sixteen. We loved each other from the first, sir, since we were mere children."

I smiled reassuringly at him "That is good to hear. You must concentrate on the best of times, Wilkin. When time has passed you will remember clearly the good times and less of the bad."

His eyes filled with tears and one spilled over onto his paled cheek.

"You would know, sir," he said self-consciously.

He referred to the death of my first wife Cecily and my five year old son Geoffrey. Yes, I too had cause to mourn.

"You were together a long time. Parting is never easy after that length of time."

"Twenty years sir...twenty years."

"No children older than the boys?"

"No, sir. God didn't favour us until a few years ago."

"You are blessed with two good lads."

"Aye, sir. Thomas, nine and Alfred, nearly seven."

There was a little silence. I drained the small beaker. The ale was too good to waste and there would be no further brews by the hand of Emma Chetel.

I stood. "You can tell me no more. No one disliked your wife?"

"No, sir. Not enough to kill her."

"No threats?"

"Never, sir."

"What do Emma, Freya and Lea have in common, Wilkin—anything?"

He stood and thought, brushing away the tear which had collected on his cheek and smoothing his long moustaches. He shook his head. "Cows sir...only cows."

"Hmmm. Thank you Wilkin. God keep you."

*****

I ducked under the door lintel and came face to face with Tova Cottar.

"Ah...just the person I want to speak to."

"Again, my lord?"

"Again, Tova."

I took her shoulder and moved her to the back of the cottage.

She stood before me, the same truculence in her face as upon the first time we'd met.

"Where were you when your mistress met her end under the Braydon oak, Tova?"

"I told you I didn't see her again that morning. I went out to milk the goats and was there for a while, and then I came back to the children."

I folded my arms and fixed her with what my wife always called my 'withering stare.'

She sighed and scuffed up the dirt path with the toe of her boot.

"Then I was here, taking apart the beds."

"The beds?"

"Mistress Emma wanted me to help with the washing."

I frowned. "Washing?"

"I was to start it and she was to carry on when she returned. I told you, she didn't come home."

I leaned forward. "Tova... I know enough about domestic matters to know that washing is not to be done when the weather is damp and cold."

"I was told to begin it. I took the sheets from the bed," she insisted.

"Bed...you said beds, all the beds?"

"No sir... it was just the one. The big one. Mistress and Master Chetel's."

There was a strange look on her face.

I walked around her. "This family is one of the better off amongst my villeins, aren't they?"

"Yes sir. Master Chetel has worked hard and his father before him and can afford to keep me as a servant and have nice things in his home."

"That's why you came here? A better home than you were used to?"

"Father is also well off, sir, as you know. He has cattle and sheep of his very own."

"And a parcel of land here in the forest?"

"Yes, my lord."

"The Chetels have a bigger house," I said.

"And real fine linen sheets to the beds, sir."

"So that morning you were washing the sheets. Why?"

"Because Mistress Chetel asked me to."

"Why do you think she asked you to do that in weather that wasn't exactly good for washing?"

She shrugged. "It was..." She looked away. I could see she was bursting to tell me something, "Stained sir. She didn't know I knew."

"With what, blood?"

Tova giggled. "No, my lord."

I frowned. Then light dawned.

"Your mistress and the master had..."

"Ah no, sir."

"What. They had not been in the marital bed and..."

"Well, no sir."

"Tova...I am getting tired of this. Had your mistress and master been enjoying conjugal relations earlier yesterday?"

I saw her face flush. She so wanted to shock me but hadn't the courage to use the words she wanted.

"No sir. They hadn't done that for a long time. They have the boys, they don't need any more children."

"They were a devoted couple I hear. Why not?"

"The church frowns upon carnal pleasures sir, on bodily lust but for the getting of children."

I cleared my throat. "I know that but...."

"So they hadn't been trying to make any more children, sir."

"What then had...they been doing?"

"Nothing sir. What does one normally do in bed? Sleeping. Because the master was... is... impotent, sir. He has been for many years."

Chapter Seven

Yes, Paul, she told me just like that. No preamble.

I walked away from that house, my mind in somewhat of a turmoil. So if Master Chetel had not been in bed with his wife that morning, who *had* been between the sheets with her?

Tova obviously thought that Emma Chetel had taken a lover. I would have to verify this piece of information. But how?

I'd asked Tova who she thought the man was. She shrugged and said she didn't know.

And she wasn't the only one for I was certain that Master Chetel didn't know either. Unless his tears that morning had been tears of regret and guilt.

I thought back to what he'd said. He had been in full view of those laying the hedges that day. No, he had not killed his wife in a passionate fit of jealousy and taken her body out to Braydon Oak.

I rode at speed for Braydon and caught up with Andrew who was searching the glade with four men.

They'd found nothing so far.

All houses bar one had been searched.

Andrew was standing in front of Mistress Lea's small cottage as I rode up.

"Nothing, Aumary," he said. "So far the place is clear of anything that shouldn't be here."

He tried the door of Lea's house.

"It's open. No one here."

"This is Ellen Lea's house, Andrew. She has gone to Cadley to family for her own safety. I sent her. It's empty but for a few meagre possessions. When I found the body of Emma Chetel, I thought it was *her* body under that oak."

"Ah. You thought perhaps that her life was in danger?"

"I did. I still do. I didn't, however, think for a moment that our murderer would stray outside this glade, that someone else from another place would die."

"The murderer's reach has extended. Now we have them in Cadley too. Did they follow Ellen Lea? *Is* she still in danger?" asked Andrew, horror in his voice.

I threw myself from Bayard's back and ducked inside the house.

It was almost as it had been when I'd last visited. The pots and treen were still laid neatly on the shelves. This time the fire was out and the hearth was cold. All had been laid in an orderly fashion for it to be lit again when the occupant returned. There was the cloak on the back of the door. The sack was missing from the chest top. The thorn stick had gone.

I looked up at the rafters and over at the goat pen. It was empty. I suppose Mistress Lea had taken the animal to a neighbour to be looked after.

Andrew had followed me in. He looked round.

"Aumary...what's this?"

He hunkered down by the empty hearth. Last time I'd looked at this place, there had been a small swaddled child lying on a sheepskin, over it. Andrew scuffed up the tamped down earthen floor with his fingers. "Blood?"

I opened the door and window shutter to let in more light and strode to the hearth.

"I didn't see this before because it was covered up. It does look like a little amount of blood."

"Old dried blood though. Soaked into the beaten earth."

"Could be anything. Mistress Lea gave birth here, Andrew. She cooks and prepares food here. The hens come in and out. It could be anything."

"Hmmm."

We shut the shutters and the door and left. Our search had given us nothing new.

*****

On the way back to Cadley I fretted over the fact that the murderer had been active in this village too.

Was it, as Andrew had said, that Mistress Lea was still in danger?

Hal told me that the last person to see Father Justin was Osmund Hart, Nod's father. He'd lifted his hand to Osmund in greeting as he entered his home a little while before the fire was discovered. No one had seen anyone enter the house and Father Justin did not exit again. Hal had managed to plot the priest's movements that day. The facts told us nothing. I called on Nod again to ask him where Mistress Lea had been staying, for he knew all the folk of Cadley.

He took me to a cottage on the eastern side of the road by the village pond. Apparently, Ellen's grandparents lived here.

The old man was deaf and frail with thin white hair and sat in the corner of the main room shaking and dribbling into his tunic. The grandmother was younger with only a little grey at her temples. I could see this poking out untidily from her head cloth as she bade me enter.

Hal stood outside and I could hear him marching up and down the small path from the pond to the house door and back.

"She isn't here, m'lord. She left the baby and went out," said the grandam.

"Does she have parents too?"

"Only us, m'lord. Her mother and father died in the fever a while back."

Many folk had died in those years. Durley too had suffered badly in the outbreak of dock fever, so called because it was believed to originate at the docks.

"Where has she gone?"

"She won't go far, sir. Not out of the forest. She knows that is forbidden."

"Hmmm. I am worried that she might be in danger, good woman. Where *might* she have gone?"

"She won't be gone for long, sir, for she has to feed the babe," said the woman with a worried expression.

"But where?"

The old lady shuffled to the other side of the table. "She didn't say."

"Think. Where might she go?"

"She has a friend who lives up the lane, m'lord. She hasn't seen her in a while. Maybe she's gone there."

"Her name?"

"Ailsa, m'lord."

I exited the house and pushing Nod in front of me yelled for Hal to follow.

"Where does this woman live, Nod?"

"Old Ailsa, sir? She lives in the last cott on the lane, just in the trees."

"Show me."

We walked up a rough track. I'd been this way before and I knew that almost at the end of the track lay a turner's cottage. This lay on the southern side. There was a gap of scrubby greenery and then a small meadow. Across the meadow we saw the rather dilapidated cottage occupied by the widow, Ailsa. The track then went on to meet the Shaftesbury Road at Granham Hill.

Hal shooed the chickens from the house front and we scratched on the leather panel which served as a door.

"Ailsa!"

I looked up at the thatch. It was patchy and in places quite bare, with weeds growing from it. The wooden and wattle bones of the house were poking out from the thin covering of daub.

Nod ran to gather up the hens and pen them behind their thorn hedge.

Hal pushed up the leather.

It was extremely dark in the cottage for there was only one tiny window and the day was still dull. I ducked and looped the leather over the stick laid at the top of the lintel, to keep the door clear.

My eyes unclouded and became more used to the lack of light.

The place stank of rot.

This was no well-kept cottage like Mistress Lea's or the houses lived in by the Cottars or Chetels. This was a poor house with only the bare essentials. From every beam and peg hung plants in various stages of drying and decay. The table was full of them, the floor littered with them.

Nod ducked under the leather door.

"Cor, sir. I meant to warn you. It stinks like a bog in here. Always does. Ailsa, you here?" he cried.

There was no answer.

Hal ducked to avoid a bunch of dried nettles hanging down a good three feet from the middle rafters and swore.

"God's cods! Here, sir!"

Nod, whose eyesight was obviously better than mine, ran around the table.

"Ailsa...mother Ailsa?"

A woman lay on her back. Her eyes stared up at the assortment of herbs and plants hanging from her roof.

Nod fell to his hocks, took her head and laid it against his knee. "Oh no. No. Ailsa."

It seemed that Nod knew this old lady quite well.

"Ailsa of Cadley, sir," he said, looking up at me tearfully. "She's the cunning woman we come to for our remedies and such."

I bent to look at her.

"Ugh!" said Nod as he brought his hand from behind the woman's head.

As his hand came out into the light we could see that it was wet and bloodied.

"Struck on the 'ead," said Hal.

"Is she dead, sir?"

"Yes, Nod, I'm afraid so."

Hal was searching the cottage for the stone with which the old lady had been struck, so confident was he that here we had another murder of the same type as our previous three.

"Oh well. Ah..." he said suddenly and bent double over the hearth at the far end of the cottage.

I looked round. "What Hal?"

"Seems like she 'it her own 'ead. Look."

The hearth had been raised from the bare earth with mud compacted into a shelf. Around this were large stones laid in a line surrounding the four sides of the space. Warm ashes sat in the very middle. There was blood on the end stone.

"The fire isn't completely out yet."

"No one's fed it have they?" said Nod, getting up from his knees and wiping his bloody hand on his jerkin.

"Hasn't been out long though," I said.

"Looks like she fell and struck 'er 'ead on this stone, m'lord," said Hal pointing. "She staggered backwards, hit her head and fell there."

"That is how it looks Hal. But...no stone?"

"No stone with flint as we've 'ad before."

"Try to dislodge that bloodied stone will you, Hal?"

Hal looked a little disgruntled at being asked to get his hands dirty but Nod beat him to it, grasping the stone with both small hands and pulling.

"No sir. It won't budge. It's set in the clay edge."

"Then it does look as if the old woman tripped and fell," I said.

"But where is Mistress Lea sir?"

I looked round the cottage again.

Something familiar took my eye. "She has been here, for look, here is the blackthorn stick that was in her cottage the day we found her husband, Hal."

The stick was on the floor, against the wall by the door.

" 'Ow do we know it's the same one? There's plenty of folks who make sticks like this. Maybe the old woman 'ad one."

"Ailsa didn't need a stick sir," said Nod. "She strode out like she was my age."

"So she wasn't unsteady even though she was aged?"

"No, sir. I think she was one of those women who looked older than she really was."

I remembered my wood warden John's elderly mother, Mildred, for whom one of my large wolfhounds was named. She had been threescore and ten but walked out like a woman of twenty with a steady and long step.

"A woman unlikely then to become unsteady and fall hitting her head on the hearth stone?"

"Anyone can 'ave an accident, m'lord," said Hal.

"True old Hal. It doesn't mean that she *didn't* fall."

"But you think it's unlikely, m'lord?" said Nod, his eyes wide.

I shrugged. "You don't think this is Ailsa's stick, Nod?"

"No, sir. I don't. I don't recognise it."

"But I do and I think it's Ellen Lea's or more properly her husband's."

"But sir, she said that 'er 'usband's stick was missing along with 'is cloak and 'is sack" said Hal, his tone disbelieving. "And 'is scrip."

"A man may have more than one stick, Hal."

"Aye, that's right enough."

I gazed over the cottage's interior again. "Nothing more to be seen. We must call the coroner and if he can be spared we must ask Johannes to return."

"What about the priest? We need... Ah no. We int allowed to do that are we?"

"As far as I understand it, Old Ailsa can be buried elsewhere but no word must be said over her."

"Anyway," said Nod "Father Justin can't do anything. He's lying at the doctors with his head smashed in."

"It's a pretty mess, I must say."

"Sir..." Nod looked a little evasive. "It's all right...about Old Ailsa."

"About Ailsa? In what way, Nod?"

"Well, she don't hold with churches and prayin' and such like."

"Did she not?"

"No, sir. She preferred to be out in the trees and worship the old way."

I closed my eyes and counted to ten. "Nod, it's all right for you to tell *me* this but never tell anyone else, all right?"

"Why sir?"

"Because the law of our land says we must all worship the same God."

"Except if we'm a Jew, sir," said Hal mischievously.

"Well, yes the Jews are... different." I sighed. "Although their God is the same as our own. We'll just keep it quiet shall we?"

"What, that Ol' Mother Ailsa was an 'eathen sir?"

"Er yes, Nod. Never breathe a word of it to anyone."

Nod stood up tall. "No sir. Never!"

"It's our secret."

"Well, it weren't exactly a secret because..."

"Nod."

"Yessir."

I cleared my throat. "Right. Lets' go outside and search around. See what we can find."

"What're we looking for, sir?' asked Nod.

"We shall no doubt know when we find it, lad."

"Right, sir."

We exited the dark cottage and pulled down the leather flap.

Hal leaned over the thorn hedge and looked at the hens scratching around the enclosure.

"Nothing 'ere."

"Is there a garden plot Nod, behind?"

"Aye sir, a big one."

We walked round the edge of the cottage and through yet another thorn hedge.

Here were some ducks dabbling in a small pond and at a muddy bank. They scattered as we approached quacking and flapping angrily.

"Mother Ailsa keeps a boar and a sow. Here sir."

"She didn't kill them in the autumn, salt them down?"

"No sir. Her boar services many of the pigs hereabouts. He's a nice little red lad, he is."

"Right we shall need to find them and make sure they're secure until it's known what is going to happen."

"It's here, sir."

We heard the snuffling as we rounded a small wattle pen.

"Ah, there you are Porknell!" said Nod smiling widely. "Safe in your little house."

He leaned over the fence. The smile left his face.

"God's wounds, sir. Quick!"

Being tall I could see into the pen. There in the mud, I could see a leg.

I vaulted over the wattle and pushed aside the two pigs which were the little bristly forest variety many of us kept.

"Hal, help here."

I lifted the woman from the mud, oblivious to the muck now staining my cotte.

"It's Ellen sir. Ellen Lea," said Nod jumping from foot to foot.

I handed her to Hal across the fence and jumped over again.

The woman moaned.

"A wound sir, to her forehead," said Nod

It was indeed Ellen Lea. Blood had trickled down her face and over her eye. Her hair was plastered in mud and her head cloth was gone.

"It's all right, mistress, we have you now," I said.

She began to shake.

"Can we carry her to the house place?"

"I'll go in first and cover the body, sir," said Nod. "She'd best not see that, had she?"

"Good thought, Nod."

I picked up the woman from the grass where Hal had laid her.

She grabbed a handful of my cotte and moaned. "A man. A man… Aah, oh!"

"A man. A man hit you on the head Ellen?"

But she did not answer me.

I rounded the cottage corner with my burden. Hal unhooked the leather panel.

My gaze dimmed again in the interior and I looked for a bed upon which to lay her.

In the corner furthest from the door was a pile of small twigs overlain with dried grass and a blanket. Despite the smell, I laid Mistress Lea on it.

She moaned again and once more grasped my clothes.

"A man…he hit me."

"Yes, Ellen, we shall get you cleaned and mended and don't worry, you are safe now."

I stood up. "Ellen, do you know who hit you?"

Her eyes were huge in the darkness and glinted in the rushlight which Hal was now lighting.

"A man…a man. M…man with a big beard."

"Maybe the man hit them both, sir, after all," said Nod.

"Only this poor creature." Hal pointed to the body under its rough blanket. "This one didn't survive."

"At least Mistress Ellen is alive, sir," said Nod.

"And when she's recovered, she can tell us who hit her," I said.

*****

105

A boy was dispatched to the town to fetch the doctor. One of my Cadley foresters, known as a riding forester, took one of the manor rounceys and rode off to Ramsbury to the coroner. We would report the death even if the coroner did not deign to record it.

After a short while, we walked a trembling Mistress Lea back to her grandparents' cottage and her head was washed and dressed. We told her that Ailsa of Cadley was dead.

I hunkered down in front of her.

"Ellen, tell me in your own time, what happened to you and to Ailsa of Cadley today in her cottage?"

The woman sniffled. "I went to see her. Tilda wasn't suckling well and I knew she'd have some remedy for that, seeing as how she knows all about babies and simples and stuff."

"She was alive when you saw her?"

"She was, sir. We talked a little while..."

"Did you take Bordern's stick with you?"

Ellen frowned and then cocked her head. "Yes, sir, how did you know that?"

"I found it in the cott. Go on."

"I took it for protection, sir."

I nodded.

"I'd only been there a moment when there was a cry from outside."

"What kind of cry?" asked Hal.

"Like someone had hurt themself, sir. I poked my head out the door and I couldn't see any one."

"So what did you do?"

"I went to the back of the cott thinking that the cry might'a come from there."

"Ailsa was still alive then?"

"Yessir."

The woman moaned. "I heard a kinda scuffling and then nothing."

"From inside the cottage?" asked Hal.

"Yes sir and then I went right round and poked my head into the door hole. I didn't know any more till you found me, sir."

"You were clappered on the 'ead, lass," said Hal.

Mistress Lea lifted a shaking hand to her forehead.

"But you did see that there was a man in the cottage and that he had a beard?"

"Yes, sir, a big black beard and lots of black hair... oh and he grinned as he hit me and so I saw he had a broken tooth."

"A broken front tooth?" asked Hal.

"Yessir. Then you found me. Thank the angels you did, sir."

"Did you know the man Ellen?"

"No, my lord."

I turned to Nod. "Nod, do you know him?"

He looked puzzled. "No sir. No one from Cadley."

I turned to ask Ellen's grandmother but she didn't know anyone like this either.

"Nor in Durley neither," said Hal.

"Nor as far as I can say from the wider forest but we shall ask about."

I stood up.

"Nod can you run back to Mistress Ailsa's and fetch the stick I saw on the floor by the wall?"

The lad nodded and we heard his running footsteps crunching up the trackway.

"I must feed Tilda, sir," said Mistress Lea. "She's overdue."

"You have had a terrible shock. She is quiet for the moment. Leave it for a while, mistress."

It was true, for Tilda Lea was lying in a rush basket before the fire in her great grandparent's cott, fast asleep.

"Have you seen this man before, perhaps at Braydon?"

"No sir."

"You don't think he knew your husband Bordern, Ellen?"

"I don't know, sir. He must be a wolfshead."

"Hmmm." I looked down at her "Did you know that Mistress Chetel of Henset has been killed, Ellen?"

Her face registered shock. "No sir. Oh no, sir."

"The same. The same as Mistress Cottar, hit with a stone."

"I didn't know her well of course," she said. "She seemed like a very nice woman."

"Hmmm."

"Of course—she were a redhead too."

"Yes, she was, Ellen."

"I know that the priest has been hit, sir."

"How did you know that?"

"The neighbour, here. He's Alan Small. He was the one who fetched out Father Justin from the fire sir. With Nod's da."

"Yes, Osmund Hart."

"Is he dead, sir?"

"Father Justin? No, sore hurt but no, he isn't dead."

"Has he been able to say what happened?"

"No, he is unconscious and is likely to be so for a while."

"Oh. That's terrible, my lord."

"He has been taken down to the town to be cared for by Doctor Johannes."

The woman didn't seem to hear me but swayed on her stool and her grandmother grabbed her arm and righted her.

"I do feel queer, my lord."

"I have asked for the doctor to come up here. He helps me in cases like this and he can have a look at your wound Ellen, make sure you are all right."

Granddaughter and grand dam exchanged a look.

"We have nothing with which to pay the doctor," said the older woman. "We are poor people, my lord."

"The doctor does not charge for his services to me, mistress."

She blinked as if that was something unheard of. Well, I suppose it was. She was a simple soul. To her something for nothing was impossible.

"We can give him a few eggs, sir," she smiled.

I smiled back, "I'm sure he would be more than pleased with those, mistress."

"Come Ellen, we shall get you from these clothes...all muddied and shite stained with the pigs." She helped Ellen Lea rise from the stool and go behind the screen of a blanket which had been erected over a rope strung between two beams at the far end of the main room. This would give Ellen some privacy.

Nod ducked under the open doorway.

"The stick, sir."

I took it from his hand. This was definitely the same stick I'd seen in the Lea house.

I took it to the light of the open door. "Hal... look."

Hal stared at the handle end of the stick. "Blood sir?"

"Blood and hair."

"Mistress Ailsa didn't wear any head cloth, sir. Well, not inside her house at any rate. Nothing to protect her skull from a blow," said Nod.

My brow furrowed in puzzlement. "No, Nod?" I looked at Hal and his eyebrow raised. "The stick that hit Mistress Ailsa?"

"I thought we'd established that she had 'it 'er 'ead on the stone fire surround?"

"Pushed by this strange man?"

"But this 'air is grey sir. Steel grey..." Hal freed a strand of the hair from the end of the stick and held it up to the light."

"Mistress Ailsa, Nod... to confirm, her hair was dark grey? I didn't see well in the light of that cottage."

"Grey and long sir. Down to her bosom. She had a thing about not cutting it."

"Hmmm."

"Do we think this is the murder weapon which killed her and then struck Mistress Lea?"

"No sign of Ellen Lea's hair sir," offered Hal.

"Sir," said Nod. "The woman was struck on the forehead. There wouldn't be any hair would there?"

"Well done, Nod."

I looked at the curtain which shielded the dressing woman and her grand dam.

"I must look at that wound again when Johannes gets here."

*****

Andrew was just finishing his final searches of Cadley village when we emerged from the cottage.

"You're right about there being a pile of these flint stones here, Sir Aumary, right by the new church building. Look." He hefted a large flint.

"So that is where our killer found the weapon with which he attacked Father Justin."

Andrew nodded and threw away the stone. "And the house is now safe. Want to have a look?"

"I do."

We trudged through the growing greenery of the space between the priest's house and the new building.

Hal sidled through the doorway. "It's a squeeze but you can just get through," he said.

The room was mostly intact but the wall by the door was scorched and blackened and the heat had cracked the daub of the inside lime plaster.

Ashes littered the floor by this wall and burnt thatch was left in clumps all over the earth.

The table was intact and the surface was pitted with ashes.

A gaping hole in the far wall showed where they had taken the axe to the daub and fetched out the insensible priest.

I crunched my way over to the wall and crouched over the place where Father Justin had lain.

"Here Nod?"

"Just there sir. Lyin' like this with his head to the corner."

"What had he been doing here? Why had he turned his back on his visitor?"

"Well... 'e must'a known 'im because 'e wouldn't do that else," said Hal. "Even a priest is goin'a be careful with a stranger in 'is 'ouse."

"If it *was* our black bearded fellow, Hal."

I looked around.

"Sir..." said Nod standing on tiptoe.

"What?"

"Is this what Father Justin was looking at... or tending to?"

Suspended from the rafter at the unburnt end of the cottage where lay the things which the priest might use to store food, was a small basket.

It had been pulled up to a distance of about seven feet at the gable end.

I released the rope which had been tied to a beam and lowered the basket.

Nod peered in.

"Eggs sir."

"Eggs, Nod?" I said retrieving the receptacle.

"Father Justin is very fond of eggs."

"Is he?"

"So," said Andrew from the doorway, "maybe someone had brought him some eggs which he went to store at that end."

"As he always did," said Nod authoritatively.

"And as he tied the rope, someone struck him from behind."

Hal picked up an egg. "Hah! The heat will'a cooked 'em for 'im won't they?" he chuckled.

Johannes arrived at the priest's house about the ninth hour of the day. He reassured me that Father Justin was still hanging onto life and that the burns he'd received, although grievous, could be managed by careful doctoring. I'd seen him treat burns before when one of the castle guards had suffered bad scorches to his leg. I knew he could help. The wounds turning bad was his major worry and Johannes was being very careful with the priest's injuries.

Father Justin had not yet spoken.

Jem Chadwyk, a young soldier from the castle garrison had arrived to guard the patient. The doctor had left him in his capable hands and those of Little Agnes, his housekeeper and helpmeet.

"I would not have left him, Aumary, if Jem had not been on guard."

"I think we have need of yet another guard, Johannes."

"Oh?"

"Mistress Lea was attacked. She too survived and has given us a description of the man who hit her."

"Does she know him?"

"No, he cannot be identified by anyone."

"Then we are indeed looking at a masterless man of the forest?"

I shrugged. "If that's so then he has kept very low. There have been no complaints of this man stealing food or attacking anyone for goods or money anywhere in my demesne or forest. No one passing through the trees has been attacked or robbed."

"And why murder innocent peasant women? What can they give him?"

I shook my head. "None of it makes sense. Anyway, might you just go to have a look at Ellen Lea, to satisfy my mind that she isn't going to topple over and die of her wound. I need her guarding. Although she doesn't know the man, he might think another attempt on her life is necessary."

"Assuredly I can."

"Nod will take you there."

Johannes strode away.

I called to him, "And then might you come home with me? Lydia and I have some questions for you."

"Questions?" His voice held a puzzled note.

"It's about Phillip.....we need your help."

Johannes called, walking backwards from me to join Nod a distance away. "Is he ill?"

"No. We just have some concerns about him and need your advice."

"Then I will most certainly come home with you."

Chapter Eight

"Hal, we need to have Mistress Lea guarded."

"I was wondering about that, sir."

"If word gets out that she is still alive and can identify her attacker..."

" 'Er life won't be worth a snotty sneeze, sir. Even though 'e don't know she can't say 'oo 'e is."

"Johannes is looking at her now to make sure she is all right. I think the best thing would be for her to go down to the town and stay with Johannes and Agnes. That way we can have all our folk in one place and they can be guarded. We know Johannes' house is safe and can be secured easily."

"Not so these flimsy forest cottages m'lord."

"No indeed. One swipe with an axe and the wall can be breached, as we have shown."

"Want me to take them down to town sir? Her and the baby?"

"No, she can go down in one of the Cadley carts. I believe Osmund's neighbour has one. Andrew can drive it and his horse can be tied behind."

Andrew was going home to Marlborough and might as well drive Lea's widow to the doctor's. Agnes would accept his word and things would be well organised by my friend and fellow castle man.

"Right you are, sir."

"Then when Johannes is finished we shall all go home. It's getting late."

The wind got up as we rode home to Durley. It found its way into every crevice of clothing, every gap at neck and sleeve. We were all perished as we clattered through the gate house and left the horses to the grooms.

I looked up at the sky. The grey clouds were clearing and it was going to be a starry night.

We ran up the manor steps and into the warmth of the hall.

"Before we talk to Lydia, Johannes, come into my office and I'll tell you what we found at Father Justin's and what happened to us at the woman Ailsa's. Then you can let me know what *you* think happened."

I stirred my brazier into life and whilst we waited for warmth to thaw us, Hal brought us some warmed ale from the hall fireside.

He closed the office door behind him.

"Ailsa of Cadley. What can you tell us?"

"A blow to the back of the head killed her much the same as the other women, Johannes answered.

"We found no discarded stone this time," I said.

"No?"

"We made a search but there was no bloodstained and hair smeared flint around the area."

"Did you see the hearth stone?" asked Johannes.

"Aye we did," said Hal.

"The woman Ellen said that she heard a noise outside and went to investigate. When she returned Ailsa was dead on the floor and a bearded man struck out at Ellen with the blackthorn stick which she had left in the cott. There was blood and hair on it too."

"The blood and hair on the stick was the old woman's, you tell me?" said Johannes.

"We think so. So she didn't fall backwards and hit her head on the hearth stone? However there was, as you said, blood there too."

Johannes moved closer to the warming brazier and held out his hands.

"Trying to work out what happened and in which order is akin to working out which animal God made first before Adam and Eve, Aumary!"

"The snake..." said Hal with authority.

We smiled.

"We must try to understand it."

"'Ow's this sir?" said Hal "The murderer picks up the blackthorn stick and bashes the old lady over the 'ead..."

"Why Hal?" asked Johannes.

"Maybe *she* knew 'im."

"Hmmm. I suppose so."

"She 'int dead but then Ailsa falls and cracks her 'ead again on the fire stone. Cer-runch. Out she goes like a blown taper."

"Then Ellen comes to the door hole and she too is hit. This time on the forehead," I said.

"The wound to her head is certainly one received by being struck by something solid like such a stick," said Johannes."

"And out she goes too," added Hal. " 'Cept, the murderer can't finish her because he hears us coming..."

"The old woman certainly hadn't been dead long at all," said the doctor. "She was still warm, the blood was not yet fully congealed and rigor had not started."

"Hmmm. The fire was not out quite....though as Nod pointed out, it hadn't been fed for a while."

" 'E picks up the woman and dumps 'er in the pig pen?" continued Hal.

"Hmmm. Why move her at all?" I asked.

"Why not just drag her into the house from the doorway, step over her and be gone?" said Johannes.

"He wasted time getting her to the pig pen at the back."

"Aye that's a foolish waste 'a time. There's no way I would spend time doin' that," said Hal shaking his head. "I'd be off sharp."

"Pigs have a certain reputation don't they?" said Johannes.

"They aren't particularly fussy about what they eat," said my man at arms. "Maybe this man was hoping that Mistress Lea would be silenced, good and proper. P'raps 'e 'oped we wouldn't find 'er and the pigs'd eat 'er, sir."

"Or at the very least trample her."

"Hmmm," said both Hal and the doctor.

"Thank you for taking Ellen in, Johannes. It's by far the easiest solution to our problem."

"Happy to be of use. Agnes will be kind and helpful."

"Yes, I know."

"So what did you find at Father Justin's?"

"Nothing which tells us very much. He knew his attacker, for he turned his back on him."

"They all do," said Hal. "This man is known to all the victims, 'cept the Widow Lea."

"Ah. We don't know about Bordern Lea. As Johannes has pointed out, that death was different from our others."

"'E must'a bin known. No one would let anyone they didn't know get close enough to stick a knife in their eye."

I rubbed my aching forehead.

"No motives..."

"No cui bonies sir. Like 'Ol Master Quimper used to say."

"No, Hal. The victims knew each other but no one had a reason to murder any of them it seems."

"You've often said, Aumary, on our late night musings when we have been chewing over the wicked things people do to each other, that revenge is the common thread which connects folk, have you not?" said the doctor.

"Yes, but here, what possible motive for revenge could there be in these little peoples' lives?"

Johannes shrugged. "I don't know but maybe it would be worth looking at that common thread. What is it that connects all these people?"

"Cows, Johannes," I said jokingly.

"Ah no, sir. Not old mother Ailsa," said Hal. "Not the priest, neither."

We lapsed into silence and drank our ale, staring into our cloudy pots.

"It's as clear as a muddy pool 'int it?" said Hal at last.

The waters were very muddy. Very muddy indeed.

*****

Later that evening saw us all staring down at the sleeping form of my second son, Phillip.

"And so, to recapitulate..." I said. "He doesn't seem to respond to noises. He watches faces very carefully and responds to smiles and gestures."

"And to being picked up, but..." said Lydia shrugging, lost for words.

Johannes stooped and gently scooped up our son from his crib. Phillip woke quickly but did not cry. His little arms threw backwards in a reflex I'd seen before in babies and his legs kicked out.

"He is a well formed little chap," said Johannes, smiling and cradling him in the crook of his arm. "And apart from the quietness and the inability to react to sound, he is very much as all babies should be at this age?"

"I think so," said his mother. "He suckles well and has grown. He has strengthened his neck and can hold his head up."

"Hawise and Lydia put him on a sheepskin on the floor on his front and sit by him," I said.

"Hawise lies with him on the skin so that he can see her and he lifts his head well," added his mother."

"He kicks and moves his arms about?"

"He does," replied Lydia. "Though he doesn't turn his head when you call his name, speak to him, or when you move about him."

"Hmmm."

Johannes sat on the bed edge and moved Phillip to his knee.

"I can see nothing obviously wrong."

"Watch, Johannes."

I walked to the other side of the bed and stood behind my son, now being dandled on his great uncle's knee.

I clapped my hand loudly behind his head.

Johannes looked up at me. "No, he did not hear it."

"He doesn't jump or flinch, the eyes do not grow larger. He just doesn't hear it," I added.

Lydia came up to me and put her arm into mine.

"Whatever can we do?" Her face was pale and there were tears in her eyes.

Johannes moved closer to Phillip and put his lips to his ear. He sang a long base note loudly to the side of his head, into the bony place behind his ear.

Phillip stopped moving and stared.

Then Johannes whistled a high note close to his ear.

Phillip jumped.

Lydia's face crumpled, "Oh. Oh Aumary, he heard. He heard!"

Johannes smiled and handed our son to his mother.

Lydia cuddled him as if he'd been missing for months.

"I have seen this before, though not at such a young age. I have seen this sort of thing manifest but when the child is older."

"He *is* deaf," I said. "But...?"

"The deafness is selective. He will hear some things and not others and it depends on the proximity."

Lydia kissed our son on his forehead.

"Does this mean that he will not be the outcast I thought he'd be, Johannes?"

"Lydia, he will be no outcast. Not as long as we live," I said.

"Nor Hawise neither," said Johannes. "She, I know, will look after him. She adores him."

"What do we do? I am so afraid for him", whispered Lydia again.

"It will take a deal of work. He will need a lot of attention but I think he can be made to understand us."

"How, uncle?"

"Much time must be spent with him. Teaching him, talking to him, so that he can see our faces. We must use gestures as Little Agnes does."

Little Agnes was Johannes' dwarf, mute, maid servant. She had been educated at Amesbury Priory and could write and did so every day when she needed to be understood. Johannes and she had a special code which they used to understand each other.

"As I say it will take time but I am sure we can look after him."

"He will not be considered possessed of demons, uncle or the result of the sins of...of...?"

"His parents?" I said. "What can we possibly have done that God would punish Phillip in this way? There may be some who will think him an unnatural product of the devil but it's not as if he is living in the village and is the son of a labourer. He can be protected."

Lydia sighed.

"We will do all we can to help him and safeguard him," I said. "This I vow."

*****

Early the next day Johannes, Hal and I travelled through the forest into town to see Father Justin. The trees were alive with bird song and we heard the woodpeckers drumming deep in the forest. Good news for this meant spring was certainly on its way.

When we arrived the man was barely conscious and Agnes indicated that the poor priest was wandering a little in his wits.

Johannes went off quickly to see to his patient, exchanging a few words with Jem as he passed him in the hall corridor. Hal stayed to chat to the young soldier. Mistress Lea was sitting in the kitchen with her baby, Tilda and now she was a little calmer, I talked to Ellen again.

"Do you remember anything further, Mistress Lea, about yesterday at the cottage?"

I took a good look at the huge abrasion and purple bruise on her forehead. There was no doubt she had been struck forcefully.

Ellen Lea shifted on her stool with little Tilda held to her decently covered breast.

"I... I dunno, sir. I can't think of anything else. The man who hit me was big and black haired and bearded."

"No one knows him, Ellen."

"Then he's an outlaw, m'lord. There must be these men lyin' about the further parts of the forest. Wicked men with murderous hearts and terrible bloody minds."

I sighed. "My foresters are out in each baily today and we'll comb the thicker and most inaccessible parts for these bloody minded men as you call them, Ellen."

"And then I can go home, sir?"

"Yes, maybe you can."

She smiled up at me. "Thank you, my lord and thank you for looking after me."

Overriding her thanks was a determined banging on the front door.

I strode out into the passage and shouting over my shoulder to Johannes in his work room, I called out, "Hal who is that?"

He opened the door to one of my foresters, Rob Hartshorn.

Rob took off his coif. "Sir, you should come."

"Good morning to you Rob." I said, smiling "You're a long way from home."

"Aye, sir. Good morrow." He looked embarrassed. "Master Brenthall sent me."

"Did he now?"

"Please don't tell me that we 'ave another corpse?" said Hal grimacing.

"Don't know, sir." Rob shoved his coif back on his head.

He looked over my shoulder as Ellen Lea came into the corridor and watched us.

He whispered. "I think it's something else, sir."

"Very well. Where are we going?"

"La Verme sir. Braydon Oak."

"There again?" Hal looked surprised.

"Yessir."

I nodded to Jem Chadwyk and popped my head into the workroom where Johannes was scampering around his work table.

"Called to Braydon, Johannes. Can you come too? The boys have found something. We might need your help."

"Aye - a moment."

I walked into the room. Father Justin was on his front on the pallet which Johannes reserved for patients who were bedridden.

"I'll wait for you. How is he?"

"Sore, very sore and very groggy. However he will live to name his attacker, I think."

"Good. Can you leave him?"

"I can. The dressing has been changed and there is little more I can do for the moment. Sleep is his best medicine. However I must be back soonest for it is market day and I will be busy."

"I'll go and saddle Titus for you," I said.

*****

"This sir, we found this."

"Hmmm."

"We were trying to get the oak away from the path and cut off the branches so it wouldn't foul the way through. We dragged it here and then we found this under the tree's roots."

"It's been burned."

"But there's enough of it to tell us that it's a dark brown cotte, sir."

"Yes. Where exactly was it, John?"

John Brenthall strode over to the old Braydon oak, now denuded of its branches and many of its roots.

"You may not remember, but there was quite a hole in this old tree."

"Yes, I do remember, John. It was quite hollow in places, had been for a while and latterly there'd been a big enough hole for a badger to tunnel there."

I chuckled remembering the times I'd crawled into the centre of the tree to hide from my friend Percy, when we were lads.

"You can see where Brock has been active, sir, in the soil... there."

"Ah yes."

"The tunic was found in one of the holes in the bottom of the tree. When the wind brought it down it exposed the roots and a bit of the fabric. Wilf saw it and pulled it out."

"Was there charring on the tree itself?"

"No, sir. The garment was burned and then when it wasn't completely destroyed the rest of it was shoved into the hole."

"The person doing it didn't count on the tree coming down did he?"

"No, sir."

"So, do we recognise it?"

"It's a plain piece but worn and not very special. However, the most important thing about it is this, sir."

John stretched out the piece of material carefully. The whole thing measured no more than about eight inches by ten. I looked at it attentively.

"There's nothing to say it's an item of clothing, John."

"Ah sir, if you do this...."

He teased out the under layer of the cloth.

"I didn't realise it was double," said Hal looking over my shoulder.

John slid his hand between the two layers. "It's the end of a sleeve sir."

We all bent to look.

Johannes took the piece from John.

"It's the sleeve of a cotte and it is bloodied from what I can tell," he said.

"Hard to see because of the colour. It certainly looks like blood."

"John, do you have any water?"

"Certainly sir." He lifted a leather flask from his saddle bow and handed it to me. I poured some water over the piece of fabric and then Johannes squeezed it.

The resultant ooze was a brown red.

The doctor put the material to his nose.

"Blood," he said, nodding.

"Does this mean we've found the garment?"

"Or what's left of it," said Hal.

"Which our murderer was wearing when they killed Mistress Chetel?" Johannes frowned.

"Is there any sign of something being burned around here?"

John looked over to his foresters. They all four shook their heads.

"Then it was burned elsewhere and brought here."

"I wonder if this is what remains of the clothes worn when Mistress Cottar was killed. You remember there was much more blood in that attack," said Johannes.

"It could be."

"We must ask around for a brown tunic or cotte then," said Hal putting his thumbs through his belt and rocking on his heels. "Though it's goin'a be 'ard, fer so many folks 'ave tunics o' that colour."

"Indeed. There's nothing very special about it as John said."

"Best to ask about though. Someone once 'ad a dark brown garment who no longer 'as it," said Hal. "Want me to ask around Braydon, 'Enset and Cadley sir? "

"Yes, Hal. Begin with Master Mount. I'm still not sure about him."

"I'll make sure I ask if anyone recognises it," said Hal, "if someone 'as lost a garment suddenly."

"I'll meet you at home later Hal."

"Right you are, sir."

*****

Our return to Marlborough and the doctor's house was not what we expected. The place was in uproar.

As we jogged in the back gate and left the horses in their comfortable stable, we heard an almighty noise coming from the house.

I ran in the kitchen door.

"What on earth is all this about?"

The priest of St. Mary, Father Torold was comforting a loudly screaming and weeping, Mistress Lea by the kitchen fire.

Jem was sitting on a stool, blood oozing from a wound on his head attended by Johannes' neighbours Mistress Prys and her daughter.

Nick Barbflet, the town reeve, was standing in the kitchen doorway talking to Gabriel Gallipot the town apothecary.

Two townsmen were standing behind them in the hallway muttering.

Everyone was speaking at once.

"What has happened here?" I yelled.

Silence descended.

"Oh Sir Aumary, thank the Good Lord you are returned," said a flushed Gabriel Gallipot.

"Gabriel," nodded Johannes. "What's the matter?"

Nicholas Barbflet, the town reeve and the man responsible for the smooth running of the town and a good friend of mine, now came forward.

"Jem has been attacked, my lord."

I strode up to the soldier and looked down at him. He seemed grey in the face, groggy and uncoordinated.

Johannes came up behind me.

"What happened, Jem?"

Jem opened his mouth to speak but Mistress Prys butted in. "The young man was hit on the back of the head, my lord."

"With this, we think," said her daughter.

This was one of the logs which Johannes kept in the kitchen for feeding the fire.

"We found it in the passage."

Johannes leaned over and parted Jem's hair.

"You didn't have your mail coif upon your head?"

"No sir. It was too hot in the house," answered Jem groggily. "And there seemed no danger, for it was just me and the doors were locked."

"He has a huge bruise and bloody lump at the back of his neck," said Mistress Prys.

"Thank you, mistress," I said. "We are very grateful for your help but now I think we can manage." I gestured to the kitchen door.

The woman harrumphed, gathered her skirts and, grabbing her daughter by the arm none too gently, she stalked off out into the courtyard. We heard the back gate bang shut. I jogged out to bar it.

"How did *they* come to be here?" I asked when I returned.

"They came in the kitchen door when Mistress Lea started to scream," said Gabriel.

I looked around, "Where's Agnes?"

"Market sir," said Jem. "It was just me and Mistress Lea." He stretched his neck and put a hand to the back of his head.

"I will see to you, Jem," said Johannes reaching for his medical bag.

The two townsmen nosily pushed their way into the kitchen.

I looked up. "Thank you, good men, for your help. There is nothing more to do now."

The tallest man, a man whom I think worked in the Marsh down the hill; I'd seen him there several times, touched his forelock.

"My lord, we heard the screaming when we were coming in to see the doctor and then noticed that the front door was open. We came in and found..."

"Thank you. We shall perhaps need to speak to you later."

"I'll see you later Walter," said Johannes smiling. "Come back in a while."

I ushered them too, out into the courtyard, let them out, barred the gate again and closed the kitchen door.

"The work room? Was the door locked?" I asked.

"Yessir," said Jem feebly, "I was only out of my senses for a heartbeat. It wasn't a really bad blow. No one could have forced the door in that time. Mistress Lea heard the noise when she came back in and found me."

"Where had she been?"

"The privy, sir."

Nick reached for me.

"Aumary..." he took hold of my arm and walked with me into the corridor.

"This has not long happened and…" He gestured.

I traced the direction of his hand and looked at the door to the workroom. Johannes had followed me out of the kitchen and was reaching into his scrip for the key. His face fell.

The door seemed open, for a key sat in the lock.

We looked at each other in horror and treading on his heels, I followed him into the work room.

Father Justin was still lying on his front, his head turned to the side. His eyes were closed and there was a small trickle of blood from his lips.

Johannes leapt up to the priest.

We all held our breath.

"No, he's gone, I'm afraid." He ran his hands over his hair.

All present crossed themselves. Silence came down again and we heard Mistress Lea weeping in the kitchen.

I looked at the body of poor Father Justin, a man whom I'd known for many years. A man I'd liked.

In his back was a knife; a knife I knew, a knife I recognised.

Chapter Nine

"That's my knife..." said Johannes. "My knife. The one I use to..."

"You leave it here in the workroom. Anyone in here could have picked it up."

Johannes felt for a stool and lowered himself onto it.

I patted his shoulder.

I called out to Gabriel. He came trotting into the doorway.

"Oh my! Oh merciful Heaven." His already pale face paled even further. He crossed himself.

"We had tried to keep quiet about the fact that the priest was here," I said.

"Certainly. I did not know he was here until Nick and I found him dead."

"What happened that you were here, Gabriel?"

"I saw the front door open and came in, looking for Johannes. The two townsmen followed me shortly after, looking for the doctor for it is market day and we found Jem groaning and bleeding into the flagstones and..."

"Mistress Lea?"

"I saw her. She came into the kitchen, through the outer door, from the courtyard, saw Jem through the door and started to scream."

Nick Barbflet now joined the conversation.

"We were passing just after the moment when she began to scream. Father Torold and I. We came in to see Jem leaning against the wall with Gabriel holding him up."

"The workroom door was closed?"

"Aye it was."

"Then once Father Torold had satisfied himself that Jem was all right, we went to see this Mistress Lea, I think you called her?"

"Yes."

"She was hysterical," said Gabriel. "Master Barbflet followed us all in."

I looked back at her through the open door. Ellen Lea was now calmer and Father Torold was speaking to her gently.

"Then Jem said something about Father Justin. Naturally I remembered that you'd brought him here for his safety and I realised that the door, although closed, was not locked. The key was there as it is now. I looked in and knew he was dead," continued Nick. "Gabriel and I went in for a heartbeat to make sure and then we closed the door on our exit. It was then that you arrived."

I nodded.

"Johannes, can you lock the front door so no more patients come through?" I asked.

He acquiesced as if in a daze and went to do my bidding. Market day was always a busy time for him for many people came from the villages around and visited him for help. He was a wealthy man and it was known that he would turn no man away and did not charge for his services should people be unable to pay. Many's the time I'd seen him take eggs or vegetables, herbs or other items, as payment in kind.

Nick and I went to the back of the kitchen.

Father Torold stood. His deep bass voice underpinned the hum of the room and the noise from the street.

"My Lord Belvoir. A tragedy sir. May I go into my brother in God and give his soul solace?"

"If you feel you can, Torold."

He nodded. "There is nothing to say I may not. He is after all a man of God."

I smiled. He left quietly shutting the door.

I perched on the table edge and looked down at Mistress Lea.

"Ellen, what can you tell us about all this?"

"I thought it'd be safe here, sir," she whispered breathlessly, her nose runny, her voice nasal.

"Yes, I know." I sighed "So did we."

The woman wiped her eyes and nose on her sleeve. Her gaze flicked to the baby lying kicking its legs in a basket on the floor by the table.

"I left Tilda here, sir and went out to the privy, I hadn't been gone more than a heartbeat, when I heard the kitchen door bang shut hard."

"What did you do?"

"I was a little afraid but I knew it must be someone coming in because the doctor had told me that people come in and out all day to see him on market d..."

"They come through the *front* door Ellen."

"Ah well... I was unsure and so I came in quickly to make sure that Tilda was all right.

You hear of babies being stolen don't you, and devil children being substituted, all the time. I was just a little bit afraid."

"What did you see?"

"I saw the man with the beard sir, he was leaving the house through the front door and then I saw Jem on the floor. Oh sir...if I had been in the room.....I might've been dead too."

I turned to Gabriel Gallipot.

"You were quickly on the scene, Gabriel. Did you see this mysterious black bearded man?"

The apothecary's brow creased and he became pleated about the eye with puzzlement.

"No sir. Most assuredly, no."

"Nick?"

"No, m'lord."

Johannes came back into the kitchen and sat wearily on the bench. "The key, the spare key to the workroom. The one I lend to you now and again. The intruder must have known where it was kept."

"And where is that?" asked Nick.

Johannes stood and lifted a pottery jar from the potboard on the wall by the outside door.

"Here. Inside."

"How did he know it was there, so well hidden? Has this man been here before?"

"I don't recognise the description but if he has been here before and this is a disguise, I still cannot see how he knew where to find it. Patients do not come in here."

"Who knew where it was?"

"You did, Sir Aumary. Gabriel. Agnes of course. I think Roger does too. Gabriel?"

Roger was Gabriel's journeyman.

"No one else?"

"I try to keep it quiet. Jem probably knows."

"Aye sir, I do."

"It's unlikely this man knew."

"Unless someone told him," said the doctor.

We all digested that unsavoury fact for a while.

I paced up and down a little.

"Nick, can you go out into the town and have it cried that I'm looking for a man, black bearded...and. How old is he, do you think, mistress?"

"Hard to say...he isn't old and he isn't young...about as old as this man sir."

She pointed to Nick. He was almost the same age as me.

"A man of thirty or so. Is the man tall, big of build...small?"

"Yes sir. Quite big, though not as tall as you." She bent to pick up her baby. "We had a lucky escape didn't we, Tilda?"

Johannes wiped a shaky hand over his forehead. "You did, mistress. From now on we must secure all the doors, all of them. All the time."

"I'll get a search underway for the man," said Nick and he was gone.

"Jem go back to the castle and rest and send down Castleman if he's on duty or Pearson, to take your place."

"I'll go with him," said Gabriel, looking worried. "It's a long walk down the High Street for a man with a broken head."

"Thank you Gabriel. Before you go Jem. Can we have your story?"

Jem sniffed and pulled himself up.

"Yes, sir. And can I say I am right sorry that I wasn't able to protect Father Justin."

"Our murderer is very determined, Jem. Think yourself lucky that he didn't kill you too."

"Aye. Well, I was standing outside the locked workroom door as I usually do," continued Jem. "Mistress Lea opened the kitchen door and said that she was just going out to the privy and might I mind the wee baby for a heartbeat. It was no hardship for she was fast asleep, bless her, in her rush basket. She went out leaving the yard door open and I turned back to my task. Then I heard a knock on the door."

"The front door?"

"Yes, sir. I very carefully opened it a crack. Bearing in mind what happened last time someone opened this door to someone when guarding a man, sir, I was, I don't mind saying, a little cautious."

"Good man," I said. The last man who'd opened the door like this was another of the castle guards and he'd died of a knife thrust up into the heart.

"I poked my head out. There was no one there. I looked left and right. No one. Then as I came back in and shut the door, I was hit from behind with that log."

"And when you came to, who was here?"

"Master Gallipot was bending over me sir and Mistress Lea was screaming. The others came in shortly afterwards."

"No sign of your attacker?"

"No, sir."

"Thank you, Jem. You may go."

Suddenly the room was empty. Only Johannes, Mistress Lea and I remained.

"We need to get Father Justin to—oh no, we cannot lay him before the altar can we?" I said. "Then we must put him in the crypt until he can be buried."

"He would, I think, rather be buried at Cadley," said Johannes. "It was his village after all."

"Aye. I'll get a cart to take him there."

"Simon Smith will no doubt oblige us again."

The farrier across the road had a small handcart, big enough for a body. He had helped us on previous occasions.

"Shall I go and ask him?" asked Johannes.

"Later, there's no hurry; we wait upon the coroner."

"I cannot see patients with a dead body in my workroom, Aumary."

"Ah no. No indeed."

"I'll see people in the parlour."

"If you think that will work."

"It's better than nothing."

"Lock this door then," I gestured to the kitchen door, "and open the front door again. I will stay until the castle guard returns," I said.

At that moment there was a banging on the courtyard gate.

"That will be Agnes, I suspect," said Johannes, "back from market."

"I will unbar the gate. Poor girl, she will wonder what's been going on."

I tripped across the yard and pulled up the locking bar. Agnes' little face peered at me under her eyebrows. Her brow furrowed. She curtsied and, shifting her basket on the crook of her arm she put up two hands in a gesture of 'what is happening here?'

She then made a sign which indicated that there were people waiting outside the front door of the house...a tail of them.

I shook my head.

"Oh Agnes...you missed the upset. Thank Heavens you did for if you'd been here, you too might have ended in a heap on the floor."

Her face creased and she came in the gate. Putting down her basket she traced her face with her finger and then rocked an imaginary baby in her arms.

"Ah no. Mistress Lea is safe. Jem was attacked and though he is hurt he lives still and has walked down to the castle with Master Gallipot. No, it's Father Justin..."

Agnes' mouth formed a small 'o' but no sound came out of her.

"Father Justin is dead, Agnes."

*****

It was to be a day of comings and goings.

No sooner had Agnes settled herself in the kitchen than Hal came bowling through the back gate on his favourite grey, Grafton. He jumped down quickly and jogged to the back door.

"I thought I was to meet you at home, Hal?"

"Aye well...I thought I'd better come and let you know straight away what I found."

I brought him up to date with the news about the wounding of Jem and the murder of Father Justin.

"God's holy teeth, sir! This black bastard is gettin' a mite too daring int 'e?"

"What brings you back to town?"

"This sir."

Hal reached into the breast of his gambeson and with evident distaste brought out a charred lump of fabric. Fastidious as ever, he brushed the black from his clothes and looked over my shoulder at Agnes and winked. Then he took me nearer to the door and turned his back to Mistress Lea, whispering "Found it, burned and shredded in Braydon."

I took it from him and we went out into the yard. The better light there showed me a piece of dark brown fabric with an edge turned over and sewn with yellow stitches. I teased it out. It appeared to be the back of the neck of a cotte much like the one we had found under the roots of the Braydon Oak.

"Where, Hal"

"In the garden. A fire at the cottage of John Mount."

"Mount? A fire?"

"He'd been burnin' summat in the garden, maybe just this clothing and I thought it was odd. I was looking through and found it."

"Well, done, Hal." I exclaimed. "We must find Master Mount and encourage him to answer some questions for us."

"Think he's our black avised man, sir?"

"If he is then he is in disguise, Hal," I said. "No one could mistake him for a bearded man with thick black hair. His hair is thin and mousey."

"Don't rightly recall him having a broken tooth either," said Hal, preening his own perfectly manicured beard.

I turned back into the kitchen.

"Mistress Lea, this man you saw. Did he have a limp at all?"

The woman looked up from feeding her child. "A limp? Well...no I don't think he did. I didn't see him proper. Why, m'lord?"

"No matter." I turned away "We shall still fetch him in, Hal. We shall go down now to the castle and collect our men. Master Mount will answer for this."

*****

John Mount was not at home. Hal, my two men at arms and myself tracked him down to the barn at Red Vein Bottom.

He saw us coming into the glade and without a second glance, bolted. Despite his badly set leg, he could run.

He set off across the glade, dropping his tools in the grass and made for the safety of the trees at the further side.

He jumped over tussocks of scrubby grass and smaller outlying furze bushes like a Greek athlete of old.

We rode across the meadow. I threw myself from Bayard's back and shouted over my shoulder at Hal.

"This I hadn't expected, Hal!"

We pursued on foot. Into the shrubby trees we ran.

At last the man tripped, swore and rolled in pain, his knee twisted. He grabbed his injury with two hands and swore again, roaring and rolling around in the undergrowth.

Stephen Dunn, one of my Belvoir soldiers, grabbed him by the tunic neck and hauled him upright. I came up shortly after and stared down at him, Mount puffing and grimacing and standing on one leg.

"Why did you feel it necessary to run, John?"

"I knew you'd come for me. You got two soldiers. They came fully armed. You obviously thought me guilty. I wouldn't stand a chance if you caught me," he wheezed. "I'd be guilty without a doubt."

"And you didn't think that your feeble attempt at escape might make us believe in your guilt more firmly?"

"I'm a man of little worth to you and your sort. You'll hang me as soon as spit on me, guilty or not."

"The Lord Belvoir is not one to 'ang a man with no evidence," said Hal. "You should know 'im better. "

Mount sneered at him but did not reply.

"Besides I do not hang men. The sheriff does that.....or Sir Hugh."

Calm returned to the woodland glade. The birds began to sing again, further off than they had been before, it's true, but I heard the beautiful cadences of the wren and the thrice repeated call of the thrush.

"Right, let's get him back to the horses."

Mount couldn't put his foot to the ground and so Stephen and Peter held him between them and practically lifted him the whole way back to the barn at Red Vein Bottom where they threw him into some straw in a cattle stall.

"Peter, Stephen, guard the door."

"Aye, sir."

"Now," I said. "We shall have a little talk."

Mount licked his lips.

"And I will have the truth this time. Did you see Bordern Lea after the evening of the day he disappeared?"

"No, my lord, I swear it."

"Did you see anyone else with him upon that evening?"

"No sir." Mount rubbed his hand across his lips. "I was staying behind and when Cottar and Lea left, I saw no one until the following morning when Cottar returned."

"How did Cottar seem?"

"No different."

"He wasn't agitated nor seemed upset."

"No, sir."

"Hayward. When did you see him?"

"Two or three days later my lord."

"You didn't report to him that Lea had gone missing. Why?"

Mount sighed. "We thought he'd return soon enough. We thought he'd gone to....to his lady love somewhere."

"Who is—was his lady love?"

"Aw my lord Belvoir—please. He's dead. It will do no good to rake it all up."

"Had he done this before, gone off to see her?"

"Aye sir. Now and again," said Mount, sullenly.

"Did he go off to see many women?"

"NO, SIR!" John Mount looked shocked that I had even entertained the thought.

"He might not have been the most loyal of husbands but he was not spreading his favours will-I-nill I about the forest, sir. It was just the one woman," he said. "God rot him," he added under his breath.

"Just this one woman? Always this one?"

"Yes sir. We helped him to keep it quiet. He told us he loved her sir. We thought that it would fist out soon enough but - it didn't."

"Who is we?"

"Alwyn and I."

I nodded.

"How long had it been going on?"

"About nine years sir."

"For Heaven's sake! Nine Years! Who is this woman?" exclaimed Hal.

Mount hung his head and his long hair fell over his cheeks. He mumbled.

I grasped his chin and forced it up. "Who?"

"It was Mistress Chetel, my lord. Emma Chetel."

"And now *she* is dead," I said.

I walked to a three legged stool which was standing by the partition of the stalls and sat down stretching out my long legs.

"Well...this is a pretty pickle, John," I said. "An adulterous herdsman, dead, his lover battered to death. A secretive Cottar alive and his wife dead. The old wise woman at Cadley, dead. The priest of Cadley...dead today."

"No, sir!"

"I can assure you, John, that the man was murdered today in the town."

"Oh Lord save us," cried Mount crossing himself. "It can't have been me, sir. I was here all day and yesterday. I have been nowhere. I go nowhere."

"Witnesses?" asked Hal, folding his arms.

"Master Cottar my lord. He was with me."

"All day...every moment?"

"He could not have got into town and back either m'lord. Some of your foresters saw us too."

"Hmmm," said Hal unconvinced.

"Jesu," said Mount, crossing himself again. "No one is safe."

I held out my hand to Hal who fished in his gambeson.

"This was found at the rear of your cottage Mount. What do you say? Burning the evidence were you?" I shook out the scrap of material.

135

"What is it, sir?"

"It's a piece of a brown tunic and it has yellow stitching at the neck. We already have the bloodstained sleeve. That was shoved into the bole of the Braydon Oak and when the tree came down, it was found."

John Mount screwed up his eyes. "'Tis burned you say?"

"Both pieces are burned. Hal found this piece in your bonfire at the back of your cottage. Is it yours?"

"No sir. I don't, I don't own a b - brown tunic of any kind. I haven't burned anything recently anyway," he stammered.

"Do you know who it might belong to?"

"I...." John licked his lips again. "No, sir. I do not know who might have owned it." There was a catch in his voice which I didn't quite trust. "I didn't burn it."

"You are sure you don't know who wore this garment?"

"No, sir."

"We shall speak again about Mistress Chetel. Did Mistress Lea know that her husband was seeing her?"

"No, sir. She cannot have known. We kept it so secret from her. Besides, Ellen is a simple woman, my lord. She would never think ill of her husband."

"And Master Chetel, did he know what was going on?"

John Mount shook his head vehemently. "No, sir."

"How can you be so certain?"

"Master Chetel adored his wife, sir. He's another one who would never think ill of her. It simply wouldn't cross his mind. And really...she adored him too..."

"And yet she was unfaithful?"

John sighed. "Yessir. She was, but on her part it was for a good reason."

"Good reason...whatever is a good reason for not keepin' yer marriage vows lad?" asked Hal.

"I cannot tell you, sir. Only please believe me it was not how it seems. This was no mere dalliance, sir."

"If it was serious then you must tell us what you know."

"No, sir. I cannot. I have sworn an oath."

My heart gave a wobble. An oath. I too as a seventeen year old, had sworn a solemn oath and even now nearly 15 years later, I still felt uncomfortable thinking about it.

Ah yes Paul. You remember my oath. We wrote about it in the first of my tales.

"Did you kill Freya Cottar because you were jealous that she had, in the end, married Alwyn Cottar?"

"No sir! It was her choice. We spoke on it. We came to an agreement about it. There was no ill will."

"Why were you skulking in the bushes on the day Freya died?"

"I...." The man looked away. Then he covered his face with his hands. "It was dreadful."

I leaned forward, "Tell me."

"I had gone for water sir, to the river when I got home. If only I'd been earlier.... gone in the morning. When I got there, Freya was lying at the water's edge. I could see that there was no way she was alive, sir."

"You heard no one with her?"

"No, sir, but then, just as I had decided to go up and see her, I had to pluck up the courage. It was not something I wanted to set my eyes upon...up came Alwyn, calling her name."

"You saw him arrive."

"Aye, I did."

"And what 'appened then?" asked Hal.

"I heard him yell. I saw him fall down beside her. I knew that if I'd been found there...as the first finder...I might be accused so I..."

"Ran?"

"Yessir. I am not pleased with myself but I was scared."

"And no doubt very upset."

"Aye sir, I was. I loved Freya Cottar. I could never have done *that* to her. Oh my God!" and he put his hands over his face again and wept.

Hal looked at me askance.

I shrugged.

"Mount, both you and Cottar are to pledge for each other. I will have neither of you absconding into the forest. If you go...your friend will be imprisoned and if Cottar runs, the same will happen to you."

"You will not...take me up to the castle now then, my lord?"

"Not at the moment but it doesn't mean I shall not in the future. John, you and Cottar may be in danger. It would be best if you two stayed together from now on."

"Danger, sir?"

"We have had a report of a black bearded fellow roaming the woods. He may be our murderer, though God knows where he comes from and why he is disposing of my villeins one by one. At this rate I shall have no one to take care of my cattle."

"I have not seen this man, sir."

"He is medium height, thirty or so, black bearded with a profuseness of hair."

"And he has a chipped front tooth," added Hal.

John Mount shifted slightly in his straw.

"I do not know him, sir. I... I... have never seen him about the forest."

"John if I find that you have lied about anything more. I will personally string you up high."

"Yes, sir...I have told you all I know." The man looked away, his brow furrowed.

"Think on it a while and if you remember anything, let me know. Meanwhile, stay at Braydon with Master Cottar. Be companions for each other and if you must leave there only travel together. Oh, and take care."

"Yes, sir. I am free to go?"

"For the moment Mount. We shall take you back to Braydon and you will, along with Cottar, swear to remain together."

Hal sighed. I knew that he didn't agree with me.

We turned away from the glade and walked our horses onto the path, John Mount followed hobbling behind me, beside Hal's saddle. Stephen and Peter brought up the rear.

"He'll run. If you let him go. He'll run."

I looked back at the man. "I don't think so Hal. He knows that we will search and find him. His best chance of remaining free and of survival is to do as I ask, stay with Cottar and both of them be on their guard."

"And if Cottar is our felon?"

I shook my head. "No, Hal. I do not believe it."

"Well. If this one…" he threw a thumb back over his shoulder in the direction of Mount, "is killed, you'll know you were wrong."

"Then I will suddenly have become a very poor judge of men, Hal."

Hal scoffed.

We walked on in silence until we reached Braydon and we let John Mount enter his house. We told Alwyn Cottar that they must stay together and extracted an oath from them both that they would not run away. As we left, Mount looked back at us once, his face puzzled as if he didn't understand what had just happened.

Along the way, I went over the facts of the day in my head and turned up one or two things which greatly puzzled me too.

When I reached Durley I would, as was my custom, write everything down. This always cleared things for me and often led me to an understanding of the little details with greater clarity.

John Brenthall was waiting for me in the hall.

"Ah sir. We are glad you've returned."

"What might I do for you, John?"

"Your black bearded fellow."

"You have located him?" I asked with hope in my voice.

"Not exactly, my lord."

"Speak then."

"The description that the woman gives…"

"Ellen Lea?"

"It matches one which Bird Forester gave to me about a week ago."

"Bird has seen this man?"

John chuckled. "In a manner of speaking, sir, yes."

"Then where has he seen him and when."

John tucked his thumbs into his belt and laughed. "He grew up with him, my lord."

"I don't recall…"

"Ah…" said Hal on a long note.

"It's his brother, sir."

Chapter Ten

I sat down with a bump.

"Tolly? Tolly Forester?"

"Yes, sir."

"But he left the forest a good few years ago. Bird's half-brother."

"He went off to work for… Who was it, Hal?" asked John.

"I think it was the Lord Canteloup up Calne way. He went to his fortified tower up there."

"Yes, that's right. He's a free man and he took service with them up there because he'd met a girl and wanted to be near her to get married. She was in service to the Lord Walter. He went as a man at arms, sir," said John.

"You let him go, sir" added Hal nodding.

"I remember and if I remember it all - that was when we took young Edward on as a groom."

"Aye…we did an exchange. A groom for a man at arms - well he started off like his brother, a woodsman a' course," said Hal.

"So what would Bird's brother Tolly be doing back here terrorising the forest and killing my cattlemen?"

"That's what we wonder, sir," said John with a quick look to Hal. "It doesn't make sense."

"What does Bird say?"

"That his brother and he met in the town last week. They hadn't seen each other for a long time and they thought it a good time to do it, for Tolly was passing through on his way with his Lord…."

"Walter…yes. He came to the castle last week. He stayed a night and was off again. His men rode through the forest last Wednesday on their way to join the king in Porchester." I affirmed. "Straight through on the Salisbury Road."

"That's right sir. They just met for a while…you know, have a jar or few, wander round the market, catch up on the news and then Tolly was off back with his lord in the castle."

"And so Bird reported that his brother had grown a long beard?"

"It was apparently a source of much amusement between them," said John grinning.

I pictured my forester Bird; a short man with a dark complexion, long black hair and a small beard to his chin.

"He didn't know him at first, he was so changed but his brother Tolly it was."

I stared out over the floor of the hall also picturing the man Olivier, Tolly Forester as I knew him and imagining him now with a well grown beard. A man of perhaps thirty five and not the youth I had known all those years ago.

"I ask again, why would he be out in the forest killing my herdsmen, menacing the priest of Cadley and...?"

"Ah well, he can't, can he, sir?" said Hal. "He was far away when Father Justin was attacked. And he weren't anywhere near when Bordern Lea was murdered. He was still in Calne."

"Unless he stayed in this vicinity."

"But why, sir?"

I threw up my hands. "It's too much of a coincidence."

" 'Oo else has seen 'im?"

"You wouldn't forget him if you had," I said.

John chuckled. "Last Wednesday sir. Damnable cold, remember?"

"Ah yes, John. It was, the wind went right through you. It's been like that for a week or so on and off."

"Folk marching through the forest would have their cloaks fast around them and their hoods up."

"If they'm 'ad any sense," chortled Hal.

"Hard to spot a man with a long beard and black hair," said John. "Even if you were watching the procession."

I ran my hands through my own dark hair. "I'm damned if I know how this man fits in."

Everyone was silent.

"Ah well. Let me think on it. I'm sure if I think about it, I shall begin to see some chink of light shining around this sorry chain of events."

We all went off to our suppers.

Shortly after that meal, I was in my office writing down everything

I'd learned that day about the tangle of people in this series of murders, when there was a scratching on the door.

I called out, "Enter."

Nod poked his head around the jamb.

"Sir, can I have a word with you?"

"Certainly Nod. You're back with us now are you? Now Father Justin is no longer....Tell me, how is your mother?"

"She still has the cough, sir, but she's much better thanks."

I nodded. "So what can I do for you?"

"It's about this, sir."

Nod reached into the breast of his tunic and fiddled there carefully for an instant. Eventually out came an old and stained buff coloured, sueded bag with a leather strap wrapped around the top. Nod laid it deliberately on the table before me.

"I was out today in Cadley before I came home to Durley. I thought I'd just go and have a last look at Old Mother Ailsa's place, sir. I reckoned we never really had a good look there and it's such a mess, well, it would be hard to find anything amongst all that rubbish..."

"And you found this, Nod?"

"Aye sir, I did. Now I know it int 'ol' Ailsa's, sir because she had an old grey cloth bag and she was still wearin' it when she was killed."

"I remember it at her waist, Nod."

"It was. There was nothing much in it as when they came to look at her, the coroner said..."

"Ah the coroner has been?"

"Yes, sir. I saw him. I told him it was you as found the old lady and he seemed to, well... lose interest, sir."

"Yes, Nod, he would."

"He asked me if I knew the woman and of course I said yes and then he declares that I would have to be the first finder."

I wrinkled my nose and lifted my eyes to Heaven.

"Again Nod, he would. He likes an easy life, does our Hugo of Ramsbury."

"Well, I was there so I s'posed that it was all right for me to do that and I am just fourteen so... So I told him what I knew and he seemed to be happy sir. His jury said that it was murder by an unknown felon, probably a wolfshead and that was that."

"So when he'd gone, you had a good look round? You're right, we failed to do that properly. Well done."

"I found this shoved into the space above the door. You know the place where the stick is stuck to loop the bit 'o leather over for the flap."

"I know just where you mean, Nod."

I picked up the purse, for purse it was. The loop which had fixed it to a belt was intact, so it hadn't been cut off. It was as if the bag had been taken from a belt, the loop wrapped around it and then folded up.

"It was tidily lain, like this when you found it?"

"I haven't changed what it was like. That's why I put it carefully in my breast, I knew you'd need it just as it was. I have heard you say often that things must be as they were when found."

"Nod, you are a marvel."

The young man hopped from foot to foot in pleasure. "Aw sir. I just likes to be helpful."

"So Nod, tell me. What made you look there? Just over the door?"

"I looked everywhere and then specially by the eaves. Me ma, she often puts stuff up there, important stuff, stuff she doesn't want to lose. Stuff she doesn't want my little brothers and sisters finding. They can't reach there, see." I smiled at his impish grin.

"Again, well done. Now, let us see what it contains. You haven't examined it?"

"Oh no. That's your job, m'lord," said Nod importantly. "I just found it."

I unwrapped the leather thong from the neck, opened it out and upended it carefully.

Out came: half a silver penny, a small knife in a sliver of wood of the sort one might pare fruit with, a piece of knotted hairy string, a simple bone comb with fine teeth, a strike a light box, a small piece of metal which I guessed was something with which one might get stones from a hoof. My farrier had something similar. There was also a piece of linen folded over.

I opened out the linen and carefully laying it out on my table, I brought the candle closer.

"Cor!" said Nod in a breath.

"It's a lock of curly hair, Nod."

"I'n't it pretty?"

"Yes, Nod it is."

"There i'n't many peoples have hair that colour."

"No, Nod. My daughter Hawise has red hair. One of the dead women, Mistress Freya Cottar had red hair too and so did Emma Chetel the woman who was killed at the Braydon Oak though hers was a little paler than the other two."

"Then this is her hair i'n't it sir? It i'n't as red as the Lady Hawise's."

"No Nod, it isn't. I think this is, as you say, Emma Chetel's hair."

"But I don't think this is her purse, sir."

"No, Nod. I think this is the missing purse of the man whose murder began this investigation of ours."

Nod looked up at me over the table. "Master Lea, my lord?"

"Yes, Nod. Master Bordern Lea."

Nod straightened and looked puzzled. "Why would he have a piece of linen with…? Ahhh."

"I think you have just answered your own question, Nod."

"It i'n't his wife's hair is it m'lord?

"No, Nod. It isn't."

I folded the hair back into the linen. Nod held the purse open and we put it back inside.

"So what was it doing in the house of Ailsa of Cadley, sir?"

"I cannot tell you, Nod. It's as much a mystery to me as it is to you."

"Did Old Ailsa steal it?"

He shook his head and answered his own question again "Nah... she never went anywhere near Braydon where the cow man lived. The big bearded bast... beast must'a hidden it there sir."

"Why, Nod?"

"To come back and fetch it later so he could…"

"For half a penny and a bone comb?"

Nod shrugged. "Why else would he want it?"

I felt the bag carefully. There was nothing else in it, no special lining, nothing concealed.

We looked at each other in silence for a while.

"Did you find anything else lad?"

"No sir. Nothing. Never so much as a scrap. Oh yes, I found some mouldy cheese and a bit o' bacon but that was Mother Ailsa's supper I think."

"That was on the table."

"You noticed that, sir?" said Nod with a smile. "And there was a cloak hanging up on a peg and a sack lying on the floor by the bed but it was empty, sir."

"That's all the old woman had?"

"The usual stuff sir, a cup and a kettle with a wooden stirrer but nothing special. There was something odd though. There was a shallow bowl of water which had been upended and it trickled from the table to the floor."

"Perhaps she knocked it in her fall."

"Maybe."

"Thank you, Nod."

"And sir…there's something else. When I was leaving, I saw that man from Braydon. He was skulking around on the path."

"Which man is this, Nod?"

"The one with the gimpy leg and the limp."

My heart sank. "John Mount? The cowman from Braydon? Thin man with sparse light brown hair."

"Yes, sir. I think that's his name. When he saw me come out of the cottage, he turned tail quickly and went back down the track to the main village, to Cadley Green. He looked right upset, sir, what with the coroner being there earlier and that."

What was John Mount doing at Ailsa's cottage? Had I been wrong to let him free? Was Hal right?

I reached to my waist and took out half a silver penny from my own purse.

"Here. You've earned this." I tossed it to him. He caught it deftly.

Aelfnod's eyes sparkled. "Aw sir. You don't have to pay me. I just want to help like I say."

"Nevertheless, take it. It's a reward."

Nod knuckled his forehead. "Thank you, my Lord Belvoir. Thank you."

He backed out grinning and was gone.

I sat back for a heartbeat and turned over all that Aelfnod had said.

I knew that Peter and Stephen were in the hall. I threw open my door and yelled for them.

"Back to Braydon glade with you lads. I'm sorry. Bring in John Mount. Ride quickly and take him to the castle. Get him to ride pillion. You two can stay there. Ask Master Gayle to keep him safe for me till tomorrow in the castle gaol."

My two men at arms looked at each other despondently.

"Yes, I'm sorry to send you out so late. I'll see you tomorrow."

"Right, sir."

Hal came ambling in. "What's all this then?"

"Nod found this in Ailsa's cott, Hal, hidden in the eaves inside."

He picked up the purse. "Oo's it belong to then?"

"I think it's Bordern Lea's missing bag." I rubbed my face in tiredness.

"None of this makes any sense to me, Hal, and Nod has just told me that John Mount was at Ailsa's cott the day the coroner came to call."

"Ha ha! Now what was 'e doing there then? I told you there was something fishy about 'im."

"That man infuriates me. He knows much more than he's telling. Oh I don't think him guilty of the murders but for some reason he..."

"All that nonsense about never leaving Braydon. The man ranges all over that part of the forest."

The smile suddenly left Hal's face. "Ah sir—what if—?"

"Yes, Hal, the thought had crossed my mind. What if he knows something about these murders and our murderer guesses he's in possession of some of the truth about them?"

"Then his life too won't be worth a snotty sneeze, will it, sir?"

"No, Hal, it won't. That's why I've had him taken to the castle. Though we don't tell him that."

*****

The skies that night were clear and bright with stars. Before I retired, as was my routine, I stood on the top step of the manor stairs looking out over the courtyard and up at the heavens. The pinpricks of light were as bright as the day the stars were minted. I pulled my cloak around me, for it was very cold. My breath steamed out in front of me and it wasn't long before my ears and nose were frozen.

"Shall I lock up, sir or will you?" asked Hal behind me.

"I shall Hal. Do you want to sleep in your room tonight or shall you stay by the warmth of the hall fire?"

"Aye, it's a cold night. Enough to freeze yer eye balls out."

I chuckled.

Hal went back into the hall calling over his shoulder. "I think I'll stay 'ere."

I turned back into the screens passage and locked the hall door. Then I went to bed.

I'd had an idea.

*****

The promised cold came down before dawn. A frost of great beauty rimed the forest. The paths glistened with myriad jewel like droplets. The water at the river's edge crackled with ice. The puddles in the courtyard left by the grooms cleaning out the stable the previous day, iced over. Everything was white and beautiful.

I descended the manor steps pulling on my gloves and shouting up to Henry Pierson, my steward, that I would be back for dinner.

I crunched across the yard. My chief groom, Richard Marshall came sliding out of the stable and bumped into me. The hardened puddle beneath his feet cracked.

"Oh m'lord, I'm sorry, I slipped. I was coming to ask you which horse you wanted today."

"Saddle Fitz, Rich. It's time he had a trip out to the town. Hal will have Grafton as normal."

I stooped to pick up my right glove which I'd dropped when Rich had collided with me.

"Ouch!" The shattered puddle was a mixture of slivers of ice and ground down lumps. I put my finger into my mouth.

"Sir?"

"Cut myself, Rich, on the ice."

"Aye, it's surprising how sharp and hard ice is, m'lord," he smiled.

I laughed. "And how much it hurts when you cut yourself on it. Such a tiny thing."

We laughed together.

"Get the boys to smash the puddles and brush it away will you Rich?"

"Aye sir."

I stopped and stared down at the puddle. Something had occurred to me but it was gone as soon as I thought about it.

We rode through the spring forest, suddenly turned back to winter by the sharp frost. It seemed odd that just days before, we had been commenting on the signs of spring: the pairing birds, the greening trees, the burgeoning undergrowth, the warmth in the sun. Now we were back in January. This, the last day of March would eventually return spring to us and by midday the frost would nearly all be gone. The trackway steamed where the sun warmed the earth, and the new leaves dripped on us from the canopy.

We rode on, our horses' breath snorting in columns of white.

"So what do you think Mount wanted at Mother Ailsa's then, sir?"

"The hidden purse?" I answered.

"Why was it there?"

"I must be truthful and say, I don't know Hal."

"You saw 'is face when you asked 'im if 'e knew anyone with a cotte like that piece we found. That set 'im a thinkin' I reckon. And again when you mentioned this black bearded devil. His face betrays 'im it does."

"I think he is safer at the castle than anywhere. We have already lost one of our informants..."

"And if he's our felon?" said Hal.

"Then he is in the best place."

"By our informants you mean Father Justin?"

"Aye, the good Father. His death lies heavy on my conscience. We should have been more careful." I slapped my thigh in exasperation.

"Especially after the last time...the last time we left someone in the safety of Johannes' house."

"Why do you think he was killed then?"

"My guess...and it is only a guess, is that he was the person who passed on the message to Mistress Emma Chetel, that someone wanted to see her at the Braydon Oak. Father Justin travelled freely through the forest and was able to come and go to Henset and Braydon. He also knew about the infidelity of Bordern Lea, though he was unable to confide it to us."

"Ah no, a priest can't tell the secrets told to 'im, in confession."

"He told me to ask others. That I would eventually come upon the truth."

"But *he* knew."

"He knew and I think that got him killed."

We approached Cadley and watched as the village folk went about their early morning tasks. Smoke drifted straight up into the clear air from the cottage smoke holes and the thatches were rimed with frost. Cadley pond was almost frozen over. People were smashing the ice to dip their buckets into the water. The ducks were sliding around on the sheet of ice and falling through in places, where it was not so thick. The plants to the edge were white with frost.

"So what do we do today?"

"To begin with we talk again to Master Mount and we see what he remembers about this man with the black beard."

"Andrew will have seen him too in the castle with his Lord Walter. Walter de Canteloup."

"Yes, he too can confirm the man was there. I have no doubt that Tolly Forester is the man with the beard but...I'm not so sure I believe he was at Mother Ailsa's."

"What do we do about it?"

"We do nothing about him. But after a visit to the castle gaol we shall go down the High Street to Johannes and sit before his warm fire and thaw out our toes Hal."

****

149

"You are asking me, my lord, if I remember this man? This man with a big black beard?"

"Yes, Mount, I am. And I want you to think carefully and answer truthfully. The man will have marched through Cadley on the main road to Salisbury, through the forest, last Wednesday."

"Cadley sir? I haven't lately been to..."

"Mount you were seen in Cadley, in the vicinity of the cottage belonging to Ailsa the good-body, the cunning woman. You have been to Cadley on the day the coroner visited."

John Mount was shivering in the cold air of the cell under the keep of the castle at Marlborough. Gayle had given him a blanket and I asked him if he might fetch another, for the day was still very cold. Once he'd unlocked the cell for us, Peterkin Gayle hurried out to do my bidding.

John Mount stared up at me with chattering teeth.

"You were seen, I tell you. Answer my question."

The man licked his lips and shook his head.

"I didn't kill the woman. I didn't see the man there."

"No, I don't think you did but it might help us to know what you *were* doing there."

Mount made a strange noise, half sigh and half cry of frustration.

"If I tell you why I was going to see her, you will not believe me. You'll think I lie."

"Tell me and let me be the judge of that."

Mount pointed to his poorly set leg.

"She made me simples, my lord, remedies which I used on my bad leg. She helped many folk, sir. Her remedies, helped the aching. It was a great many years ago, my hurt, when I broke my leg, but I have never been free of the pain of it and Old Ailsa made me a special remedy which helped. I went there that day to get some more from her."

"But you never went in?"

"No, my lord. I didn't. I have told you before what a coward I am. I'm not proud of myself for it. I saw the coroner's men, though I didn't know who they were then. I felt it would be best if I kept out of the way. I didn't know what had happened until later. I didn't know the woman was dead....murdered, I swear it."

I took the purse which Nod had found in the cottage, from the breast of my cotte. "Do you recognise this John?"

John gave a small almost inaudible gasp. "It's Bordern Lea's my lord. Where did you find it?"

"You did not hide it in Ailsa's cottage?"

"Why would I do that?"

"You didn't ..."

"I didn't go near the cottage. I kept to the trees. There was too much going on and I was too afraid to approach."

"You didn't take this from Lea."

"No sir. I knew it was missing. It was in Ailsa's house was it?"

I didn't answer but asked "And the black bearded man?"

Peterkin Gayle came back into the cell with another blanket and tossed it to John Mount. John threw it around his shoulders.

"Why do you ask me about him sir?"

"Did you see him?"

Eventually he answered me with a sigh.

"Yes, sir. I did. I thought I knew the man but my eyes must have been playing tricks for the man I knew was not so bearded. And yet..."

"Tolly Forester?" I folded my arms.

John Mount looked up, his face a picture of confusion.

"I *did* know him... Ah yes... It *was* Tolly. We knew each other many years ago when he was in Savernake. You will know he's a Durley man sir and was a woodsman."

"Think carefully John. Did you tell anyone, anyone at all about the man with the big black beard and the bushy hair? Did you speak to anyone about the fact you'd seen Tolly in the forest, albeit it just marching through?"

John Mount threw his head into his hands. "Yes, I did. Why... why is that significant?"

"You did tell someone that you had seen Tolly Forester once more in the forest and that he had grown a huge beard?"

"Aye, sir. Before, last week, I passed along the road and this was when I saw the column of soldiers coming up the hill. Many Cadley folk had stopped to look, to watch the men pass by."

"It was quite a spectacle, I suppose," said Hal.

"It was not something we see every day...no. Though the King rides often enough through the forest, he doesn't travel as slowly nor does he usually have so many men with him."

"No, the King often rides swiftly and leaves his baggage train to trundle along after him," I smiled.

"So John, whom did you tell?"

"When I returned to the village on my way back to Braydon sir?"

"Yes. Before you returned to Braydon. Whom did you tell?"

John Mount looked carefully at all our faces in silence. I could see the indecision there.

"John." I sat down on the stone bench which ran around the edge of the cell. "I think I know the person who owned the burnt, brown tunic. Think on it...it might be that they have murdered several people. I think you know too, why they might want to implicate you, for there's no doubt they would be more than happy for you to hang for these crimes."

Tears sprang into Mount's eyes. "I simply cannot believe that, sir."

"Tell me. If you do not, I fear you will hang for these crimes."

But he would not tell me.

Hal growled.

There was a long silence.

"Very well, the last thing I *must* ask you. I will have the truth." I paused. "Mistress Chetel?"

His eyes became wary. "I've told you, sir."

"No John, you have told me part of the tale in the hope that I will work out the rest. Well, I think I have but I need you to confirm it for me." I rose and looked down sternly at him.

"Mistress Chetel had an affair with Master Lea."

"Yessir."

"The girl Tova tells me that Wilkin Chetel is not capable of... shall we say, fulfilling his husbandly duties to his pretty wife."

"Ah..." said Mount quietly.

"Yes, indeed. And yet the man has two vigorous young sons. It cannot always have been so, now can it? That Chetel was impotent?"

"Er, no sir."

"Thomas and Alfred. How old are they Mount?"

"Erm Thomas is nine I believe and Alfred six."

"Master Chetel told me that he and his wife have been married twenty years, since they were but sixteen, Mount."

"I think that's true, sir."

"No children early in the marriage?"

Mount looked down at his confined ankles in their metal gyves.

"No, sir."

"I put it to you, John Mount, that Master Lea was the father of these boys. That once it became apparent that Master Chetel was unable to perform his husbandly duty, Emma Chetel turned to someone else, to take over that role?"

"And that person was Lea, sir?" said Hal at a whisper.

"Yes, Hal."

"So she was killed because she was playin' the two backed beast with 'im and Lea was killed because he'd..."

"No, I don't think so."

"No, Master Hal," said Mount at last. "If you think that, then you do Master Chetel down sir for you must think that he killed both his wife and her lover."

"And that isn't true, is it Mount?"

"No, my lord. Master Lea loved Mistress Chetel, it's true. Mistress Chetel simply took him as a lover in order to get her children."

"And her husband knew. He connived with his wife. He would not be..."

"No, he wouldn't be jealous, sir, for it was what they'd all agreed."

"Wait a minute!" cried Hal grabbing and throwing off his coif. "Master Lea was dead by the time you were told that Mistress Chetel lay with a man the morning she was killed, m'lord."

I smiled at him. "Yes, Hal. It was not he who had been in the big bed of the Chetel house that morning, was it John?"

John sniffed.

"No sir...it wasn't."

"Then who the bloody 'ell was it?" said Hal, his eyes wide with confusion.

"It was me, sir," said John Mount.

"You?" cried out Hal. "But you loved Freya Cottar."

"Have you never in your life, Master Hal, done anything which you cannot quite explain? Have you never been in so much pain, pain of the heart that you have sought solace where you would never think you would, were you whole and hearty? Do not think I was proud of it."

"Well, I'll be buried in Burbage!"

"You are quite right. I did love Freya Cottar with all my being. However we decided that it was in her best interest to marry Cottar for he was a man of means and Freya wanted, needed, nay *deserved* to live a life of relative comfort and I could never give her that."

"Cottar is much older than she, it might be that in the fullness of time, Alwyn would go to God and you and the widow might be married," I said.

"And you would marry a wealthy woman."

"Yessir, with your permission of course. I suppose that is what we thought."

"Or he might be eased into his grave," said Hal under his breath.

"So when Freya died you were distraught."

"Aye sir. I was beside myself. I passed through Henset on my way to the barn and saw Mistress Chetel very early, as soon as her husband was gone to his work. I was to join him at the barn, you see and I saw Emma and one thing led to another."

"Tova Cottar didn't know it was you but she did know a man had been with Mistress Chetel that morning. She was puzzled, for although she knew about the relationship between Lea and Mistress Chetel, she could not imagine who Emma could have become entangled with now. Or why."

"Just the once sir. Just the once. I would never have..."

Hal put his coif back on his head and stroked his twin pointed grey beard.

"So all this about Lea putting himself about the forest...?"

"It is true sir. He did flirt with the village women but the only two women he ever bedded were his wife Ellen and his love Emma."

"And Mistress Chetel?"

"Chaste sir, apart from Lea..."

"And you," said Hal

"Just the once...I swear it. We were both so very upset about the deaths of Bordern and Freya. We took solace in each other."

Hal sat down with a bump on the stone bench which ran around the gaol.

"So you say it's not Chetel having his revenge."

"No sir."

"And Mistress Lea for she knew nothin'?"

"No sir. I promise you, she is ignorant of anything."

"You are quite sure?" I asked.

"Yessir. It's just not possible that she knew about the children."

"So that leaves us with Cottar and 'Ayward and 'is wife," said Hal

"Or someone entirely different in the forest. As Ellen Lea has reported sir," said Mount.

Hal drew his hand across his brow.

"Why would any of them want to kill the priest and the old lady?"

Mount shrugged. "People kill for many reasons. All I can say is, it wasn't me."

We all looked at each other in the gloom of the cell.

"You will stay here for your own good, Mount. I will put it about that you are here and that you have a deal of information yet to be discovered."

"But sir..."

"This may flush out our murderer, John. I can say that you have given me the name of the person you saw kill the old woman Ailsa that day."

"You think the murderer might get jittery then, sir?" asked Hal.

"It might be so, Hal. When people are afraid they do stupid things. They make mistakes and then, we shall be there to see them make those mistakes."

"If the murderer thinks you know something sir, then surely, will you not be in danger yourself?" asked Mount.

"Won't be the first time, John."

Hal scoffed. "Last time was nearly the end of you."

I had been poisoned by a particularly vindictive murderer in the spring of the previous year and my wife, friends and Doctor Johannes had despaired of my life—but I am made of tough stuff it seems.

Susanna M. Newstead

Well, Paul, I am still here at 73.

I recovered and although my stomach rebels now and again, now I am aged, I was as I said at the beginning of this tale, as fit as a butcher's dog.

"I am not worried about this murderer, Hal. I don't think they will want to take it out on me, if it's indeed who I think it is."

"You know who it is?"

"I think I know, though I am unsure how it came about and my mind is still a jumble when it comes to the first death, that of Bordern Lea."

Hal and Mount looked at each other.

"No, I don't think I'm in any danger from the murderer."

How wrong I was.

Chapter Eleven

At last we found ourselves sitting as I'd promised Hal, in front of Johannes' fire.

I told mistress Lea that she could now go home as we thought we were very close to arresting the man responsible for the murder of her husband.

Her face registered relief as she bobbed a curtsy.

"I've come to tell you, Ellen, that you may return to your home at Braydon."

Her hand went to her throat. "Oh, sir. You caught the brute then?"

"We have John Mount in the gaol and he is helping us to find the murderer. He knows who the killer is, though at present he still satys silent on the matter. However after a little while sitting in the cold there on short rations with nothing to do, I feel sure he will tell us. We shall be able to catch up with them very soon. I think you are no longer in danger."

"Thank the blessed saints, my Lord Belvoir." Ellen Lea crossed herself. "I'll see if there is anyone going up the hill with a cart, sir. We might be able, Tilda and I, to hop on the back."

"You don't mind walking alone through the forest?"

"Oh, it's no worry, my lord. I've been doing that since I was a child."

"Do you feel well enough to walk all the way to Braydon? That is a very nasty bump on your head. Are you sufficiently recovered?"

" 'Tis nothing sir. I'm sure we'll manage. Us forest women are as tough and strong as the forest oaks, my lord."

I smiled. "You are indeed Ellen."

"Ellen, don't forget to take back the basket in which you brought little Tilda," said Johannes pointing to a rush basket sitting by the table leg.

"That's all right, sir. I prefer to strap her to me and I have my cloth bag for the things I brought with me."

"Then if you set off now, you'll reach Braydon well before dark."

Agnes helped Mistress Lea to organise her things. The woman wrapped her baby in a large piece of cloth and tied it firmly around her waist and neck so that the baby's head was just visible between her breasts.

In this way she could walk into the forest and have two free hands, in one of which she carried her cloth bag.

"Godspeed, mistress," said Johannes.

We watched her go out of the front door, down the lane to the junction with the Oxford Road and stride out down the hill to the Marsh.

Here were situated many of the trades of the town; trades which might have a cart full of leather or baskets, wooden items from the turner, or cheese perhaps travelling up the protracted and steep gradient known as Forest Hill on the long road to Salisbury.

We came back in and settled by the fire again.

"Is this true, Aumary, that you know who the culprit is?" asked Johannes. "That you are near to a solution as you told Mistress Ellen?"

"I have many ends to tie together but, yes, I think we are very close to a solution to this whole terrible business. There are just a few things I don't understand."

I told Johannes about the finding of the scrip, the naming of the man with the beard and about the arrangement which Masters Lea and Chetel had contracted.

"It wouldn't be the first time that a woman took a lover to get children for her husband, nor the last I warrant but with the full connivance of her husband? That takes some beating."

"Father Justin, I think, knew about the arrangement. I suppose that he will have thought it God's will that the Chetel's remained childless and so, a terrible sin, to have remedied it, in such a way."

"He was a man of the cloth and a worldly one at that but I doubt even he could turn too much of a blind eye to such goings on."

"But 'e couldn't tell, could 'e?" said Hal. "And so they remained safe. So why suddenly kill 'im, after all this time?"

"I have puzzled over this, Hal," I said. "And one of the motives which I can attribute to his death is revenge."

"Revenge... on a priest?"

"He has known for some time. He has given absolution to those involved. Once the boys were conceived, the meetings between Mistress Chetel and Master Lea ceased...."

"The sin was an old one," said Johannes. "Why bother?"

"And then...Master Lea is killed."

"Then it might all come out you mean?"

"I do. People...like me will start to dig."

"So best get rid of anyone who knows about it."

"Then it must be Wilkin Chetel for 'e doesn't want it known 'is wife was cuckolding 'im and that 'is boys are little bast..."

I chuckled. "Yes, Hal, that's one interpretation. But it's not mine."

"Well, then what's yours?"

"I think that our good Father Justin, not only knew about the arrangement for Chetel's wife to be serviced by Lea..."

"Like a prized cow!" said Hal grinning.

"But he also worked out who it was who murdered Mistress Chetel for I think he carried the message to her from the murderer. I think he may have confronted our killer, urged them to make a confession and..."

"Boof! On the back of the 'ead with a stone."

"Precisely."

"So why don't you just go and confront the murderer and have done with it all Aumary?" asked Johannes.

"Because I need more evidence. And the best form of that would be Master Mount's testimony about the brown cotte and the black haired man."

"You think he'll squeal?" asked Hal.

"I think he will when he is threatened with hanging," I said.

This came quicker than I had anticipated.

But I race on Paul...things happened before we can tell that part of the tale.

We returned home in the afternoon. I heard through the gossip of Marlborough town that the Sheriff, Sir Geoffrey de Neville, had ridden into the castle that afternoon. I was not disposed to go and meet him that day.

Instead I rode for home to spend some time in my manor and with my wife and children.

I took the steps up the manor stairs two by two, leaving Hal to sort the horses and emerged breathless in the hall.

Father Crispin was sitting with his back to me on one of the benches, idly turning over an empty wine cup. He was alone.

I slapped him on the back.

"Ah well met, Crispin," I said. "I have been meaning to talk to you."

I threw off my cloak and went to the fire to set on another log.

He looked up at me languidly.

"Have you heard, Aumary?"

"Heard what?"

"That many of the clergy have abandoned ship. Taken sail. Sailed to foreign shores."

"Ah."

"It was bound to happen of course. Richard the Dean of Sarum has gone to France…you know he taught at Paris before he came here?"

"Herbert's brother, yes."

"York has gone as you know. Quite a few have died and are not replaced. Rochester and Herbert Poore are in Scotland. There's hardly anyone left."

I sat down slowly beside him.

"Are you too thinking of fleeing abroad?"

Crispin started to chuckle and after a heartbeat allowed himself a full belly laugh.

"No…no, not at all. It's just I feel as if it's all falling apart and after having been in the centre of things for so long…I am cast adrift…I feel useless. I have no role. Tossed about on the waves." Crispin had once been a senior servant of the Bishop of Salisbury, Herbert Poore.

"Nothing to anchor me."

Where was Crispin getting all these nautical ideas from?

"Then I have a role for you."

"Oh?"

"This state of affairs will not last forever. You *will* be priest of Durley church once again."

"God willing one day—though I never cease to be so—just I cannot act as such in the same way as I did."

"Then oversee the building of a porch Crispin."

Crispin drew back and looked at me as if I were mad.

"A porch?"

"I have for some time now been thinking that we should build a porch on the church. A proper place for our folk to be married. A two storey addition so that you might have a room above for a school. I promised dear Cecily I would do it. And I shall."

Crispin blinked. "I run a school...such as it is."

"Yes, I know but how much better might it be if you had a room all of your own, a room devoted to your teaching?"

A while ago I had determined that I would have the priest teach some of the village children, for I realised how few of my people could read. I had wanted to remedy this and Crispin had been teaching the favoured few children in the church in early mornings on some days. Aelfnod had been one of them.

"There is no doubt that a special room would be most agreeable."

"Then we concur?"

Crispin grinned. "Just like that, Aumary?"

"It is something I have been considering for years, since Swithun was priest here and I glassed the windows of the church."

Crispin frowned as if he disbelieved me.

"And I have another role for you."

"Another?"

"You are bored. You have little to do, you tell me."

Crispin sighed. "With nothing happening in the church, yes I am feeling rather lost. I cannot even pray in the private chapel as I did...keep the offices as I did at the monastery."

Crispin had been a monk at Sarum and so his day, even when he came to us as our priest, was made up of prayers from dawn till dusk and dusk till dawn again. It was his habit.

"Then take on the very important role of tutor to my son."

"I teach Simon, you know I do. And Hawise too—Paternoster and the Creed."

"No. I know you do. And you do it very well."

"I give them both religious instruction."

"I mean Phillip."

Crispin's eyes grew round "Phillip is still but a babe in arms."

"He is Crispin and in sore need of God's help....and ours, for we think that our Phillip is deaf."

A silence stretched between us.

"Deaf?" whispered Crispin.

"Johannes thinks he hears little but not enough to learn normally, as a hearing child would. We all need to put our heads together and work out a way of devising some method to teach him so that he might learn to read and speak and yes write, even, one day."

Crispin looked at me, puzzled.

"You have the time to devote to Phillip. Now...you have the time."

"He's a baby..."

"He will not be a baby for long and we need to begin soon, says Johannes. Children start to pay attention to their surroundings at quite a young age."

"I know nothing of babies."

I laughed. "Naturally Lydia will be on hand. She too will be instrumental in the teaching. She is his mother. She must be involved. And all the servants."

"I-I do not..." he stammered.

"Johannes too will help. I will do what I can, when my duties allow."

"But..."

"Everyone with whom Phillip comes into contact will have to be part of this learning process. It will not happen else."

"But..."

"I want you to lead us."

Crispin rested his elbows on the table. "And as a reward I get my porch? You drive a hard bargain, Aumary."

I chuckled. "No, the porch will be built whatever you say."

"I shall be floundering around in the dark, Aumary...you know this."

"Nonsense. I have watched you. You are a good and patient teacher. And you are a clever and quick witted man."

Crispin then looked at me with wide intelligent eyes. His gaze raked my face, his look searched my very soul, it seemed to me.

"I will...I will try."

We shook hands. "All I ask is that you do your very best for Phillip."

"If it is his will that Phillip be taught then God will guide me," he said.

I thanked him and ran up the solar steps.

Lydia was there with all three of our children.

Hawise was lying on the floor with Phillip, Simon was sitting on Lydia's knee chewing a small wafer of which he was very fond.

"Dada!" he cried and put up his arms. I lifted him from Lydia's knee.

"Crispin has just agreed to help."

"Good. It will maybe stop him mooning about the place like a lovesick boy."

I laughed. Crispin had never been a lovesick boy.

Simon threw his arms around my neck and gave me a hug then he threw his hands down my neck and into the breast of my cotte and rummaged around.

"Ah no, my lad. That you cannot have."

I pulled out his little hands and I tickled him.

"That is evidence."

Simon wriggled away.

I threw the purse on the bed and Lydia picked it up.

"What's this?"

"Bordern Lea's purse, found at Old Mother Ailsa's by Nod. It's been identified by John Mount."

"What was it doing there?"

I shrugged.

Lydia did not attempt to open it but brought it up to her eyes.

"Hmmm. It's seen better days."

"It was shoved into the eaves of her cott."

"No, I mean it's stained and worn."

I looked at it over her shoulder. "Aye it is but then..."

Lydia sniffed.

"It smells."

"Bordern Lea was a cowman," I chuckled.

"No, it's..." She put the scrip to her nose again. "It's..." she sniffed once, "well, I may be wrong but it smells like milk to me."

"Milk?"

"Old milk. You know that sour smell it gets."

"Why would Bordern Lea's scrip smell of...?"

I took it back and sniffed.

Then I closed my eyes and sat on the bed.

"Of course! Of COURSE!"

*****

The castle was bustling with men when I trotted under the gate arch alone after noon the next day. The sheriff's men had augmented the castle garrison for a day and the bailey was full of carts and men, arms and chests of possessions. The field to the western side of the castle was full of tents. Sir Hugh's office had been taken over by the sheriff.

Andrew Merriman cornered me as I took Bayard to the stables.

"Aumary...here to see your prisoner? Or the sheriff?"

"I'll have a few words with him - yes. However I am not desirous of seeing the great man himself. He can go and whistle."

"I ought to warn you, the sheriff's men have been to see Mount."

My eyebrow rose. "And...?"

Andrew swung his sword onto his hip and balanced his hand on the pommel.

"I hear that your prisoner is pleading guilty to the murders."

"He isn't."

"Hmmm?"

"Guilty."

"Then why do you have him locked up?"

"His life may be in danger and he knows something about the murderer. I am trying to get it from him."

"Well... the sheriff's men got it."

I sighed. "I suppose he was bullied into a confession?"

"Peterkin said that the sheriff said that this man has no rights...he's a churl."

"He's *my* churl."

Andrew clapped me on the back. "Ha ha! That is what I told Pete you'd say!"

164

"What?"

"That no matter what, the man should have a fair trial, churl or free man," he said. "That evidence, proper evidence must be provided. Pete made a complaint but..."

"He tried to see fair play?"

"As yet, torture is illegal is it not in this realm?"

"Oh spare me Andrew. We all know it goes on. And as you say Mount has no legal rights."

"You say he's innocent?"

"I do."

"You know that the sheriff will disagree."

"I don't care what the sheriff thinks. Or Hugh de Neville."

"Well. You have until tomorrow to get to the truth. Thought I'd warn you."

"What?"

"I'm sorry, Aumary. The sheriff marches out tomorrow for Sussex."

"What the devil will he be doing in Sussex?"

"The King has called him there."

I sighed fiercely.

"He will hang Mount tomorrow before he leaves."

I ran up the steps of the castle keep and ducked into the cell underneath. Andrew watched me from the bottom of the steps, shaking his head. Peterkin Gayle, the gaol master was just re-locking the door.

"Pete. Can you unlock it again please?"

"Sir Aumary...I..."

"I know what's happened. I just need to speak to Mount for a moment."

"He's been..."

"I know. And thank you for lodging an official complaint. You're right he's my prisoner and not the sheriff's."

"But I cannot go against the sheriff's will, Sir Aumary."

"No, I know that."

He turned and unlocked the cell door once more.

"Here's the key. You can lock up after yourself." He winked at me.

I smiled. "Thanks but no, I shall leave the prisoner where he is. I have hopes of his release soon. His official release."

Peterkin's white eyebrows rose to the fluff of his sparse white hair. "You know who murdered these people."

"I certainly will when I've spoken to Mount."

"I had Dr. James look at him." He was the castle doctor but no match for Johannes.

"Thank you, that was kind."

I stepped down into the cold and dark cell.

"John?"

Pete followed me in and lit one candle which was sitting on the bench running around the cell.

Light flooded the immediate area but the rest of the room stayed in darkness. Our breath steamed out, white in the cold air.

"John? It's the Lord Belvoir." I took a few faltering steps in the darkness.

There was a rustling of straw and an inarticulate murmur.

I took up the candle and passed the light from it around the furthest wall space.

Into view came John Mount lying doubled up on the bench, covered with his two blankets. He was shivering violently.

"My lord." He tried to rise but was unable and sank back moaning.

I could just make out the words "Now you have the truth. It's what you wanted. Leave me to die."

"I didn't send the sheriff's men in to you. Though I must admit I was sorely tempted to beat you about the head myself for your stupidity."

"They roughed him up, Sir Aumary," said Peterkin Gayle. "Dr. James said he probably has a couple of broken ribs and there's much bruising. A split lip, a broken tooth, excessive beating to the mouth."

"Well, that's a fine way to get a man to speak…beat him so he can't."

"I stayed."

"Thank you."

"To make sure they didn't do anything too damaging."

"Why? Why did they want to?"

"You said it yourself, Aumary. He's your man. Your property," said Andrew from the doorway.

"Ah...I see."

I had fallen foul of the sheriff and his cousin Hugh de Neville back in the autumn of 1207 when the King had taken my part against the two of them. I guessed this was a petty form of revenge.

I looked down on my tied villein.

The side of his face was swollen and puffy. His left eye was closed. Both lips were split and bruised almost beyond recognition. His nose was broken. Blood seeped from his mouth and as he breathed a rasping sound came from his lungs. He obviously had great difficulty breathing. I sat beside him and lifted him gently to a sitting position.

"You have brought this on yourself, you foolish man."

There was a chuckle...if I could call it a chuckle and blood bubbled up into his mouth. He spat into the straw.

"Always...was...stubborn."

"You know that they threaten to hang you tomorrow?"

"All over...all over...all the hurt and torment." At least I think that's what the man said.

"Listen to me. I want to know the name of the person you know wore that garment. The brown one with the yellow stitching."

Mount struggled to laugh again and coughed, a terrible sound and doubled up in pain. "Jesu. It hurts."

"Tell me what you know, John, and I will make sure you don't hang."

"You...against the sheriff, sir?"

"Me against the sheriff."

Mount lifted his head painfully to my face and stared with his one not so good eye.

"I will get Dr. Johannes to come and look at you, John. Tell me."

"If I tell, you must make sure that ..." Mount took another breath and moaned again, "that the person confesses. I can't have their death on my conscience. If I am wrong..."

"You aren't wrong, Mount. I don't think you are wrong."

"I simply cannot believe it. And I don't know why, sir....." Mount sobbed, "I don't know why."

"You don't know why the killer did it?"

"No, sir. No. Why Lea?"

"I think I know why, John, I just don't know how. Who was it you told about the bearded man? Someone who didn't see him marching down that hill at Cadley but said that they had? Someone who was busy at the time and couldn't get out to see?"

"Aye, sir. You're right. They were." I saw Mount's tongue flick out to lick his lips but it was dry and swollen.

"Pete—some water."

Andrew leapt down the few steps and reached into the corner where there stood a small barrel of water. He plunged the wooden dipper into it and filled a small beaker. I heard the water slopping about as he disturbed the surface but couldn't see it, for it was so dark in the gaol.

He handed me the cup.

I managed to put my arm around John Mount to steady him and I tipped the wooden beaker up to his mouth. His lips and tongue were so swollen that he could hardly swallow nor take in the liquid.

It took us quite a while.

There was much coughing and retching and he lost more than he swallowed but it was enough.

"Swear to me, my lord. Swear you will make sure they are really guilty?"

"I swear to you."

I saw Andrew's face crease. He was not used to a villein coercing his lord to swear to him.

"Tell me, John. I swear that I will make absolutely sure that you are right before I do anything. I will get Doctor Johannes to treat your hurts. Tomorrow I will get you out before the sheriff has even risen from his bed."

John Mount's eyes rose to mine.

And he told me what I needed to know.

*****

I ran down to the stable, grabbed Fitz from a startled groom and saddled him myself.

I walked my horse out into the bailey and put my foot into the stirrup.

"Belvoir!"

168

I recognised the deep voice of the Lord of Raby, Sir Geoffrey de Neville.

I heaved myself up into the saddle and saw out of the corner of my eye, the sheriff standing in the doorway of the Lord's office, his hands on his hips.

I judged my moment and put spur to flank. Fitz leapt forward like he'd been stung by a gadfly and raced for the gate.

"Belvoir," bellowed the sheriff.

"I am sorry, my lord," I yelled as I passed him, "I have no time now," and I was out on the drawbridge, Fitzroy's hooves clattering on the wooden boards. I scattered a bevy of pigeons feeding on spilt grain from one of the delivery carts and startled a man with a pack on his back coming into the castle. He leapt for the side with an oath. I didn't look back but rode on, over the Pewsey Road, past the king's garden with its closed gate, between the houses at the end of the High Street and the church of St. Peter and on into the wide street and the marketplace.

I rode at speed the whole way, scattering chickens and matrons, children and some laymen who served the Gilbertine monks of the priory and rattled to a halt on the gravel outside Johannes' house front. I threw myself from Fitz's back and dived for the front door. It was mercifully open. I raced down the passage, glancing quickly into the work room. The door was open but Johannes was not inside.

I grabbed the kitchen door and fell into the room.

"Gods, Aumary!" yelled Johannes. "You frightened us to death. Is the devil after you?"

I laughed then.

"Nah! But the sheriff is...and that's worse."

Johannes put down the bowl of porridge he had been eating. "What's happened?"

"Can you go up to the castle gaol? See to John Mount. Don't let them dissuade you. You have my full authority and that of my warrant. I think he has a damaged lung. Tell Peterkin."

I fished for my warrant in my purse and brought out the leather pouch in which I kept it.

"Here. Your authority."

"What the devil?"

"They beat him. For the sheer fun of it, because he's my villein."

Agnes crossed herself as she came from the door of the pantry. I hadn't realised she'd been in there. I nodded to her.

"They managed to get a confession from him. Of course they did. They beat him to a pulp. Please, Johannes, do what you can."

"I will." Johannes looked round for his cloak. "I will just fetch my pack from the work room."

"I am off into the forest to apprehend the real killer. I will be back before supper. I'll meet you back here."

"Mount?"

"Do what you can but he must stay where he is until tomorrow. The sheriff wants to hang him and I've a mind to thwart him. He needs more warmth, Johannes. I fear he will take some kind of a fever if he stays as he is."

Johannes nodded. "And your true murderer?"

"I'll bring them back with me. To the castle."

"Where is Hal?"

"At Durley. I didn't bring him."

"You are going out to arrest a felon, all alone Aumary. Is that wise?"

I chuckled. "I should have no trouble, no trouble at all, Johannes. I'll be back for supper, Agnes," and I ran out into the passage, out of the front door and threw myself onto Fitz's back again.

I took the Oxford Road at a gallop and the end of Barn Street. Then I slowed. I looked back. No one followed me. I crossed the wooden bridge over the River Kennet.

I slowed even further. I met Master Glover coming from his fine house into town and nodded to him, and then I veered right and started the ascent up the Forest Hill.

I looked up at the skies. It was another of those grey, dull, cold days of which we had many in these parts. The sun was barely visible through the clouds and there was a slight misty rain in the air. I noticed a sheen on my cloak. It had started so cold and frosty and now it had all gone.

The Forest of Savernake loomed high above me on the hill. The trees came down to the road and stopped short about ten feet. Here we had cleared the side of the road of vegetation. No man could lurk here unseen.

Fitz and I made our ascent up the hill and into the forest proper. Large trees now surrounded us—oak, ash, holly, birch, hawthorn all well into leaf—the beech trees of the west baily to my right were dotted about the ground. Amongst the mature trees, only they were devoid of any leaves.

The understorey had now begun to grow seriously with ferns and bracken, gorse, in places and with a few of the wildflowers of the chalk hill and forest.

Despite the gloom, birds sang high in the canopy and lower in the undergrowth. The whitethroat grizzled from his thicket of blackthorn, now in full blossom. The robin chirruped in anger at an interloper. The blackbird warbled in answer to his cousin the wren, whose song rang out like a bell across the glade on Forest Hill.

I saw in the distance a man on a mule; his feet dangling down the sides and panniers filled with goods on either side. We passed each other after a while and I gave him a 'good day'. He doffed his cap and looked surprised. His servants walked behind with an open mouth.

I made the descent into Cadley bottom and up the other side of the hill into the village centre.

Here I stopped to think.

Did I look here, or did I go on into the forest?

I settled on the latter and turned Fitz back onto the main road through the trees, taking the path which passed by the fallen Braydon oak.

I looked down to the pit made by the fallen tree as I passed.

The tree itself was dragged away now and lay rather forlornly shorn of its branches at an angle some way off.

The red earth of the root place where the tree had lain for perhaps a thousand years was churned and dug where we had fetched out Mistress Chetel's body. The soil was good and friable.

I bade Fitz stop for a moment and I gazed down into the pit thinking. I imagined the murderer standing here in conversation with the dead woman.

I saw in my mind's eye Mistress Chetel turn her back. In a flash, the rock was in the hands of the murderer...and Emma Chetel turned to see....what? The stone making for her brow? Surely she would duck? Then

I imagined it done in another way and was satisfied that I had it right.

I shook my head. I would have the truth soon enough.

I heard the goat bleating as I approached the glade. It was tethered in the middle of the grass, before the large barn now devoid of cattle. It lifted its head to me and went on munching whatever it had been eating.

I steered Fitz between the barn and the first house, Mount's house. I passed and looked down into the garden. Yes, there was the pile of stones and half made wall. It would need to be much higher to deter Mistress Lea's goat.

A mangy cat came screeching out of the open door of the Cottar house making me jump. I dismounted and left Fitz to crop the grass outside the garden.

I poked my head into the interior. No one was home. Cottar would be out in the meadows at Red Vein Bottom or Luton Lye, or perhaps on his plot in the glade behind the house.

This was once a place where six people had lived. Now there were only two. Three I supposed if Mount returned. I hoped Johannes could help him and that the wounds he'd received were not fatal to him.

I called out.

There was no answer.

I trod carefully over the grass, across the small path and up to the door of the cottage lived in by Mistress Ellen Lea and opened the door.

Chapter Twelve

Ellen Lea was bending over the fire. She looked up quickly.

"Oh my Lord Belvoir, you startled me. I didn't hear you come up." She bobbed a perfunctory curtsey.

I looked around the small cottage. Little Tilda was lying on her sheepskin by the central hearth, kicking her legs into a blanket placed over her.

Mistress Lea removed the pot she'd been stirring and set it on the trestle.

"Have you come to tell me that you have solved the mystery, sir?"

"Yes, Ellen, I have," I said, pulling off my riding gloves and laying them beside the pot on the table. I swung off my cloak and laid that too on the table's surface beside my gloves.

"May I?" I gestured to the bench pulled up to the furthest wall.

"I have no ale to offer you, sir. I haven't been home long and..."

"No. Indeed. You have some water in your barrel. We could have a cup of that."

"I get it every morning from the river sir. I've not been there yet. The water in the tub is stale."

"I hope you'll not get it at the same place as poor Mistress Cottar met her end, Ellen?"

"Oh no, sir. I don't think I could go there," she said quickly. "I'd have to go upstream a little."

"Hmm. You know then, where that was, Mistress Lea?"

Ellen Lea licked her lips.

"Have you caught the black beast, sir? The man who killed the priest of Cadley?"

"We have identified him, yes."

"Good."

She picked up her daughter and sat on a stool opposite me. Her eyes ranged around the cottage.

"So what happened, my lord? Do you know? Do you know who

killed my poor Bordern?"

"Oh yes, Mistress Lea. I know." I stretched out my legs and sat with my back against the wall of the cottage.

"Shall I tell you from the beginning, what I think happened?"

The woman swallowed and then smiled sweetly. "Oh yes, sir. I don't think I could sleep at night not knowing what happened."

"Our story begins nine years ago."

"Heavens...so far back?"

"How old were you then, Ellen?"

"I think I must have been about sixteen, sir...I don't rightly know when I was born, you see."

"That was before you married Bordern Lea."

"I was about seventeen I think when we got together."

"And he was about twenty two? Is that right?"

"I think so, sir. He didn't rightly know how old he was either."

"He was at that time, very much in love with the woman now known as Emma Chetel. He had loved her since they were young, since she was plain Emma of Henset."

"Oh no, sir. He never loved anyone but me. He told me that, he....."

"No, Ellen, he didn't tell you about that, did he? He kept that from you. They all kept it from you. That he loved Emma."

She pulled the child to her breast.

"I must feed Tilda, sir; it's past her feeding time."

"Go ahead, Ellen. I have no objection. My wife, Lady Belvoir feeds our children herself. I'm quite used to watching a child suck at the breast."

Ellen Lea stared at me and then pulled her blue veined breast deliberately from her cotte and set Tilda to suck.

"Emma married Wilkin, you married Bordern. But there were no children for either of you. Not for Emma, nor for you."

"Oh no, sir. That is where you are wrong. Bordern and I had a son but he didn't live beyond a few months and I miscarried a few times."

"Very well. No living children."

"God didn't see fit to let our little Harold live sir. But Tilda... Tilda is healthy and the image of her father," she smiled.

"Oh...she no longer has a problem suckling then, Ellen? Ailsa of

Cadley managed to give you a remedy for Tilda's affliction before she was killed."

There was a momentary silence as the child sucked on. Sucked vigorously, I might add.

"Yes, sir. She did."

I nodded.

"So everything went well. For years. Then came this winter. Bordern went out to work."

"And he didn't return, sir."

"No?"

I stood and took a turn around the cramped space.

"I put it to you, Mistress Lea that your husband *did* return. That evening; he came back at his usual time."

"No, sir."

"He came in with his purse attached to his belt. The stick with which he had walked through the snow and the sack in which he kept his daily food."

"No, sir. He didn't come home."

"He took off his belt. He removed the purse, laid it here, as I have laid my gloves and cloak. He stood his stick up against the wall and threw the sack onto the chest in the corner. He then replaced his belt."

Mistress Lea stared down at her child.

"And then he ate his supper. How long you sat here together I don't know but I'd say it was well after dark when your husband told you that he had had a love affair with another woman in the forest. That he loved her deeply and that he didn't love you."

"No, sir....Bordern didn't love elsewhere. He wouldn't do that."

"He told you that evening that he was going to leave you and go and live separately in the forest, so he could be free for his... I expect he called her something like his red headed beauty. I don't think he gave her a name."

Ellen Lea's eyes were as large as the moon and glistening with tears.

"Now I cannot be absolutely sure what happened next because it could be so many different things. There you were, distraught. Pleading with him, I suspect, not to leave you, for you were big with child and you just didn't know what to do."

"Nooo."

"You were angry, upset."

"I was no such thing."

"You were a good wife to him, he said. You kept the house well. It wasn't your fault. It was just that he couldn't love you. He loved someone else."

"You are making this up," said Ellen Lea.

"No, I don't think so. So you pleaded. You clung to him. He probably said something like, 'I'll go and sleep in the barn tonight.' He opened the door to leave. You followed him out and stood in the doorway. It was a very cold night, the stars were bright. The snow was frozen..."

I opened the door of the cottage and stood in the doorway as they both must have done that evening and I looked up.

"I can see him standing here, telling you that he was going now.... that he would not be back to live with you. He would build his own cott somewhere out in the trees. He would return for some things."

"You are deluded, m'lord. The devil has got into you," she said.

"No, Ellen, I think the devil at that moment, got into *you* for I think as he stood here you reached up to the eaves...like so."

I lifted my hand to the thatch of the outside just beside the door. It was easily reached by me for, as I have explained I am a tall man. However a short woman like Ellen Lea could have reached it too, for the thatch came down quite a way just by the door hole.

"You pushed your way beyond him."

"NO!"

"You broke off one of the pointed and extremely sharp icicles which had formed there over the week and telling him he would not leave you, you argued with him, brandishing the icicle as a weapon I suspect. Then as he tried to calm you, in a fit of anger, you plunged it into the eye of your husband."

I was reminded suddenly, as I said this, of Hal of Potterne's words to me a few days before; that the cold was enough to 'freeze your eyeballs out.' Ah well, yes....it had.

Ellen Lea took in a shuddering breath.

"I do not think you meant to do it, Ellen. Passion, anger and fear and disappointment made you lash out with whatever came to hand. You have no sharp and long knife here in the house. You have no need for such a weapon but ice is hard and can cut as well as any knife, as I found out to my cost today, when I sliced my finger."

I looked at the cut made on the side of my forefinger by the ice from the smashed puddle.

"And the eye is vulnerable. It was an action made in haste and anger but it was one of accidental accuracy."

I went back into the cottage and closed the door.

"Nooo... No..."

"A vulnerable spot. You jabbed out in anger. You wanted to hurt him like he was hurting you. But your aim was too good and he fell dead, the point of the icicle embedded in his brain."

Ellen stared up at me and the child Tilda stopped sucking, perhaps sensing that something was very amiss.

I bent to pick up the sheepskin upon which the child had been laid.

"Here is where he fell. He was dead before he hit the ground. There was very little blood but what blood there was is here beside the fire where he landed. This is a small cottage; it's no distance from the door to the fire. Perhaps he staggered a little but this is where he fell and this is his blood."

I saw Ellen Lea clench her teeth.

Tilda began to grizzle. I replaced the sheepskin.

"So we know, Mistress Lea that your husband did indeed come home that night."

"NO, sir. It isn't true."

"The sack we found was indeed your husband's. The stick too was his." I lifted my hand and pointed, "And the cloak was the one he left hung up before you killed him."

"No, no, it's all lies!"

"Mistress Lea, please will you take that cloak and put it on."

"Why, my lord?"

"Why? You tell me it's yours."

"Yes, yes that's right, it's mine."

"Then put it on."

Ellen Lea fiercely clutched her daughter to her bosom. "I..."

"I will hold the child."

"You, my lord...hold Tilda?"

I chuckled, "Yes Ellen. I have three children of my own and I am used to holding babies, never fear."

Ellen Lea wrapped her docile daughter in a blanket, laid her gently on the sheepskin.

She stepped up to the peg on the door, lifted the cloak and swung it over her shoulder.

"There..." she said.

I stood looking at her as she remained before me; the cloak touching the ground round about her feet and bunching up a few inches.

"That is the cloak of your husband Bordern, Ellen, for it is far too long for you."

Ellen angrily tore the cloak from her and threw it on the corner chest. "That one is Bordern's. I forgot."

I carried on. "And so you must get rid of the body. But you are heavily pregnant. It would not be easy."

"Then what did I do with this very silly weapon sir?" she asked, the cut of her chin pugnacious.

"Oh that was very simple."

I crossed to the large bucket of water. "You pulled it out of your husband's body and dropped it in here, mistress, where it would melt away."

I stood by the door and folded my arms.

"So now you must somehow get rid of Bordern but you couldn't take him far, being well advanced in your pregnancy. So you carefully, in the dark, slowly and with difficulty, dragged his body to the back of the cottage and let the snow and ice and then the thaw do the rest."

When enough time had elapsed and you had had time to think, you let it be known he was not at home and sent Cottar to me for help. We might not have found him until the thaw but Ben my dog discovered the body."

"This is all nonsense, sir."

I shook my head. "Oh no mistress." I came to sit once more on the bench.

"I can almost forgive you for the killing of your husband for it was a crime of the spur of the moment. As I said, you didn't mean to do it. It was almost an accident. But I cannot forgive you the murder of three innocent women and Father Justin the priest."

"Why...why would I kill him?"

I chuckled. "I don't think you had intended to kill anyone. No, not even your husband. But after you killed Bordern your mind began to worry and churn, like a bubbling pot. And you were so angry. Not only angry with Bordern but you were angry with the red headed beauty whom he had taken as a lover. Who could this be?"

"No, sir...no." Ellen Lea thrashed her head from side to side.

"Freya Cottar. It must be Freya Cottar for she was red haired and a strumpet. Had she not loved John Mount and then proved a traitoress to him and married Alwyn Cottar?

"You bide your time. You give birth to Tilda. You build up your strength once more.

"You take the sack which had lain in the cottage and into it you put one of the large flint stones from the plot at the back of your garden. And then you wait for Freya by the river."

"No, sir... I could not have done that killing. I am a small woman. It took some power I hear..."

"Where did you hear it Ellen?"

"Oh there's gossip in the village. I heard it said that the murderer was strong and a small woman like me...could not..."

"Oh come, Mistress Lea! Have you not told me yourself that you forest women are strong and tough?"

Ellen Lea's eyes narrowed.

"And besides. You had the sack."

"And what did I do with this imaginary sack?"

"It would not be difficult for you to approach a friend, like Freya. You must have met by the river countless times when drawing water. Mistress Cottar was bending to her task. She saw her friend and neighbour, Ellen Lea approaching holding a sack...not a strange thing to do. She probably spoke to you. You probably answered her to put her at ease and then, you swung the sack very hard at the back of her head...the holding of the sack had given you more power, you see."

"And then what did I do in your fanciful tale, my lord?"

"Why then you removed the stone from the bag and you struck her again and again and for good measure again and again until there was virtually nothing left of beautiful Freya Cottar. You were *so very* angry with her for taking your beloved Bordern from you, weren't you?"

Ellen Lea smiled. "No, sir. It cannot have been so for Freya Cottar was not Bordern's lover."

"No, that's right. You made a terrible mistake. You killed the wrong red headed woman."

Ellen smoothed down the skirt of her yellowish green tunic, smiling.

"So then I suppose I murdered Emma Chetel?"

"Yes...yes you did."

Again the woman smiled. "And why would I do that?"

"Ah, this time you got the right woman."

"And how did I, as you put it sir, get the right woman? She was nothing to me. I hardly knew her."

"You didn't have to."

In the ensuing silence Tilda Lea gave an enormous burp.

I looked down at her. Her large grey eyes stared up at me and she smiled.

"You probably heard Artor and Mistress Hayward and John Mount talking about the arrangement which was made between your husband and Mistress Chetel. They had kept this from you because, although it was a long time ago, Bordern still loved Emma and he had hoped that she would come away with him, maybe even quit the forest and run away."

"She wouldn't."

"No, I know that. She loves....loved her husband and only settled upon the course of action with Bordern to get Chetel two sons, for he was unable to sire children himself."

"Poor deluded Bordern."

"Aye...he was. How did you learn that Emma Chattel's sons were Border Lea's?"

Ellen stood and stared down at Tilda.

180

"Bordern was a charming man sir. You cannot know how handsome and charming and perfect he was. When he....had gone to work, I heard the three of them, Cottar and Hayward and Mount, whispering in the large barn about how my husband had serviced that bitch to get her sons and that it had been with the permission of her husband. What kind of man would do that, sir?"

"Get sons for another man?"

She looked up, shocked.

"No! Stand by whilst his wife was tupped like a ewe, serviced like a cow at the bull. Let it happen. Allow it to happen."

"So she too had to die."

Ellen Lea bit her lip and tried to nod but it never happened, just the ghost of a head movement.

"You saw Father Justin at some time about then didn't you?"

"I see the priest a lot, sir. He comes and goes through the forest."

"And he knew what had happened didn't he? He knew about the bargain made by Lea and Chetel. He knew but he was unable to speak, for a priest, cannot break the law and tell of the confidences of those he confesses. He could not tell, Ellen."

"But he knew that Emma was no more than a strumpet for she had confessed it to him."

"He could not tell, Ellen," I repeated.

"No, sir. This is not how things happened."

"You asked him to tell her that you wanted to have a word with her at the Braydon Oak didn't you?"

"I did not."

"And she came all unsuspecting for she didn't know that you knew what had happened all those years ago and she didn't know that Bordern had confessed his love of her to you recently, albeit that he had not given you his lover's name."

"I knew it was her but no, I didn't kill her."

"And so you approached her as she waited by the recently felled oak. What a clever piece of work that was, Ellen. A ready-made grave."

I shook my head.

"This time the murder was well planned. You put the shovel there the day before, I suppose and tested the earth. We found that shovel and I recognised it as being one in your shed. Somehow my brain wouldn't quite let me make the connections at the time. What happened?"

"I did not meet her there."

"Yes you did. You had a rock carried in your sack. I suppose she gave it a little glance."

"Hah! She wouldn't have liked to have known what was in it! She faced me, the brazen hussy. Oh I was sweetness itself. She asked me about Tilda. I spun some yarn about her being ill. She said that her two boys were strong and sturdy. She was looking at me as I swung the bag."

Ellen looked up quickly "No, sir. It... it was not like that." Suddenly the woman was taking it all back.

"You hit her in the same way as you hit Freya?"

Ellen's face wore a faraway look as she whispered.

"She fell but not quite into the hole so I took out the rock again and finished her with two more blows."

"Not quite so angry were you this time though?"

The pugnacious look was back.

"Angry enough. Then I tipped her in the hole and shovelled the earth over her," she said more loudly.

"After that you went home to Tilda."

Ellen Lea picked up a small branch. I watched her carefully. She prodded the fire and then laid the wood on top.

"Father Justin?" I asked.

"I visited him...when you sent me to Cadley."

"We found the eggs you took him. They'd come from your grandparents' house."

"Ah yes...he was fond of those."

"So what happened there, in his house?"

Mistress Lea sat once more and settled her head cloth more firmly around her hair as brown as a mouse's back.

"I went in to see him and give him the eggs. I wanted to know what he knew."

"You had asked him to pass on a message to Emma Chetel. Did he suspect you'd met her and killed her?"

"He told me that I must confess for it was a mortal sin and that I would burn forever in hell for the death of such a woman."

"Do you believe that's true?"

She shrugged. "The priests tell us this but no one has ever proved it, have they?"

I smiled. I'd heard this argument long ago from my own brother.

"You will burn in an even hotter fire, Ellen, for the deaths of Mistress Cottar and your husband, not to mention the priest, if you do not confess."

She shrugged again. "I will confess when I have to."

I looked her over; she seemed totally unconcerned for the state of her soul.

"So what happened?"

"I am sure I don't know."

"Mistress Lea. I know you killed him."

The woman looked away and then took in a deep breath.

"He was still wittering on when he turned his back to me to store the eggs. This time I had no bag and I just hit him with the stone I'd found in the yard outside. I had hidden it in the folds of my cloak. He fell and I thought it would be a good idea to burn him as he'd said I would burn."

She giggled. "That would be fine justice, I thought."

"But he was saved."

"Hmm and you had him taken to the town. I don't mind saying I was in a terrible state not knowing if he would be able to speak out or not."

"Let's talk about the woman Ailsa of Cadley."

"I didn't kill her; she was killed by the man..."

"Ellen...there was no man."

"Oh yes there was."

"John Mount spoke to you about a person he'd seen marching through the forest, a man he knew. He described him and that caught your imagination didn't it? You thought he'd be a fine man to blame for all this misfortune. He looked evil... black bearded..."

Ellen Lea looked at me severely then and at last sighed.

"Oh all right. There was no man. I made it up. Did John tell you?"

"He did and he also remembered where he'd seen the brown tunic with yellow stitching before. It was yours. The kirtle you wore when you killed Freya Cottar. You burned it in his yard when he was out at his work at Luton Lye but I think you were probably disturbed and so hid the rest of it at the Braydon Oak."

"I knew there was a hole in the tree but I wasn't to know the tree would come down the next day."

"Let's go back to Ailsa. Why did you feel the need to get rid of her?" Ellen Lea folded her hands between her knees.

"I'd gone to her to hide Bordern's scrip in her house. I didn't know how to get rid of it. I'd carried it in the breast of my cotte all the way from Braydon to Cadley. She wouldn't see me for she was practically blind in the darkness of her house."

That, I thought, was why Lydia had smelled milk on it.

"Why didn't you simply throw it into the forest?"

"Your foresters go everywhere. They might have found it. Besides, I thought it would be fun to blame Ailsa, if it were ever to be found there."

"Like you tried to blame John Mount for the burning of the tunic?"

"He knew about Bordern and Emma. He kept it quiet. I wanted to punish him and that stupid man Cottar."

"The poor man *has* been punished, for the sheriff is convinced that he is guilty of these murders and will hang the man at dawn tomorrow."

"Good."

"Ellen, you would let a good and honourable man go to his death just..."

"He lied, my lord."

"He is a loyal friend, Ellen, for he suspected that you had killed your husband and Freya and Emma and did not speak out for he couldn't believe it of you. It took a beating from the sheriff's men for him to confess to the guilt of these crimes himself."

"Then let him hang."

I rubbed my hand over my cheek in exasperation.

"Ailsa? What happened at her house?"

Ellen Lea giggled. "She was an amazing woman, you know. There were things she knew which...well... no man without the help of the devil, could know. I went to see her, for I wanted to know if the priest would die and if I would be safe."

"How can Ailsa have known this, Ellen?"

"I told you my lord, Ailsa *knew* things. She used to take a bowl of water and gaze into it with her milky eyes and... She just knew things, she could see things."

"And did she do this for you, Ellen?"

"I made a pretence of worrying about our priest. I asked her to scry—that is what she called it sir. Looking to see. She got a bowl of water...."

"Ah we found it upended and empty."

"And I asked her to see if she could see him alive. She would not, for she said that she knew I had tried to kill him."

"How did she know this?"

"I *told* you sir...she knew things."

"So you hit her."

"We struggled for a while, for she knew what I was there to do. I fell and I hit my head on the hearth stone."

"Ah the blood there was yours!"

"Then I took Bordern's stick and I hit her with it."

"We found her blood and grey hair on the stick you tossed away." I thought back to that day at the cottage of Ailsa of Cadley; the spilt water, the discarded stick.

"Then I suppose you heard us coming down the lane and thought it would be best to get you to the back and feign..."

"It wasn't feigned. I felt proper sick. My head hurt like the devil. I shoved the scrip into the eaves and then I scrambled round the back and hid in the pig pen."

"Where we found you."

She looked at me with a brazen stare. The bruise on her forehead was now just a fading brown and blue mark.

"Then sadly, something happened about which I will suffer and do penance for the rest of my days. I took you to Marlborough and placed you just where you could do the most damage."

Without warning Ellen Lea laughed out loud. "Oh that did make me scream with laughter, my lord. My safety....ha! I knew then that I had a chance to get rid of Father Justin once and forever."

"Let me see if I can piece together what I think happened. You may correct me if I am wrong, Ellen."

She smiled and settled on her bench. I swear she was enjoying this.

"You went to Doctor Johannes' house with Tilda. You knew, for you'd heard me say so, that the good Father was still alive and had said nothing. Whilst we were all away, you peeped out of the door of the kitchen, making sure that young Jem was at his place by the workshop door in the passage."

"I took the key which I had seen Mistress Agnes use and hide again in the pot on the pot board..."

"And you ran around the front after telling Jem that you were going to the privy in the yard and would he mind little Tilda."

"Yes, sir...that's right."

The woman seemed very pleased with her handiwork.

"Tell me...surely Jem would recognise you when you scratched on the front door...how did you...?"

"I hid in the passage close by the front door."

"Ah yes."

I remembered an episode when I too had poked my head from that door. An assailant had been hiding in the darkness of that very passage and I had escaped death by a mere inch.

"He looked left first, then right...I had my head cloth pulled up over my face so should he decide to look my way, he wouldn't see who it was sir but he didn't...he looked up the hill."

"So poor Jem fell foul of your sack and rock? How did you get those into the house?"

Ellen Lea chuckled low in the throat. "I hid them in the basket I carried Tilda in, my lord. Underneath her. And threw the rock later into the dung pile."

"Ah. That is why you refused the basket and didn't take it home. You no longer had need of it."

"It was a good basket and not to be discarded lightly but...no I didn't want it any longer."

"So Jem falls stunned."

"And I dropped a branch in the passage so you'd think that was the weapon."

"Ah yes."

"I didn't hit him so hard. He's a nice young man and I didn't want to hurt him too much. I didn't want to kill *him*."

I scratched my nose. "That's very good to hear, Ellen."

"I pulled him in the passage and took the key to the lock. I found a nice sharp knife and..."

"You stabbed the defenceless priest with it."

The woman shrugged. "He deceived me and he was going to tell... Then I came back out, ran round into the backyard again and waited for my moment so that I could come back into the kitchen when it was all over. I saw the man with white hair..."

"Master Gallipot."

"Yes, him, come into the passage and then I started to scream."

"You had everyone fooled, Mistress Lea."

"But not you, sir."

"Oh yes...for quite a while, you had me fooled too, Ellen."

*****

Silence stretched out between us like a taut rope.

"So what will you do now, sir?"

"You have confessed to me, Ellen. I must take you to the castle. You are one of my tied women and so you could be taken first, to my manor court but, at Durley I have nowhere to keep you and your small child and these crimes are those which should be tried by the justices. So I think the castle is the best place. There you will tell again to a scribe of my choosing what you have told me and he will write it all down."

"Why, sir?"

"Because Ellen, you must make a confession."

"Why must I?"

I sighed in exasperation.

"Your words will be written down so that others may read what you say and make a judgement of you."

"Why should I say all that again?

"My word is enough, yes...but I would not..."

187

"Why would I confess?" she laughed.

"I will lay all the evidence before the justices. You must plead guilty to the charges which I will lay against you...."

"No, sir. I will not confess and I will not plead guilty."

"Ellen, it will do you no good."

The woman walked around me. I did not allow her to get behind me unguarded.

"You and I know what happened, my lord. No one else will know."

"The man you know as Hal of Potterne, he knows much of what I have guessed."

"But that is it, sir. Guesses. You cannot prove it."

"With the testimony of Master Mount and the evidence of your clothing and proof of your lies, mistress...we shall validate it."

"No, sir. You will not."

"Ellen, you cannot escape your punishment. Neither in this world nor the next."

"You will hang me, sir?"

"No. *I* will not hang you. The sheriff or someone of higher authority than I will hang you, Ellen. Or if they see fit, they will burn you."

Ellen's eyes suddenly flared huge. "Burn me?"

"You have killed your husband. The punishment sometimes meted out to women who do this, is burning. I will do what I can to make sure that they hang you and that they do it quickly."

The punishment for the crime known as petty treason, the killing of one's lord and master is one which was becoming more common for women. No man could be safe if his wife could murder him with impunity and only suffer the lesser punishment of hanging. It was intended to keep women in their place, for it was considered totally unnatural for a woman to be so vicious as to murder her husband, her lord. The law didn't catch up until a little while later and it was possible to argue the case, at that time, with the justices that it was not strictly legal.

I had tried to do this in a previous case and failed. Up against the Lord de Neville, I had been powerless.

"And Tilda sir?"

"I will make sure she is cared for, Ellen. After all she is my property."

"And Master Mount?"

"He will be set free."

"But he cannot say anything against me if they hang him, can he?"

"When we arrive at the castle I will tell them to release him."

"Do we need to go now, sir?"

"Yes, Ellen, if we are to reach Marlborough by nightfall," I said.

Ellen Lea stood in front of me and smoothed down her skirts.

"I will fetch some things."

"I will stay and watch you until you are ready. I'll put out the fire. Then you can strap Tilda to you and you shall ride before me on my horse to the town."

I saw her go to the chest in the corner and take out some clean linen. She took a large canvas bag from a peg on the wall and stuffed it with the clothes. She rummaged about here and there collecting together various things I supposed she needed for the child. They too disappeared into the bag.

I watched as she took up Tilda, washed her and changed her breechclout, all the time mumbling and crooning to her in an inarticulate way.

At last she was ready and her infant lay sleepily on the sheepskin once more.

I bent to douse the fire.

I leaned over to find something with which to rake over the ashes and extinguish the flames.

"I tell you again, sir, I will not make a confession."

"That is your choice, Ellen. It will not matter."

Ellen Lea reached for an iron tipped wooden rod which was lying against the wall. I put out my hand to receive and quickly take it from her in order to rake the ashes. We could not leave the fire burning untended for this was a danger to the thatch and to the other houses and the barn in the glade, should it rekindle and burn the vulnerable thatched roof.

Ellen kept the poker and bent and drew it through the fire slowly. I reached for the turves which would extinguish the flames properly. I laid them down and stood to retrieve my gloves and cloak.

All the while my eye was on the woman. I didn't trust her an inch.

She turned her back to me and attempted to lean the poker back against the wall.

Suddenly revolving, gaining momentum as she did so, with great strength and two hands she struck me in the side with the poker.

I do believe I heard a rib crack.

My sight dimmed momentarily. I could still see Mistress Lea but as if through a pink haze. I managed to step back as she tried a second blow.

The third blow caught me on the upper leg.

My brain said, 'If she runs, you will catch her, for she will be encumbered with a small child and will not run fast.'

She barrelled into me as I doubled up, short of breath and pained and I fell to my knee, wheezing, shaking my head to clear my vision.

A shaft of light fell over me as Ellen Lea cleared my body and opened the door. I felt the brush of her skirt as she leapt over me and she was out of the door hole.

I glanced to the sheepskin.

The child still lay there unconcerned, bubbling froth from her mouth.

After a heartbeat I was able to rise and staggered out into the rapidly decreasing light of an early spring evening.

I heard the blackbird singing somewhere in one of the trees at the far end of the glade and the answer of a chaffinch from the birches by the river.

I heard a scraping sound and a dull squealing.

Of Ellen Lea there was no sight.

Chapter Thirteen

Where might she have gone? Painfully I circled the house. The door to the small outhouse was open. Ah yes...it stuck didn't it? Berating myself for my stupidity in trusting the woman even as little as I had, I looked through the door. The shed was empty.

I ran on, past the place where Bordern Lea had been found and back to the front of the cott.

The glade was silent but for the birdsong.

I glanced through the open door. I must pursue the woman but I must make sure that Tilda was found.

I scanned the glade. From the trees on the track to the Braydon Oak a covey of partridge flew up noisily, clucking and clattering in a whirr of wings.

I made off in the direction of the noise.

My breathing slowed, the pain in my side settled to a dull throb with the occasional stab. My thigh stung. Thank Heavens for my padded gambeson which I wore underneath my cotte at all times when out in the forest. This garment absorbed much of the damage a blunt instrument might inflict.

I stopped to listen.

A noisy magpie went up with its horrid cackle and I veered off into the undergrowth at the base of the trees, the place from which it had flown.

Everything was silent. All I could hear was my stertorous breath and the crackle and swish of the stems and stalks as I broke them with my tread.

The blackbird's song fell behind me. The forest closed in around me.

I fought on. Once or twice I thought I caught a glimpse of a woman's yellow dress amongst the greens of the forest plants but I could not be sure, for the colours all merged at this distance in the crepuscular light.

I heard a coughing shriek and followed in the direction from whence it came. Either the woman had fallen or she had become annoyed at the greenery dragging at her skirts and had cried out.

"Ellen!" I yelled. "You will be found and Tilda will not do without you."

Ellen Lea laughed. Her voice rang out. "She will have to, won't she, if you hang me?"

I paused to gauge how far ahead of me the woman was. The swishing of skirt in bracken and fern, briar and bramble ahead, continued. I heard mistress Lea again shout in annoyance as her skirts were snagged.

I ploughed on.

A rabbit startled by my invasion of his home bobbed off into the bracken. I tripped on a root and righted myself. Holding onto my side, I ran on.

Yes. There was the woman ahead of me nimbly flying over the ground and leaping the fallen logs and higher plants like a deer. She had grabbed her skirt with one hand and bunched it about her waist, leaving her legs free. I saw them, white in the failing daylight.

I made in a straight line for where she ran like a hound after a hare.

She looked back at me once and increased her speed.

What was it she had in her right hand? I screwed up my eyes.

She swept this thing harshly over the brambles and plants standing in her way and there was a crunching sound. Thus could she pass quickly over the ground.

I caught up with her handiwork a few moments later.

She had taken a shovel from the small outhouse behind the cottage. I wondered if she'd thought to use it as a weapon. Perhaps she had simply panicked and had reached for the first thing which would facilitate her passage through the undergrowth.

No, this woman did not think like that. She had a purpose for it. I would find out what, later.

I heard a forest raven call out, a raucous and loud 'cark'.

Ellen Lea faltered and looked up. Ah yes. She was a superstitious woman I remembered. The raven was the symbol of death in the forest.

She leapt onward.

Our noisy passage through the dusky woodland had awoken many of the inhabitants and they now fled before us in fear.

A disturbed pair of courting barn owls flew before me for a few yards. The female's call low and harsh, the male's higher and tremulous. They wove and twisted, turned and eventually were lost in the darkening evening.

Startled, Ellen Lea looked back.

I caught her face as she saw me coming through the gloom and I saw determination take hold of her again.

Then I lost her and all was silent.

I walked on carefully, aware that the woman had a weapon of sorts and that I knew she was not afraid to use it.

I came out into the glade where lay the Braydon Oak and the pit into which its roots had once anchored it.

I stopped to get my breath.

I walked forward scanning side to side and frequently looking behind me.

Secretly I released my knife from its scabbard. If I was to be attacked, then I too would be armed.

The glade was in silence. No animal scurried out from the ground plants. No bird fluttered from the branches.

A fox barked at a distance and then all was silent again.

I called but not too loudly, "Ellen."

My voice echoed around the glade.

I made it to the proper path which passed the tree and saw the holly, which clung tenaciously to the edge of the pit, shake once.

I took my knife from its scabbard.

"Ellen. I do not want to hurt you but if I must..." My voice rang around the glade again, rising in volume. "I will."

I reached the holly.

There was a swishing sound and I ducked as the spade came for me. I felt it catch my shoulder edge. Again my gambeson saved me from injury.

It was growing quite dark now and the woman blended into the background as a dunnock does in an oak tree. My cotte was undyed wool. I was easy to see.

I couldn't see her, only hear her breath and the movement of her feet in the grass.

She swung again and missed. I managed to grasp the edge of the wooden shovel but it was sharp; it had a metal edge. I'd left my gloves behind in the cottage; I'd had no time to put them on. The sharp blade caught my palm and I let go.

It was enough to turn her though and I saw her pale face in what was left of the light. I stepped forward.

She swung again.

This time she caught me on the upper arm and although it did not cut or pain me it made me stagger sideways a little.

My foot hit the soil at the edge of the pit and I stumbled as the earth gave way.

I scrabbled to keep my feet.

The woman came up and hit me again, this time with the full, flat, force of the blade of the shovel and I went down, the knife flying from my hand.

She kicked me and I felt my poor rib bruise again.

I staggered up and lurched for the woman but disorientated as I was, I missed and grasped thin air.

Then Ellen Lea pushed me.

I was falling.

Falling.

I hit the earth, the impact driving all the breath from me and everything momentarily went black.

There was a trickle of earth and then a deluge.

I scrabbled and wriggled in the soil. The holly tree perched so precariously at the edge of the hole wavered and came crashing down. I looked up to see Ellen Lea, pushing for all she was worth, rocking the remaining trunk of the tree, at no small cost to her, for I saw her hands and face were prickled and bloodied by the sharp spines of the leaves.

Then I too was prickled and I put my hands over my head to protect myself.

Soil tumbled down into the hole. I thought it would never stop.

I took in a breath to yell.

But into my mouth came the fine, red earth of the Savernake. I coughed and spluttered. Soil trickled all around me, over me, into my eyes.

And then all went quiet and I lapsed into a semi consciousness.

*****

I say semi consciousness, for I was aware of the weight of the holly
tree bearing down on me and the thump of soil being thrown onto my
body.

Again, I think, I tried to cry out but only succeeded in getting more
soil in my mouth. I wriggled, trying to stand but the thorny bush pinned
me down. I curled up as small as I could and waited for the soil to stop
falling.

Above me, Ellen Lea continued to dig the earth from the edge of the
pit and throw it onto me.

Great gouts of red soil came down as she drove the metal edged
shovel into the earth. The ground was so easy to dig that one small
movement caused a landslide. The mizzle had made the soil sticky. The
weight increased. I found it difficult to draw breath.

I wriggled as much as I could further under the holly tree, hoping
that there would be pockets here which would allow me to breathe more
easily, where the soil had not become so deep.

I managed with great difficulty to get my hands down to my mouth
and nose and cupped them before my face, allowing a space where soil
could not penetrate. How long would I last before the air was gone?

Through my brain, passed images.

One might surmise at a time like this I would think of my wife and
children at home in Durley, blissfully unaware that I was drowning in soil.

Perhaps you think a great event of my existence might pass through
my mind as I slowly suffocated? Maybe, an incident from my eventful life?
My first marriage, meeting my Lydia, the day I became Lord of Durley
or first became a father?

No. What came to mind, unbidden into my brain was the smell of
the tiny wild, red sweet earth berries of the forest floor; the bright blue
of the speedwell flower at the base of the great oaks, the call of the Jay
as he lifted off into a bright blue sky, the skylarks singing high above me
on the downs, above the close cropped chalk, the sound of sheep as far

195

as the eye could see.

I was sweating and very hot and at the same time chilled, for the earth above me was cold. I struggled for breath.

Eventually, I think I passed out to the trickling of little stones and rivulets of red earth as the soil settled.

My last thought was of flying high above the downs, the strips of the villeins' land below me. I soared like a buzzard, free and unencumbered, wheeling where I wished, in utter peace and silence, the wind whistling through my ears.

Chapter Fourteen

I now know that Ellen Lea ceased her digging and shovelling. She had jumped into the pit; now much filled in and began to tread the earth down over me with her small feet. We found the evidence of her tramplings later.

Then she hefted her shovel and trotted home.

No, Paul, obviously...I didn't die.

Though I was almost dead, they told me, when they dug me out.

Alwyn Cottar and Artor Hayward dug with their bare hands, with sticks, with anything they could find to reach me below that holly tree and the soil.

It was fortunate that they had seen me exit the house of Ellen Lea in a hurry, they told me. And they'd followed.

As I sat in the Cottar house before the fire, shivering in my filthy cotte, my hair plastered in mud, my hands and face scratched by the holly, a blanket round my shoulders and another over my knee, my two cowmen told me what had happened.

"I owe you my life," I said.

"Ah sir. We thought as how something was funny," said Hayward.

"Aw, not funny what you can laugh at," said Cottar looking askance at Hayward.

I chuckled and coughed. I think the soil would take months to clear my lungs.

"No—no—not that odd. You see, we saw Ellen disappear to the back of her cott. Then we saw you, a bit groggy like, yes groggy, follow her."

"Artor here peeped into the cottage and there was Tilda laying a burblin' on her bed. Well... why would Ellen leave her like that? If she leaves her, she always puts her in her basket or her box bed, so she can't roll into the fire and such like."

"I waited for a heartbeat," said Artor. "But neither of you came back.

So I picked up Tilda, put her in her box bed and came back for Alwyn."

"It's a damned good job you did," I said weakly. "If you hadn't seen me I would be dead now."

"So why were you chasing Ellie through the forest, sir and why did she want to bury you?"

"I will tell you, my good man. First you tell me what happened, what you did, what you saw."

Artor stirred a pot over the fire and then ladled a beaker for me. It was good, warming ale.

I wrapped my fingers around the wooden cup.

"We followed you both. Obviously you had a bit of a head start but we could just at first, make you out, for your clothes were pale and in the failing light, you showed up like a white windflower against the grass. Yes indeed."

"We heard you yell that Tilda couldn't do without her."

"And we heard her answer summat about you hanging her, sir," said Artor.

I nodded "And then?"

"We saw you get to the Braydon Oak. It was getting real dark, *real* dark then and it was hard to see much but again, with your light clothes, we could just see you..."

"A bit of a blur but you showed up," said Cottar.

"We heard scuffling and couldn't quite work out what was happening."

"Then you disappeared, sir."

"Aye, into the pit."

"Well, we didn't see that, we weren't quite close enough," said Cottar. "Then..."

"Then we heard the tree shift and fall."

"And Ellie, we think, started shovelling the earth on top of you."

"We were just about to come into the glade and stop her when she finished shovelling and jumped on top of you and trampled the earth down....well that's what we thought she was doing."

"Did she see you?"

"Oh no, sir. Though she might have heard us come a stompin' through the bushes," said Hayward. "But she was making a deal of noise herself."

"We had been some way behind you, you see and only got right into the glade as the earth was settling" said Cottar. "By the time we got to the hole she was gone and we thought it best to look for you."

"We were a bit puzzled, I can tell you as to what had been going on."

"If it weren't for old hawk eye here." Hayward flicked his thumb at Cottar, "We wouldn't have known for sure you were in the pit. No, we wouldn't."

"But a bit 'o light just caught your knife, sir. It was lyin' on the grass by the edge of the pit and that's when we knew where you were. So we jumped in and started digging."

"I thank you both for your prompt action. A few more heartbeats in that soil and I would have been food for the Savernake worms."

Both men smiled.

Their smiles left their faces. "Sir...what's going on?" said Artor Hayward.

"Where is Ellen Lea now?" I asked.

"Not sure, sir. There's a light in her cott so I suppose she's gone back to Tilda and is at home."

"Good."

I rose. "Keep an eye on her please."

"Aye, sir. What do you want us to do?"

"Later, I want you to pin her in her cottage. Secure the door. Somehow. Do not let her out."

"All right sir...if you say so. She did try to kill you...we think..."

"Yes, Cottar, she did." I shivered.

"Your horse is at the back, sir. He's a good lad. He just waited for you to return and never moved."

"He's been taught to do that," I answered. "I am going home. I'll be back tomorrow with some men."

"Yes, sir."

"On no account let that woman out of her house, you understand and keep an eye on the cottage."

"Yes, sir."

"But first....we face her."

I winked.

*****

We walked quietly across the glade. As we approached the door we heard Mistress Lea singing softly.

I whispered to the two cowmen, "Wait here in silence and listen."

Gently I pushed open the door.

Ellen Lea had her back to me. I noticed she had folded up my cloak and set it to one side of the table, my riding gloves neatly positioned on top.

I looked around. No sign of Tilda. She must be in the loft in her box bed.

I stood there and waited.

Ellen was chopping some greenery with a small knife. Mine was back in my scabbard but I had released it, in case of need.

She looked up from her chopping and then slowly, very slowly turned and saw me.

Her eyes grew huge and frightened.

The knife left her hand and clattered to the beaten earth floor. Her face registered surprise and then abject terror.

She hurried behind the table putting the board between us.

"Noooo!" she cried vigorously making the sign against evil with her fingers.

"Ellen Lea, I charge you with my willful murder! You will burn in hell forever," I said in the most croaky voice I could muster. Well, it wasn't difficult with half a ton of Savernake soil in my throat.

The fire light flickered in the draught from the open door. I must have looked ghostly, for I was covered in soil, my face plastered in mud, totally wild and as my two cowmen had said, pale in my disordered cream woolen cotte.

"Noo—you are dead—" she said, hysteria in her voice. "Dead!"

"I am dead and I will bring with me those others whom you wickedly murdered. They will come back to haunt you Ellen Lea. Torment you!"

She staggered backwards to the wall of the cott.

"Nooo!"

"You will never escape."

"No....I didn't mean it...no I didn't mean to kill them. I just...."

"Confess...." I said. "Confess."

"No… no. Don't."

"Confess for the good of your soul or the devil will come and drag you down to Hell."

I heard from Cottar and Hayward later that even they were impressed by my ghostly impression. I must say I think it was worthy of one of the little plays we always get at Christmas, played out by our mummers at Durley.

Mistress Lea collapsed in the corner weeping. "I killed them," she said. "I killed them but I didn't mean to."

"Name those you killed so you can make amends to their souls. Name them!"

"I killed Bordern. Oh, I didn't mean to, he knows that! Ask him... he knows that."

I pointed at her. "Speak!" I said in a very sepulchral voice.

"I killed Freya and Emma and the old woman Ailsa and then the priest...Oh God...Help me God," she coughed and cried. "Help me."

She put her knees to her chin and folded her arms over her head and wept.

Then I stepped forward into the light. "And you almost killed me." I said in a normal voice. "But you failed."

Her head snapped up. Her snivelling face creased in an expression of utter venom.

"You!"

"Artor, Cottar." I called. "Have you heard enough?"

Shakily Artor Hayward and Alwyn Cottar came into the door hole. Alwyn was as white as a sheet.

I turned back to them.

"You heard?"

"Aye sir, we heard," they said.

"I will tell you all about it tomorrow. Do not Alwyn, take the law into your own hands. I see you are shocked but—the woman will hang and Freya will have justice."

I left them nailing boards across the door of the cottage and Ellen Lea cursing them from inside. I rode for the Cadley Road and stopped to ask Osmund to go down into the town and let the doctor know I was all right. I had promised to be back for supper and I was not going to be able to keep my word. I was exhausted and needed to be at home.

I mounted Fitz and turned his head for Durley.

My welcome there too was just as surprising.

I left Fitz to Cedric who gasped when he saw me. "Sir, is everything all right?"

"Nothing a bath, a change of clothes and sleep won't remedy, Cedric."

I staggered up the steps of the manor stairs and into the hall. I paused on the threshold to take in the view.

Hawise was playing backgammon with Hal who had his back to me. She was grinning. She was obviously winning.

Crispin sat with Lydia, Phillip balanced on her knee and they too were grinning.

Simon was racing around the table on his cock horse and the children's nurse Felice was chasing him telling him to be quiet.

He saw me first.

He stopped stock still.

"Dada?"

"Yes, Simon. It *is* me."

Felice screeched.

Lydia turned. "Who's that? Merciful Heavens!" she exclaimed, "Whatever have you been doing, Aumary?"

Hal turned too and Hawise looked past him, her eyes unconcerned.

"It's Dada. You look like some kind of gargoyle, father," she said. It was true; the mud had caked on my face.

"Well, I'll be..." said Hal. "There's a tale to this I'll be bound!"

Crispin jumped up and came down the hall as I tripped over the threshold of the doorway and skidded to a halt. He caught me.

"Are you hurt, Aumary?"

"No, just tired and rather muddy and drowned in soil."

My little white gazehound, Holdfast, who had been sleeping by the fire raced up and launched herself at me.

At least she knew who I was and was pleased to see me.

*****

Early the next morning Hal, my two soldiers, who were normally billeted at the castle, Stephen Dunn and Peter Devizes and myself rode up to the house of Ellen Lea. The day was raw with a biting easterly wind which rustled the trees in their new spring finery. I'd planned to be up as the sun was coming up but I was so tired that I slept on so we were later getting to the glade than I would have liked.

All was silent. Then Alwyn Cottar came racing out from his cottage, pulling on a tunic of dark blue. He dragged it over his head and the arms waved about until he pulled it down and settled the neck. He ran back in for his belt.

"We kept an eye, like you said, m'lord," came his voice from inside.

"Can you undo the door now please, Alwyn?"

"Yessir. I'll just fetch some tools." He ran over to the large barn which dominated the glade.

Master Hayward came out of the cottage and bowed.

"My Lord Belvoir. All has been quiet."

"Thank you, Artor."

Between us we managed to prise off the wooden boards which the men had nailed across the door, the previous evening.

I warned Peter, Stephen and Hal to be on their guard and I entered the cottage.

Mistress Lea was sitting on a stool by the table. Her child was at her feet on the sheepskin.

"Ellen Lea, I have come to take you to the castle where you are to be confined until your guilt can be proven and your punishment arranged."

She rose slowly.

"Hal, can you bind her hands please."

"My baby...I must take Tilda," cried Mistress Lea. "I cannot hold her if you bind my hands."

I looked her over carefully.

"Very well, tie Tilda to your breast like I have seen you do before and we shall put you up in front of Hal on Grafton."

I nodded to Hal of Potterne.

"I doubt she can misbehave with Tilda tied to her."

Hal wrinkled his nose. "I'm not so sure about that but...."

Mistress Lea took a length of cloth and, as I'd seen her do before, she bound the baby to her, tying knots at the waist and the neck.

"It's cold. You'll need a cloak. We will not travel at a fast speed, you may feel the chill."

Ellen Lea reached for her cloak, this time a grey blanket-like one and not the dark brown of her late husband's which was back on its peg behind the door.

"I'll need my bag, for some clothes and extra things for Tilda."

"You packed it last evening."

"It's still here."

"Search it Stephen. No weapons. Not even a small eating knife."

Stephen took the bag and upended it on the table. There were only clothes and things which the woman would need for her enforced incarceration.

"I have some bread here. I would like to take it. It will go to waste else, and I don't suppose I will be well fed at the castle."

I nodded. It went into the bag.

We lifted her up to Hal and he settled her in front of him. Wrapping his arms around her and the confined Tilda, he picked up the reins and we began our journey to Marlborough.

"Alwyn, Artor, I need you to come to the town and make a statement to my scribe. Will you ride Artor and allow Alwyn on your stirrup? On the way I'll tell you what happened and why."

"She killed my Freya, didn't she?" asked Cottar.

"You heard her confess it."

"Aye, I did but what I don't understand is why."

So, on the journey to the castle, I told Artor Hayward and Alwyn Cottar what mistress Lea had done and why. I kept Hal in front of me. Stephen rode at the head and Peter the tail with my two tied villeins beside me. I tried not to speak too loudly so that Ellen Lea would not hear what I was saying.

They asked few questions, for they still could not quite believe that a woman they had known for such a long time could suddenly become so utterly murderous.

Our early morning procession caused a few stares in the town. The matrons about their purchasing at the early market, for it was a market day, stared in silence as we rode by them and gossiped endlessly as we passed.

A few people nodded and bowed to me.

Ellen Lea stared straight ahead and saw no one.

The pennants on the castle walls fluttered and cracked in the stiff breeze. People coming and going were hurrying to be in doors out of the cold. We wove our way between these busy Marlburians at a slow pace.

At last we clattered over the castle drawbridge and Ellen Lea looked up before we entered the darkness of the gateway. There on the wall was a rope, dangling from the very top of the wall walk in full view of the town.

I saw her shiver and look away quickly.

"It's not for you, mistress," I said, "It's for Master Mount."

The moment we passed the guard, an angry shouting set up.

"No. No...." said a voice I knew. "It wasn't me. You are making a mistake." The voice was slurred and agonised and I was just able to understand the words.

I threw my legs over Bayard's ears and ran with him into the middle of the bailey scanning the walls on the eastern side.

"Peter...up there!"

My two men at arms made for the steps as fast as they could but the bailey was teeming with people and it was difficult to make headway.

Carts of supplies were lined up. Horses with decorative trappings sidled and pawed the ground, pulling at their grooms leading their reins, eager to be off.

Foot soldiers were mustering behind the knights' horses, organising themselves into their mesnies, picking up their belongings and throwing them into the back of the carts holding the baggage.

There was much noise and above this noise I heard the desperate screech of John Mount as they hauled him up the steps of the wall walk.

His hands were bound and three soldiers from the garrison were pushing him along. He was screaming, with his broken mouth.

"It's a mistake, I tell you. Ask Lord Belvoir. It's not me." His face was black and purple with bruises and his lips were swollen. His left eye was closed. "I have given information to him."

I put my hands to my mouth and yelled.

"Pearson. Stop there!"

The noise in the castle yard was prodigious but I yelled again and Stephen Dunn added his voice to mine.

"Pearson, stop!"

I shoved Bayard's reins at a befuddled groom and pushed my way through the crowd yelling back over my shoulder, "Hal stay there."

I saw Pearson locate me in the bailey. I saw his brow furrow and I saw his feet falter on the step.

"Pearson. Continue. Do as you were instructed." Another voice had bellowed from behind me.

I did not turn, for I knew who it was.

"I have the murderer, my Lord de Neville. I have brought her in this morning. There is no need to hang John Mount."

"Her, Belvoir?" The sheriff laughed. "Oh really Belvoir, this is too much."

"Pearson, wait for me there," and I carried on walking to the foot of the steps.

A few of the lord sheriff's soldiers got in my way but I pushed through. Stephen followed me.

I looked back at him. To this day I don't know why I did this, but I did. I grasped Stephen's arm and whispered.

"Go to the doctor. Bring him here. Quickly. As quick as you can." I knew Stephen was a fast runner.

Pearson was now dragging John Mount to the place where the rope had been secured to the merlons of the eastern wall walk.

He looked down at me.

"I am so sorry sir," he said, "but I have my orders."

"Belvoir!" bellowed the sheriff.

I ignored him and, passing Peter Devizes, who was standing on the stairs, I shouted for him to follow me and ascended the remainder of the steps as fast as I could.

I saw Sir Andrew Merriman coming up from the other side, from the steps on the southern wall.

I yelled to him.

"Andrew. We may need help."

I saw Andrew glance down into the yard at the sheriff.

The soldiers had now placed the rope around the neck of John Mount and were tying his feet. Father Columba the castle priest was coming along the wall at a pace. He saw me and faltered.

"My Lord Belvoir. I have been told..."

"I know what you have been told, Father but if you do this thing, it will be a gross injustice and a heinous crime. This man *is innocent*. It will be a sin for us to hang him."

"The lord sheriff..."

"Is wrong!" I bellowed.

Father Columba now walked forward much more slowly.

I saw Pearson whisper to his two companions. They too faltered and looked confused.

"Pearson!" I shouted "I have the guilty person there." I pointed down to the bailey. "John Mount is innocent. Do not hang him. The murderer has confessed."

"I have my orders, sir."

"Do you want this innocent man's death on your conscience, Pearson? When you hear the evidence and the testimony of my witnesses, you will realise that I am right."

"Pearson. Hang him!" shouted the sheriff from directly underneath us.

The two soldiers looked down at the sheriff and dithered.

I saw Andrew approaching them from behind.

I heard him say, "We'll all lose our jobs for this."

"Better than your soul," said Peter Devizes quietly at my elbow.

John Mount began to struggle and one of the soldiers gave him a gentle buffet on the side of the head to quieten him.

I came up level with them.

"Release him, Pearson."

"I must hang him, sir. Those are my orders. I cannot go against my orders. Not whilst the sheriff is here."

I watched the man's eyes carefully. There was something in them that made me nod. Again I have no idea why. Pearson was a good man, that I knew. He'd meant something by that look.

One of the soldiers finally secured the noose around the neck of a now drooping and incoherently sobbing John Mount.

Once he realised that they had tightened it, he began to buck and scream, fight and wriggle.

"John...John..." I said loudly. "Do not fight it. You understand?"

The man was dripping in sweat and red in the face with struggling. I watched his colour change as his face drained. Or rather, that face I could see amongst the bruises.

"You too, sir?"

"I will save you, if I can."

"No sir...no you won't. No."

"I will. We must hang you, do you see?"

Pearson looked at me and gave me an infinitesimal nod.

Father Columba had now come up and was reciting his prayers. I caught his eye too.

"Do. Not. Struggle. John." I said deliberately.

John Mount licked his broken lips. Tears began to course down his face,

"I am innocent sir. You know that."

"I know John. I have the real culprit. She has confessed. We shall get you a pardon."

"What use is a pardon if I'm dead?"

I looked down at the sheriff in his finery; his left hand on the pommel of his sword, his cloak thrown back to reveal the seal of office dangling from the chain worn around his neck. He had not heard me speak.

He caught my eye.

He bowed. I bowed back.

"Hang him," he said and he turned and disappeared into the throng.

We stood there a little longer.

Then the two soldiers picked up John Mount bodily. They eased him over the parapet.

"Do NOT drop him," I said firmly.

We all gathered round as if to shield Mount and gently lowered the prisoner over the wall.

Almost immediately there was a terrible choking sound.

"John," I shouted, "Do not fight." How I thought the man would not wriggle and buck in desperation and panic, I don't know.

Father Columba droned on.

After a while Andrew peered over the edge.

"He is going purple."

"Onlookers?"

"A few. Townsmen mainly."

"Can you see Johannes?"

"Yes sir," said Peter. "He's right by St. Peter's now."

I waited a few more heartbeats.

And a few more.

"He's going blue," said Andrew.

"Right now, we hold him up. Lift!"

Andrew, Peter and I leaned over the parapet and Peter and I grabbed Mount under the bound arms, grasping our fingers into the cloth of his tunic.

"He's passed out," said Andrew, digging his fore fingers and thumbs into the rope strangling the prisoner to lessen the grip.

"Good." I said.

"Pearson. Tell the men in the bailey that Mount is dead."

"Yes, sir."

He turned and in a stentorian voice yelled, "The felon, the guilty man is dead!"

There was a cry from some, a hushed sigh from others. Many crossed themselves. The priest droned on.

"Fetch him over at the very moment that the sheriff passes out of the gate and is gone up the road. If he looks up to see all's well and good or if he looks back, we shall wait for a heartbeat."

A mere moment later, the sheriff, surrounded by his entourage, passed under the portcullis and over the wooden boarded drawbridge across the moat.

We all let go of John for that moment.

Geoffrey de Neville did not look back or up.

"Quick!"

We hauled poor John Mount up over the parapet and pulled off the rope. He was very blue in the face. His mouth was open and his tongue was protruding. I chafed his rope burned neck and asked for water to be brought quietly to the wall walk.

Andrew had a small flask hanging from his belt. He upended it into Mount's mouth. Mount did not swallow.

"Please God he will come round."

Johannes came puffing up the stairs.

"Make way there! Stephen said we have a hanged man."

"We have but we held him up as long as we could. I suppose you could say he's half hanged."

I got up from my knees.

"We will now leave it to you."

Father Columba stretched his eyes to Heaven. "I cannot go to the chapel and pray that the man will survive. But I will say a prayer for him nevertheless."

I smiled. "Thank you, Sir priest. That would be of great help." Of course Father Columba could not go into the chapel, for it was closed by order of the Pope. No one seemed to want to argue.

I turned to a rather shaken Pearson. "Thank you, and to you Petty and you Farmer. This would have been a terrible miscarriage of justice."

They moved back anxiously scanning the bailey for the sheriff's men. Realising they had all gone, they sighed and made their way down the wall walk steps.

"He's not in the land of the living yet, Aumary," said Andrew smiling.

"If it's anything like me yesterday, he is riding on the air, above the downs with the larks for company, dreaming of blue flowers and earthberries."

But, of course they had no idea what I was talking about.

*****

We wrapped Mount in a coarse cloth and carried him down the steps, Father Columba reciting his prayers behind us all the way.

"We shall take him for burial in the ground round St. Peter's," I said loudly. To Johannes I said quietly. "We shall in truth, take him to your house."

"Better still," said Andrew at a whisper, "take him to my room and see to him. We can have a cart brought and we can ferry him into the town from there."

I nodded.

"Can I leave that to you? I have a prisoner to attend to."

Stephen and Peter carried Mount across the bailey. People parted to let them through, crossing themselves or grinning, depending on their point of view about the prisoner's guilt.

Hal, who had stayed mounted on Grafton with the widow Lea firmly in his grip, now handed her down to me.

I saw Master Gayle, the gaol master coming towards me at a gallop, tightening his belt and pulling his cotte tidily around him.

"Pete, can we find somewhere to put Mistress Lea and her child, in the keep perhaps until we have obtained a statement from her and decided on the course of action.

Peterkin Gayle looked down at Ellen Lea with distaste.

"Yes. One of the empty lower store rooms perhaps. I can have a pallet and stool brought down from one of the higher rooms."

I saw Ellen Lea look up at the menacing white keep on its high mound.

"The woman is guilty of the deaths of her husband, three women and the priest of Cadley, Pete. She tried to kill me last night. Watch her carefully. She's as slippery as an eel."

Ellen Lea looked up at me with wide eyes but said nothing.

Pete nodded and grasped the woman by the arm. One of the castle guards was called over and Pete, Hal and he marched her away. She looked back at me once.

"Wait for me in the keep, Pete." I shouted.

I addressed Cottar and Hayward. "I will need you to make statements. A scribe will come and take down what you know. Wait here for him."

I turned to follow Stephen and Peter with the wrapped bundle of John Mount to Andrew's private room in the southern wall.

Once there we laid him on Andrew's bed, quickly unwrapped him and Johannes ascertained that he was still alive.

"His breathing is shallow but I think you managed to hold him up long enough for him not to be totally strangled."

He put his ear to Mount's chest. "Yes, the heartbeat is weak but I think we shall be able to get him back to normal soon enough."

"Good, do so, Johannes, please. Stephen, can you go and get a handcart? I have a notion there's one in the stable somewhere."

I stood by the closed door and leaned on the wall out of the way.

Andrew came to stand beside me.

"The woman you brought in. She's the true murderer?"

"Impossible as it may seem Andrew, yes. She hit me with a spade last night in the forest as it was going dark and toppled me into a hole made by a fallen oak. She then covered me over with soil, as Hal would say, as cool as a cat."

"Gods Aumary. Buried you—alive?"

"Aye. She is tiny but she's the strength of an ox."

"How did you...?"

"Two of my villeins saw it happen, they dug me out." I looked over to the bed. "I know what it's like to suffocate."

I heard a choking sound coming from the body on the bed.

"Alive then?"

Johannes looked up. "Yes but we don't know how he'll be when he regains consciousness. Sometimes the damage is too great and people cannot function as they did before."

"How so?"

"I'm not entirely sure. I once saw a young lad accidentally hanged and when we got to him he'd been hanging there for some time I think. When he came to, he was unable to speak and understand..."

"A little like our man Foreman last year?"

We'd had a felon called Foreman who had been injured in the head by being kicked by a horse. Johannes had treated him and he'd not been able to speak nor understand, nor indeed sit or walk unaided. Johannes had thought it was something to do with the damage to the brain underneath his skull.

"Please God we don't have the same thing here."

"Amen to that," said Andrew.

We waited as Johannes pulled down his patient's shirt, chafed the man's neck and chest and listened again to his breathing.

It seemed an age before he'd finished and was satisfied.

Johannes put two drops of an amber liquid into a cup of water and dribbled it into Mount's mouth. He coughed but swallowed.

"Well, that is a good sign. He can still swallow. Just."

He then reached for a small phial and held it under the nose of my villein.

Mount thrashed and gurgled. His eyes opened. He retched as his stomach rebelled against the liquid which he'd swallowed, but he kept it down.

"Do not speak, John," said the doctor. "We must get you to the safety and comfort of my house."

Mount's throat was a mass of purple bruises and red weals in a ring around his upper throat. The huge round bruise to the side of the chin present when a man is throttled to death with a rope, was absent; the knot, which was usually responsible for this, had not been tied in a way to press here. We had Pearson to thank for that. The knot had been placed to the back of the head.

I heard the trundle of wheels, as Stephen brought the hand cart up to the door.

Andrew looked out.

"It's here."

"John, we shall move you now." I pushed off from the wall. "Do not struggle or speak. We must have everyone think you dead."

I saw John Mount's eyes flicker and I hoped he'd understood me.

Johannes wrapped the cloth around him again and with soothing noises covered over his head.

Andrew and I picked up John Mount, head and foot.

We got him through the door.

"No one's looking," said Peter.

"No one that matters," added Johannes pointing to Father Columba hurrying towards us. "The good Father knows."

"I thought..." said the red headed priest, "that I'd accompany you so far. It will look better that way."

"Thank you, Father," I said smiling.

"Does our hanged man live or will I be interring him in my makeshift church yard, since the Interdict prohibits...?"

"He lives," said Johannes.

"Praise be to God."

"Phew!" said Andrew suddenly as Father Columba began his prayers again. "What's that stink?"

"Ah yes," said Stephen scratching his bristly chin. "I am sorry about that. The only cart I could find was the dung cart."

How we laughed about that when we'd got John Mount to the safety of the doctor's house.

*****

Having settled John at Johannes' house, I walked with Hal back to the castle.

Up the steps to the mound we ran and ducked into the base of the keep. Round two lots of stairs and we found ourselves opposite a tiny cell of a room on the first floor of the building.

Peterkin Gayle was waiting for us outside.

He unlocked the door and we entered and Hal stayed in the doorway.

Mistress Lea was sitting on the stool with the child on her lap.

I walked around her. She did not look up but kept her eyes on Tilda.

"So what are we to do with you?"

I saw Peterkin Gayle shift slightly uncomfortably, by the window

"Your husband, three women, the priest of Cadley. All dead at your hand. And me too...almost."

Pete blinked and looked up at me.

"Yes, Pete. She's a murderous little liar."

"Will you have her tried by the justices, Sir Aumary?"

"I would like to say she has no right to a trial. I heard her confession as did two of my cattle men. I think it will suffice to hang her here without wasting time on a further trial elsewhere but that will not be up to me."

Peterkin's face grew serious. "You will do it, Sir Aumary?"

"Ah no. I will wait for our dear sheriff or the castle constable's presence."

"Heaven knows when that will be."

I shrugged. "Can you keep her here until such time as they come?"

"I can...but...the little one?"

"Ah yes. We need to find her a wet nurse. I don't think it would be wise to leave little Tilda in this damp and airless place for too long. Mistress Lea can take her chances but Tilda is an innocent in all this."

"And the child is your property, Sir Aumary. You will want her back at Durley."

Mistress Lea looked up at me.

"You would rip a child from its mother's arms, my lord?"

"You should have thought about Tilda when you embarked on your killing orgy, mistress."

Ellen Lea stared at me, her eyes huge as she shook her head. Was it disbelief?

"I'll find the child a box to sleep in tonight" said Master Gayle. "It can be cold of a night in these little rooms."

I knew that, for one of them had once been my office and sleeping place when I was working at the castle. I had better accommodation now.

"And I will seek out a woman in the town for a wet nurse. Oh...and I will send Alfred Clerk to take a confession from the woman and my herdsmen. Where is he now Pete? Will you remain while he does so? I don't trust her."

"Alfred Clerk? He's one floor up at the back, northerly side."

I found the young man easily enough and asked him to collect his portable desk and pens and ink. Down one floor we went, back to the little room.

Pete had now found a small wooden crate in which Tilda could sleep and be safe and a cut down blanket for warmth.

"I would not normally ask it but I think it's wise we hobble her, Pete."

"You want her ankles pinned?"

"Yes. As I say, she is as slippery as an eel and I think it would be wise to make sure she cannot escape."

"Very well. I'll do it after she has made her confession."

"So mistress, you can now tell again what you told me last night in your cottage at Braydon. Alfred will write it all down."

The woman sat on her stool and smiled a small smile.

"I will not," she said.

"Very well. I will recount what I can remember. I warn you, mistress, I have a very good memory."

"You may, my lord, do as you wish. And this young man here can go to Hell."

Alfred looked shocked and turned his dark eyes to my face.

"Take no notice Alfred," I said.

I folded my arms.

"I can make your stay here very uncomfortable, Mistress Lea. I can request that your death be a very painful one for not only did you kill your husband but you tried to kill me and I am your Lord."

The woman shrugged.

I began the tale and Alfred scratched away at his parchment, writing it all down.

The widow Lea said not a word.

*****

"Will you press her?" asked Pete when we had finished and the door had been locked behind us.

"I suppose I should," I said, "but do you know, I cannot do it. Oh not because I am afeared to do it but because she is such a horrible specimen of womankind, I cannot bring myself to give her the chance to plead. She is mine. I am satisfied of her guilt. She can hang."

If a person would not plead either guilty or not guilty then they must be made to do so. They must be pressed. This involved them being loaded on the body with heavy stones, one by one until they were forced to plead or they died.

"I never thought I would hear you say such a thing, Aumary," said

216

Pete with a chuckle.

"No. Neither did I. I am as you know Pete, concerned with justice and fairness and do not normally think of hanging as justice, but in *this* case hanging her *would be* justice. She cannot be allowed to live."

"You were very fond of the priest Father Justin, weren't you?"

"I was. I had known him almost all my life." That set me off musing and thinking and whilst I mused, Pete disappeared to his duty.

*****

He went down to the gaol to fetch up some gyves with which to shackle mistress Lea and I went down into the town to talk to my friends the Cordwainers. They would have knowledge of where I might find a woman who could suckle Tilda.

I asked in the town and not in the forest, for in Durley I knew that Johnathan Reeve's wife, Phillipa had enough milk for two children, her own Geoffrey and the orphan Algar but not for Tilda too. There were no other women who had milk, no other new mothers in the village or forest that I knew of, except for the steward of Bedwyn's wife and my own wife Lydia and that would never do.

This arranged I trotted back into the castle.

I had just organised Hal to fetch the horses from the stable for our trip home when I heard a commotion coming from the gateway to the keep.

A voice screamed, "Come no nearer or I shall drown her."

Hal's gaze whipped round to me. "That's the demon Lea!" he shouted and ran off in the direction of the wall walk to the keep.

Here the wall was pierced by an arch which led to a series of steps up which one had to travel to reach the keep at the base of the mound.

A wooden bridge led from these steps to the main bailey and standing on this was Ellen Lea with Tilda. She had stretched out over the water and in her hands she held her small daughter.

Hal came closer as did Castleman, one of the castle guards who had tried to block her way.

I slowly inched through the arch into the daylight. "Ellen, put the child down."

Her head came up and there was fire in her eyes. "Do not think I will not kill her."

"She is *your child*, Ellen. You laboured to bring her into the world."

"Yes!" she spat, "and what for?"

"She is the product of your union with your husband Bordern, Ellen..."

"PAH!" spat Ellen. "A sham—a complete sham. It was all a lie."

"What was a lie?"

For the first time since she had pretended that Bordern Lea had disappeared I saw the expression of true sadness and tears in her eyes.

"I thought he was the most wonderful man in the world."

Hal suddenly shook himself. "How'd she get out sir? Is Gayle...?"

"Peterkin Gayle! What have you done with Master Gayle?"

"That silly little old man?" She grasped Tilda harder. "No! Don't come any closer."

Hal had tried to get onto the bridge to pass her so that he might get into the keep and find Peterkin.

He drew back again.

"Give us the child, Ellen," I said again. "And we shall talk."

She shook her head vehemently from side to side.

"I knew...I knew...that Bordern loved that woman. What he told me was all a lie. I loved him so much. I loved him as if he were perfect and it was all a lie."

Mistress Lea inched forward.

"Get back!"

Suddenly I noticed that in her right hand she held a knife. A small knife but one which might do damage to a little child. It was enough to kill it.

Where had she got that from?

"Give me the knife."

Again she shook her head. Again she came on. Now she placed the knife at the neck of her child and walked off the bridge. Tilda began to grizzle. She didn't like being held in this fashion.

I drew back as did Hal.

She passed him and he ran up onto the steps and was gone in an instant up to the keep. When Lea passed Castleman he too ran up to the keep.

She passed me.

Then she darted for the steps which ran up the wall walk and onto the western part of the wall surrounding the castle.

I followed. I missed the hem of her dress by inches and sprawled on one of the steps barking my shin.

Up she went like a doe in the forest, quick and lithe and agile.

The child was screaming now, frightened and uncertain.

There was no one on this stretch of the castle wall though folk were crowded onto the southernmost side where masons were repairing and rebuilding the old walls. They were too busy at their work to give us a glance.

This wall was crumbling, I recalled and very soon the masons would begin to work here.

I saw Andrew far below me look up at the place where I stood and look puzzled. Then he saw Ellen Lea and grimaced. He made for the other steps to come upon her from the south side, behind her.

She saw the direction of my gaze and quickly moved to the wall.

"You shall not have her."

She grasped Tilda's clothes more firmly and with a steely deliberateness, she dangled her daughter over the wall.

"Ellen...it need not be like this. Come let us talk. Why does Tilda deserve to be smashed on the ground below? What has she done?"

"She is her father's daughter. She is Bordern's."

"She doesn't deserve to die for that."

Through my brain was going the thought that many would think this was merely a small girl child, the daughter of a churl, of little value and use. What did it matter that she would be dropped from a height to her death? Why should I care?

I did care. I have children, I thought. I have a daughter. She matters. She matters to God.

"She is the product of a lie," said Ellen, breaking into my reverie.

The whole world shrunk to the few feet around us. The few stones along this wall and under our feet; the ruffling of the trees by the river in

219

the stiff breeze and the snapping of the pennants drawn up at the corner of the wall. There were different flags now. The sheriff had gone and his arms were not now displayed at the castle. Now the pennants were that of the lord of this castle, the King, although he was not in residence. There would be grander flags when the King arrived.

Ellen was distracted momentarily by the sound of one of the flags clapping in the breeze. She turned her head and I sprang.

Ellen Lea lashed out with the knife but didn't relinquish the child. I managed to get my hands on Tilda and I pulled.

Ellen Lea followed me pulling back all the while trying to catch me with the small knife held in her right hand.

There was a short but undignified tussle. She pushed me hard and my back made contact with the stone of the parapet.

I was naturally stronger than the woman and eventually I managed to turn around and back her to the wall.

"Give Tilda to me," I shouted.

The knife was once more pointed at the child's throat. I backed off.

Mistress Lea looked behind me. The space was empty but she could see more folk now coming up the steps. Amongst them, Hal was making his way up with a couple of the guards. No escape that way.

Ellen Lea turned and ran south towards Andrew who was approaching stealthily from the steps in the southwest corner.

Mistress Lea gasped when she saw him and in a moment, she was standing on the top of the wall.

"Ellen, come down. The wall is unsafe." I made for her but she pricked little Tilda with the knife and the baby cried out in surprise.

"Ellen please...come down the wall is crumbling. It won't bear your weight."

"I am not so foolish...my lord," she spat. "This is a castle. Walls not safe? Pah! I am not stupid. Castle walls *are* safe, they must be." I knew she could never have seen a castle before.

And she stamped her foot on the stone block.

There was a crumbling of masonry and I watched as the woman, her face a picture of disbelief, lurched backwards, kept her footing but lost hold of the child.

I leapt forward and in one fleet movement caught Tilda as she fell and in the next threw her at Andrew who was coming up swiftly. He caught her deftly in two hands and laid her gently at his feet.

Of Ellen Lea there was no sign.

I looked over the parapet.

There was the woman dangling from the stone like a piece of lichen, her clothes buffeted by the breeze, her fingers white as they clawed the fragmenting rock.

"Ellen, grasp my hand!" I yelled and reached out for her over the edge, stretching as far as I could.

I heard her laugh.

"Ellen, you do not want to die this way. Unshriven, forgotten by God. Take my hand."

The woman looked down.

It was fifty feet to the ground.

She looked up again and with immense strength she reached up with one hand and took mine. I stretched out the other.

She grasped it. I began to haul her back.

Suddenly both her feet came up and she planted them hard on the stone of the outside of the castle wall. I staggered.

She pulled me. I lurched over the wall and my midriff caught the edge of the parapet. A searing pain went up my torso. Ah...my bruised rib again. If it was not cracked last night, it most certainly was now.

I took in an involuntary breath and pulled back.

Laughing Ellen Lea pulled both my hands, her grip as hard as any my farrier might have on his hammer. She moved her hands up to the edges of my sleeve and seized the fabric and my wrists.

'Jesus aid me,' I thought quickly. 'I am going over the wall.'

Suddenly I felt a pair of strong arms around my thighs and buttocks.

"Aumary let go," said Andrew.

"I cannot, she will not." I managed to say grimacing breathily with my face growing red.

Suddenly, Hal was beside me, stretching out over the wall. There was a grating sound and the stone over which I dangled started to shift. Andrew redoubled his efforts and strengthened his grip on me.

As deftly as a bird catcher, Hal jabbed the hand of the woman Lea with the point of his knife and she screamed letting go of one wrist.

Now she held on by the remaining hand but her grip was slackening. She looked up, then down and then all at once, let go.

Chapter Fifteen

Hal and Andrew dragged me back over the brink of the parapet. I turned and slid down the stones, my head on my knees feeling sick.

"Jesus Aumary, why didn't you let go?" asked Andrew, looking over the edge.

"I couldn't, she had a good hold on my sleeve edge."

I saw my friend grimace as he took in the body of Ellen Lea fifty feet below.

"Half in the moat and half on the ground," he said.

"Dead...?"

"What do you think?" said Hal, also looking over the parapet.

Andrew cast a glance at little Tilda and went to pick her up. She crooned to him and blew bubbles, oblivious to the tragedy played out around her.

Andrew, arms outstretched, held the baby under her arms and looked at her quizzically.

I stood shakily. "It suits you," I said.

Andrew gave me a menacing grin.

"Give 'er 'ere," said Hal "That's not 'ow you 'old a baby, yer daft loon."

"Gladly, Hal," said Andrew.

Hal took Tilda gently and settled her in the crook of his arm. He tickled her under the chin and she lay there blowing bubbles at him, her chin next to his soft woollen, buff gambeson.

"Thank you, both of you." I said.

"Ah well..." said Hal. "Saves us an 'anging."

Suddenly I remembered Master Gayle.

"Pete?" I cried rubbing my sweaty palms through my hair.

"Stabbed in the 'and with that little knife, then felled with the small stool we left 'er to sit on. 'E's all right. Doctor James is seein' to 'im now."

"Wherever did she get that knife? We searched her and her baggage before we left Braydon, remember?"

"Clever little madam that one," said Hal. "She baked a round of bread..."

"The night we left her...and baked the knife into the loaf?"

"Aye."

I risked a look over the wall.

Mistress Lea lay on her back, the edge of the moat lapping about her head, blood drifting out in lazy strings into the greenish water. Her head cloth was out in the middle of the moat and her pale brown hair drifted in tendrils about her battered skull.

Several people had now come up to us. Some looked down to the moat's edge.

I sighed. "I suppose we'd better fetch her in and get her to Father Columba. She died without confession and absolution...."

"She'll be burning in 'ell already for what she did," said Hal. "And right too."

Oh I know Paul, my scribe, Hal was a most amazing man but Christian forgiveness was not one of his stronger virtues.

"Now she's one who I won't bother about," he said "if the church can't help 'er along to 'eaven. She's got it comin' "

I struggled to the steps.

"Come on. Let's go down. If I know anything about babies, Tilda will be hungry soon."

*****

This Paul is one of the stories I have been asked to tell over and over for people cannot believe that a woman as small and insignificant as Ellen Lea could be in possession of so much strength.

It's a fallacy that women are weaker than men for forest women and no doubt villeins everywhere are tough creatures able to break the clods of the earth and carry great loads upon their backs. I have seen it with my own eyes and after this day I never underestimated a woman's courage, strength or power. No never again.

People were also staggered at the fact that she had killed her husband with an icicle. No doubt the perfect weapon.

Sharp, hard, pointed and ephemeral.

Truly I would have been none the wiser had it not been for that icy puddle in which I had cut my finger.

I have to say it was one of the most unusual murders I ever came across.

Yes, Paul. Ellen Lea was very clever. As I said, she had us all fooled.

What's that? Did Mount recover? Aye, he did and carried on his work with my cattle till the end of his days.

No, no Paul. He never married.

Later that day I jogged home on Bayard. Every step was a torment to my rib and back. How could I explain to anyone that I had been bested by a woman who only came up to my chest?

I'd left Tilda with a nursemaid in Marlborough and when she was weaned, she would come to Durley and live with a family there. That, however, is for another story.

I dragged myself up the steps of the manor and into the screens passage.

I could hear laughter and giggling coming from the hall and I peeped around the door jamb.

Hawise, Lydia and Crispin were sitting at the table with Philip held between them.

Hawise, for some reason, was pulling strange faces, gurning and poking out her tongue, crossing her eyes and generally pulling her pretty visage into odd expressions.

Crispin was encouraging her and Lydia was giggling like a child.

Phillip, our son was staring at her and chuckling with uncontrolled delight. Crispin tickled him in the middle and the laughter escalated into wild giggling.

Phillip was making sounds!

I walked into the room. Philip saw me and turned his head.

He gave me the sweetest smile a child of mine had ever worn upon their face.

I remembered Geoffrey, my five year old son, dead these many years and swallowed down tears. Phillip looked so like him. So like me, they tell me, when I was a baby, save that I have brown eyes.

The little one giggled again.

I forgot my pain and heartily smiled back. I reached for him and he put up his arms.

It was going to be alright. Even with no church.

Everything was going to be alright.

And summer was just around the corner.

GLOSSARY

Alaunt Gentile - A small greyhound dog

Apothecary - Primitive chemist

Baily - A part of the forest, an administrative unit of Savernake

Bailey - The open area of a castle within the walls

Black avised - Dark complexion

Brazier - A metal firebox

Brock - A badger

Childer - Children

Churching - A ceremony in church by which women after childbirth are received in the church with prayers, blessings, and thanksgiving

Chrism - Consecrated oil used in Greek and Latin churches especially in baptism, chrismation, confirmation, and ordination.

Clappered - Wiltshire dialect, struck

Coif - A close fitting fabric cap

Coroner - A coroner is a government or judicial official who is empowered to conduct or order an inquest into the manner or cause of death

Cottar - A man who was a farm labourer or tenant occupying a cottage in return for labour

Cott - Cottage or small dwelling

Cotte - An overgarment for both men and women. The word gives us the modern coat

Counterpane - A bedspread

Crenellations - The battlements of a castle or other building

Daub - Plaster, clay, or another substance used for coating a surface

Dunnock - *Prunella modularis.* A small brown sparrow-like bird

Evil eye - A supernatural belief in a curse, brought about by a malevolent glare, usually given to a person when one is unaware

Fist out - Fizzle out

Forest Eyre - A law court

Frankpledge - A system of law enforcement and policing in which members of society were mutually responsible for the behaviour of their peers

Gambeson - Padded jacket worn under maille

Gyves - Shackles

Hayward - An officer having charge of hedges and fences especially to keep cattle from breaking through and to impound stray cattle

Head rail - Ladies' head cloth which is worn over the hair

Journeyman - A man out of his apprenticeship but not yet his own master

Kine - Cattle

Pallet - Mattress

Paternoster and Creed - Christian prayers - Our Father and I believe in God the Father.

Pennorth - Penny's worth. Opinion.

Pottage - A stew. Peasant food which was a common meal throughout Europe in mediaeval times

Screens passage - The corridor from the outer door to the hall in a manor house

Scrip - Large purse

Solar - The family's private living and sleeping quarters so called because it catches the rays of the sun at hours of the day

Swaddle - Tightly wrap, especially a baby in garments or cloth

Tooth Drawer - Someone who pulls teeth

Tithing - A group of ten men responsible for each other

Treen - Wooden household items

Simples - Herbal medicine

Strike a light - Primitive matchbox

Undercroft - Traditionally a cellar or storage room

Wattle - A woven lattice of wooden strips

Wet nurse - A woman employed to suckle another woman's child

Wood warden - A forester responsible for the upkeep of the forest trees

Wolfshead - An outlaw

AUTHOR'S NOTE

The Middle Ages was a very superstitious time. Belief in all sorts of demons and devils, wickedly unnatural animals and the power of unseen forces pervaded all classes.

Quite ordinary events might be attributed to supernatural causes by many folk.

Naturally people at the time hadn't the knowledge we have today. Science was merely in embryo and few people could read in order to learn about the world even if the knowledge was out there.

For a long time I have wanted to write a story with a murder being committed with an unusual weapon. Here, in Wynter Wakeneth, I get my chance.

ABOUT THE AUTHOR

Susanna, like Aumary Belvoir has known the Forest of Savernake all her life. After a period at the University of Wales studying Speech Therapy, she returned to Wiltshire and then moved to Hampshire to work, not so very far from her forest. Susanna developed an interest in English history, particularly that of the 12th and 13th centuries, early in life and began to write about it in her twenties. She now lives in Northamptonshire with her husband and a small wire haired fox terrier called Tabor.

Susanna hopes to return fairly soon to her beloved Wiltshire downs where she will continue to write the Savernake series, her Kennet Valley romances and the Withershynnes Medieval Fantasies set in the area around Marlborough, Wiltshire.

ALSO BY SUSANNA M. NEWSTEAD

The Savernake Medieval Murder Mysteries

Belvoir's Promise
She Moved Through the Fair
Down by the Salley Gardens
I Will Give my Love an Apple
Black is the Colour of my True Love's Hair
Long Lankyn
One Misty Moisty Morning
The Unquiet Grave
The Lark in the Morning
A Parcel of Rogues
Bushes & Briars
Though I Live Not Where I Love

Kennet Valley Tales Medieval Romances

Forceleap Farm
Hunting the Wren
The Harmonious Blacksmith

Withershynnes Medieval Fantasy

Withershynnes : In The Dark
Withershynnes 2: Cat's Cradle
Withershynnes 3: Cheating the Wind

Illustrated Children's Books

Tabor the Terrierble: The Gardener's Dog
Tabor the Terrierble: The Dark Knight

Please visit the website for further information
https://susannamnewstead.co.uk/

www.ingramcontent.com/pod-product-compliance
Ingram Content Group UK Ltd.
Pitfield, Milton Keynes, MK11 3LW, UK
UKHW032104150325
456262UK00002B/155

9 781909 237131